IF YOU LOVE HER

Contents

To my Renaissance Man,
Thank you for being my anchor.
And to those who never fit the mold.

@kelci2D

@kelci2D

Author's Note

DEAR READER,

This book contains a few strong themes such as on and off page child abuse, neglect, foul language, bullying, suicidal feelings, on screen second degree murder, and hunting of game animals. Please consider your own mental health before starting this book.

Thank you for giving this book and these characters a chance. Like most of us, they have so much to learn, they make a lot of mistakes, but this is a story where love overpowers our past.

Prologue

Jason

EYES DON'T LIE- KINGFISHER

If the rain is a cry for help, then the snow is a peaceful slumber. The world is asleep when it snows this much. I can't explain it the way I want to but when the world is covered in white powder, it's like it's hibernating with the animals, recharging for spring. Renewing itself before the onslaught of insanity that comes with the season and the reawakened life.

But I prefer the winter. In winter, the roads close and no one can get to the house from town which is how I prefer it. I know my brother would rather have company in the winter, but not me. As much as I love my brother, sometimes I wish even he was gone between November and March. Then I would truly be surrounded by blissful silence.

Other times, like when the pipes freeze and the meat runs out and I need help keeping the cabin in working order, I'm grateful he's with me.

I took my truck hunting last night knowing the weather would worsen while I was away. While driving back through the multiple feet of snow, all I can hear is the whir of the motor and I wish it was silent so I could enjoy the deafening quiet of the snowstorm that signals the start of our isolation.

I hate people. I don't like being around them. They don't understand me. And even if I did speak to them, they still wouldn't get it. It's easier being silent. And it's easier being alone.

My brother, Dylan, understands me. But he's chatty and when he gets drunk he makes comments about how he wished I would speak to him. He thinks my refusal to talk is a direct insult to him. But I've come to learn he only thinks that way when he's had too many beers. Otherwise, he seems more understanding than most.

I was shit out of luck hunting all day, all the animals were hunkered down for the storm so I am coming home empty-handed. We still have meat in the freezer and lots of canned goods, but it won't last forever before I'll need to hunt again. Dylan wanted a new pelt for the landing upstairs since he complains about the floor being too cold when he goes to the bathroom in the middle of the night. Guess he'll have to suffer cold feet for a while.

The headlights of the truck illuminate the thick flakes coming down and they kind of remind me of stars whizzing by. I'm going as fast as I can on this thing so I can get out of the cold. It's not until I pass the black Honda Civic in a blur of motion that I even see it. In a fluid maneuver, I make a U-turn to head back for the car in the snow bank.

What the fuck is someone doing out here in this storm? Don't they know the roads will be covered in three feet of snow by morning? People don't realize this about Oregon snow, but it isn't as dry and powdery as snow in the rest of the country. It's more like slush; which means most of this will be ice in the morning.

I almost didn't see the car because half of it is buried in the snow bank as if it did a nose dive into the pile of white powder, while the other half has a light dusting of snow on the trunk that keeps getting swept away by the howling wind. I could've easily missed it, but the beams of the headlights reflecting off the back window caught my eye.

I pull up next to the car and leave the truck running while I inspect the vehicle. The front door is buried in snow but the back driver's side door looks like it could be opened with some brute force.

I pull on the handle but it's locked. *Great.* I try the driver's door to see if it's unlocked but nothing. And it's too dark to see inside to tell how many people are in there, if any. Maybe whoever was in the accident got out and walked for help. That would be a death sentence but people lose all sense of logic when the snow hits Oregon.

I decide to do the only thing left: break the window. I grab the Remington from inside the cab of the truck and bang the butt of the rifle into the glass in one sharp, controlled motion, shattering the glass enough for me to push through and unlock the door from the inside.

People always assume car windows shatter like regular windows, breaking into sharp jagged points and completely coming apart from the frame. They don't realize the design is different to prevent major injuries. The glass spiderwebs from the point of impact into millions of tiny pieces so the glass is no longer sturdy. It's flexible enough to push with your hand and crack away.

Unlocking the door from the inside, I start to pull on the handle from the outside and give it my full force to pry it open. The snow is too thick, though, preventing the door from opening further. It'll only get worse with each passing minute. Whoever was driving this car really got themselves stuck.

I start digging the snow out and away from the bottom of the door closest to the hinges since the car is on an incline down into the bank. *Fuck it's freezing.* But I think I got enough moved to pry it open. Bracing the sole of my boot against the car, I grab the handle and yank as hard as I can, straightening my leg for leverage. Thankfully, it's enough force to peel the door open wide enough for me to slip inside.

No one in the backseat, but I see a head of ash blonde hair tied up in a bun on top in the driver's seat. Whoever it is, they're the only one in the car besides me, slumped over the steering wheel and the deflated airbag.

As soon as I move my torso over the center console, I press her shoulders back to get a better look at who it is and the damage done. It takes me a minute to see past the blood and scrapes, but then the pouty lips and doll-like eyes—even closed—jar my memory.

I can't fucking believe it.

Why is Mara Meyers crashed on the side of the road in a fucking snow-storm?

Chapter One

Mara-Senior Year

USED TO BE YOUNG-MILEY CYRUS

I hate potatoes. Everyone is obsessed with potatoes in any and all forms but I can't stand them. The starchy texture, the bitter flavor. Even smothered in cheese I don't like them. This is something you'd expect my boyfriend to know.

Bryce sets a tray of cafeteria food for me on the table. I asked him to get me lunch and he brought me an egg salad sandwich, a bag of chips, and tater tots. I'm fairly certain that I've told him several times I don't like potatoes. Yet here we are. Why am I dating this guy again?

"Are you ready for prom?" He asks me.

Oh, that's right, I don't want to show up to prom alone so he is better than nothing. And it's too close to find someone else.

"Yeah," I nod, "I got my dress last weekend. My mom ordered the corsage so make sure you pick it up on Saturday before you get to my house."

"I know, you've told me already." Bryce rolls his eyes which I choose to let go. Pick your battles and whatnot.

"And you reserved a limo already?"

"Clay is in charge of the limo," he answers. Hopefully, Clay has a better memory than Bryce otherwise we're all piling in the back of his truck. And that would not be good for my hair.

I just want everything to go smoothly. No mistakes, no setbacks, no problems. I want to go to my senior prom and have fun with my friends and maybe get a little drunk afterward. I want to wear my stunning blue A-line, off-the-shoulder dress and take beautiful pictures so I can relish in what's supposed to be the greatest night of my life forever. Is that too much to ask?

"Are you going to eat those?" Bryce points to the tater tots I've left untouched while I only ate three bites of the sandwich he got me.

"No," I shake my head and sit back as if personally offended by the food. "I don't like potatoes."

"What? Everyone likes tater tots."

Not me.

Without asking if he can have them, Bryce takes the tater tots in hand and rises from our lunch table heading to a table two rows over. I don't have to guess who he's going to see.

The mute kid sits at a table by himself reading a book. Jason Alder. No one has ever heard him speak. Some say he stopped talking at five years old, some say it was at seven, and others say he's never spoken a day in his life. Who knows. Either way, he isn't talking now and that makes him an outcast. Kind of weird, really, why doesn't he talk? If it weren't for his grades in school, I'd think he was a retard. But he aces all of his classes so I guess he's not a complete basket case.

Bryce approaches from behind and I strain my ears to hear the interaction.

"Hey, mute, how's it going?" Bryce claps Jason on the back. He doesn't take the seat next to him, Bryce leers over Jason in a dominant position to assert his superiority. But Jason doesn't even look up from his book to acknowledge Bryce. The only tell he gives of his annoyance is his hand on the table curling into a loose fist.

Jason has always been a scrawny guy but just as tall as Bryce. In the past year, he's filled out a bit in the shoulders making him look a little more broad. But it isn't much compared to Bryce who's been wrestling since he was five.

"What's the matter, you don't want to talk to me?" Bryce eggs him on, clearly up to something. Jason flips a page in his book.

"We're all dying to know what you have to say, idiot." Again, Jason doesn't make a move, though I think his fist tightens at the crude name. He's been called that long before anyone started calling him the Mute. "I mean, you read and shit, so you can't be completely brain-dead. But still, you got nothing to say." A statement, not a question. Bryce isn't interested in convincing the Mute to speak. He's looking for a reaction like all bullies do.

"Well, how about this," Bryce lowers himself slightly and a nervous itch works its way up my spine. "If you don't want to talk, might as well have a good reason. How about you give your mouth something else to do." As the last word falls from Bryce's mouth, he takes the hand holding the tater tots and shoves them into Jason's mouth. It's only then that Jason reacts, falling back off the bench as tater tots are smushed into his mouth. Caught off guard, his mouth opens for just a second in shock, but it's long enough for Bryce to get some food in, the rest is smashed into his face and falls over his black t-shirt.

Bryce is laughing at himself, and a few guys on the wrestling team laugh with him in solidarity. But no one else is laughing. It's pathetic that Bryce can only feel powerful when he makes others feel weak. It's weak that he picks on the easiest targets. What did he think would happen? The mute kid would suddenly decide to talk and fight back?

Jason jumps to his feet and squares off against Bryce with furious eyes that could practically melt his enemies into lava. But before things get even more out of hand, I jump in to pacify my fucking prom date.

"Bryce," I cut in, "it's not worth it."

"You think you're stronger than me?" He taunts Jason. "You think you're above the rest of us so you won't lower yourself to speak to us?" That's not true and he knows it.

"Leave him alone," I try again with the hope he'll walk away. "The weird mute kid isn't worth your time, Bryce. Besides, he's probably going to jerk off over having your hands on him later." I know, it's a low blow, but it's better than the two of them getting into a fistfight in the middle of the cafeteria. I know Bryce well enough to know a statement like that will satisfy his need to belittle someone.

Jason's younger brother is openly gay, so it's an easy shot and one that works the way I'd hoped. Bryce laughs at Jason's expense, then backs down feeling satisfied with the humiliation he doled out.

"Yeah, go dick off with your faggot brother," Bryce spits in Jason's direction. "Fucking sickos."

Bryce backs away and turns around, pulling me by the hand toward his wrestling buddies. I take one second to look at Jason and hope he's not too offended. But the hurt in his eyes is unmistakable. I'm not sure if it's the result of Bryce's actions, my insult, or both. Either way, he looks as disappointed in me as my mother would be if she'd heard the things I just said. And I feel that down to my core, every nerve ending on fire with regret.

I try to communicate *I'm sorry* with my eyes. I don't know if Jason gets it or not because his expression doesn't change before I turn back to Bryce, trying to ignore the pit in my stomach.

"That wasn't funny, Bryce," I chastise him before we reach his friends.

"The guy is a fucking weirdo," he answers as if that's a good enough reason to justify his actions. "If he wanted to be treated better, maybe he'd talk and tell us to fuck off."

I mumble under my breath, "As if that would help."

Those piercing steely gray eyes haunt me the rest of the day, I can't get the look Jason gave me out of my head. The gnawing sensation in my gut continues as well. In seventh period English, which is usually my favorite class. During volleyball practice after school when I should be focusing. In my Jeep on the way home. Even lying in my bed face up staring at the ceiling. I see his eyes and the utter despondency in them when I did nothing to stop Bryce. And worse, I piled on the shit.

I feel like such a bitch. I should have stood up for him, I should have defended him against Bryce and told him off for being a bully. But then I wouldn't have a prom date.

And...I'd be a social pariah just as much as him. I'm almost done with high school, done with this fucking backwater town. Maybe in my next life, far from here, I'll be a better person. Maybe then, I can be the person I want to be. Until then, I'm going to live out the rest of the school year as comfortably as I can, which means not drawing attention to myself before graduation. After that, I never have to think about this place again.

Or Jason.

I don't like being that person. I wish I'd taken a different path in school. I wish I'd made different friends or something. But I'm stuck in this cycle of trying to be accepted and regretting my actions every time. I'm trying to make it to the finish line unscathed.

I just didn't think I'd have to step on others to get there.

Chapter Two

Jason

SOMETHING IN THE **O**RANGE-**Z**ACH Bryan

She's barely dressed for a calm winter day let alone the fucking storm blowing down on us, right now. Jeans, a thermal shirt and a Sherpa coat over the top. Thankfully, she is wearing some heavy snow boots so at least her feet are warm. But based on how cold she was when I pulled her out of the car, she must have been out here for a little while before I found her.

Which brings me back to the main question: why the hell is she out here in this storm? Everyone knows this time of year the snow gets too heavy for traveling up the mountain. And everyone especially knows to be careful on the bridge crossing the river on the way up. Too many cars have slipped off the road and plummeted to their death if they don't know how to drive in this kind of weather. Mara has lived here most of her life, she should know all of this.

I curl her up beside me so her head rests on my shoulder as I drive back to the cabin. Knowing today would be the first major snowfall that would lock us onto our land for the next few months, I wouldn't have been able to get home if I'd lingered much longer at the hunting spot. There's no way Mara's car would have made it up the mountain, either. Where the hell was she going?

And more importantly, what the hell am I going to do with her? If I take her back to town now I'll be stuck down there leaving Dylan stranded and alone. So I'm taking her back to the cabin but there's no way I'll be able to get back down the mountain for a few months, not until the snow melts a bit. If previous years are any indication, we'll be stuck at the cabin until March.

It takes about twenty minutes, but I finally make it back to the cabin as the snowfall picks up, even the wind is howling now. I cradle Mara into my arms and head inside, stomping up the steps to alert Dylan that I'm home before barging in with an unconscious, bloodied woman in my arms.

The warmth of the kitchen is a stark relief to the bitter cold outside. *Bitter*, that's what the name Mara means in Hebrew. I like knowing things. I like the hidden meaning behind names. I don't remember when I looked it up, but I found the meaning of her name once. Kind of fitting, really. The rest of the world saw bubbly, outgoing preppy Mara. I saw the bitter, cold, hateful side of her.

Dylan stands at the stove getting something ready for dinner, smells like the savory spice of chili if I had to guess. When he hears the door open, he starts talking without looking around. "Bout time you got back, the storm is getting crazy. I thought you'd freeze your ass off out—." His sentence trails off when he looks over his shoulder to find me standing in the kitchen, covered in crusted snow, holding an unconscious body in my arms.

"What the actual fuck," he says in disbelief, taking the chili off the stove and setting it on a hot pad, ignoring the meal to focus his attention on the problem at hand. "Who the hell...? Is that Mara Meyers? What the hell is going on?"

Without answering, I stride into the living room and use my hip to push the sofa closer to the roaring fire in the stone fireplace that takes up a third of the wall. I lay Mara out on it to warm her up before locating the first aid kit in the downstairs bathroom. She may hate me for it when she wakes up—if she wakes up—but I decide to undress her down to her undergarments to check for other injuries. It looks like her face and arms took the brunt of the force as if she was shielding herself on impact. But that doesn't mean she didn't sustain other injuries.

Without asking him to, Dylan brings me a damp rag so I can start wiping away the blood on her skin. With the dried brown-red blood gone, I can see where she has actual injuries versus blood that seeped down her skin.

"What the fuck happened, Jason?" my brother asks me. His voice is harsh but worried, not accusatory. I pause to quickly sign *car crash* with my hands before resuming my work. I don't sign often, I don't communicate at all, really, but I'm sure he's going crazy not knowing.

I did some intense first aid research when we decided to live at the cabin full time after graduating. No cell service, no internet, and no way up or down the mountain this time of year. So I knew one of us had to figure this shit out in case of an emergency like this. The only thing is, I didn't expect to use those skills on someone else.

My mind jumps directly into fixer mode, combing through everything I've learned at break-neck speed as I work. I don't like taking classes or having someone stand in front of me with a PowerPoint. So I learned through reading, YouTube, and online articles. I could probably perform surgery if I had the right resources to teach me.

It appears that most of the injuries are on Mara's face and arms, as I suspected, a few cuts and bruises but nothing that will need stitches. There's a dark bruise on her pelvis where the seatbelt kept her from flying through the windshield. That's going to hurt in the morning and take the longest to heal. But as I feel her hip bones, it doesn't feel like anything is broken, same with her arms. I wrap her right arm in gauze which has the most bleeding, and put a bandage over the cut on her cheek. I hope it doesn't scar. Or maybe I do, she was always so vane in high school, maybe this will be a good lesson in humility.

But it's then that I notice her hair isn't the bright blonde it was in high school, her nails are natural, no paint or any of that fake stuff. She's a little curvier, too, she was always stick-straight in high school. I think I prefer her like this, a little meat on her bones suits her feisty personality better than the scrawny girl I once knew.

I don't even think she's wearing makeup. I don't think I saw her step out in public without makeup the entire time I knew her in school. But, then again, I haven't seen her in two years. A lot can change in that time.

I'm a perfect example.

After the treatment she and her friends gave me in high school, I decided I needed to be able to defend myself if I was going to continue my bout of silence. I have no intention of talking any time soon. So I started lifting weights, training my body, and even taught myself kickboxing. Occasionally, Dylan will spar with me so I can get some practice with something besides a punching bag.

One thing is for sure, no one is going to push me around and humiliate me ever again. The days of being the weak mute kid are gone.

"She's freezing, man," Dylan points out. The problem is, her clothes are still freezing too. I lay them out on the ground by the fire to warm them up before wrapping Mara in a blanket that was hanging off the back of the couch. I tuck her in like a burrito before stripping off my wet outer layers and nestle in behind her on the couch, encompassing her in my warmth. She needs to retain body heat. Honestly, putting her in a hot shower would probably be quicker, but that risks waking her up with the jolt of water. As funny as it might be to watch her flail about in any other scenario, I don't think she can take much more tonight.

I still don't know how she ended up on the mountain to begin with.

I face Mara so our chests meet and bury her face in my neck, the more contact I give her, the quicker I can bring her body temperature up. It's a strangely intimate position, but, whatever works, I guess.

She's so small in my hold, I've been with petite women before but they're usually conscious, I never let anyone sleepover and I don't sleep over either. Asleep and broken, Mara feels like a fragile doll. Too bad that fragile doll has the heart of a demon and the mouth of a witch. Ya know, I kind of like her like this, unable to speak. It's only now that she's unconscious and unaware I'm holding her that I realize she's not as big and bad as she makes herself out to be.

I wonder when she got back to town. Dylan does most of the shopping cause I try to stay as far away from civilization as possible. She could've been back for months for all I know. And I wouldn't put it past Dylan not to tell me since he knows I hate her guts.

Yet here I am, trying to save her from hypothermia. If there is a God, he has a sick sense of humor to land her at my doorstep.

"Are you staying down here tonight?" Dylan leans over the back of the sofa to ask me. I nod. "Okay. Come get me if you need anything. And let me know when she wakes up. I'm sure she'll have some questions. Mainly why she's not wearing any clothes."

I get a sick sense of delight thinking about the fit she's going to throw when she wakes up in her underwear. Appearance first, safety later. That seems like her style.

"Night, brother." With that, Dylan heads up the stairs to his bedroom and turns off the lights in the process.

Under the glow of the roaring fire, I tighten my hold on Mara and close my eyes. This isn't Mara Meyers I'm holding, it's a girl in need. It's not my high school tormentor, it's a woman I found on the road in the snow. And she needs me.

"I have a fucking faggot and a mute for sons, Lois," my father screams at Mom in the kitchen while Dylan and I sit on the porch listing to the bullshit our father is spewing. "What the hell do you want me to say? That I'm happy with our life? That I'm okay with this shit? Neither one of them are right. Maybe I should send them to the cabin this winter to become men. No help from anyone except themselves."

The look Dylan and I exchange says it all. That actually doesn't sound too bad. *At least we'd be away from him.*

Mom uses her passive, tender voice that she always uses to pacify our father. "They have school, Phil. They need their education."

"Fine." I hear his thunderous steps get louder as they head our way. "Then maybe I'll toughen them up myself."

"Phil," Mom shouts. I hear her little footsteps follow our father toward us and jump to my feet to stand between the son of a bitch and my brother. He's plenty tough from wrestling, but they kicked him off the team this year when they found out he is gay. Not that he was interested in anyone on the team. But they don't give a shit. He doesn't think the same as them so he's a threat, a danger.

Our father tried to get me to wrestle too, or play football, or baseball. Hell, he even tried to get me to play golf with him, but I don't want to do anything that requires me to be around people. I started using the weights and bench press he keeps in the garage, but even that isn't enough for him.

The door flies open so hard I'm surprised it doesn't come off the hinges. As soon as our father locks eyes on me, smoke comes out of his nostrils. He drops the cigarette he was smoking inside and smashes it under his boot. He's preparing for a face-off. He's been waiting for a reason to hit me again and I just gave him one.

"What the fuck do you think you're doing?" Our father grits out in a strained voice. All the years of smoking make him sound like rocks in a blender now.

When I don't answer—like he knew I wouldn't—he takes a step closer. "You trying to stand up to me, huh? Trying to be the man, *now? Protect your fucked up brother?"*

He's not fucked up. Everything about him is completely normal except his taste in partners. Which, to be honest, isn't that weird in this day and age. But our town is a decade behind the rest of the world and they don't appreciate him leapfrogging into modern relationships.

"So what are you doing, boy? Answer me when I ask you a fucking question." His voice raises a notch in volume with each word until he's yelling at me. But that's never scared me before and it sure as hell doesn't scare me now.

"You fucking retard." My father swings his fist at my head and I stumble, but I remember a few things from my brief time in sports and tackle him with my shoulder to his abdomen, arms around the waist, trying to take him down. Even though I've gotten a bit bigger since picking up weightlifting, he's still bigger than me. Offensive lineman in high school. Probably could have gone to college on scholarship for it if he hadn't knocked up our mom.

He's caught off guard by my attack which causes him to stumble, but it doesn't take long for the bastard to shove me to the ground and stomp on my chest.

Mom starts hollering, crying for our dad to stop. But when he's like this, there's no stopping the rampage. The sad thing is he's not even drunk. I've heard about dads who get violent when they drink. But at least there's an excuse there, a way to stop it. Our dad was just born mean, bitter, violent.

He shoves me down the front steps with his steel-toed boot and I turn into the fetal position and hold my bruised rib cage hoping that seeing me wounded like a dog on the ground is enough to satisfy his taste for blood and misery.

"You thought you could hide behind your brother?" Our father turns on Dylan, clearly not satiated yet.

"No, I—." Dylan loses the power of speech when our father charges for him next.

Panic sets in. I see the pure terror in Dylan's eyes, hear Mom plead for our father to stop, crying in between sucking in lungfuls of air she can't hold onto. And my chest caves with the weight of it all. I can't see them hurting. He can hurt me all he wants, but not them.

So I do the only thing I can think of.

Chapter Three

Mara

SIREN-PEARL JAM

I was cold.

But now I'm warm.

The snow bank was coming for me as if I were the stationary object and it was a monster about to consume me. I didn't want to die, but death was just waiting to claim my life.

Is that where I am now? Is Heaven warm and comforting?

Or maybe I'm in the fires of Hell. I probably deserve it. I didn't do enough good in my lifetime to deserve Heaven.

Restraint, that's the next thing I feel. Something is wrapped around me to keep me from moving. A steel band locks my arms in front of me where my hands are laid on something hard yet soft. Not squishy soft, more like soft to the touch, cozy fabric lining a structured form. And there's a smell to it as well, I can't quite place it but something invites me in like a crackling campfire and evergreens. I've never been camping but that's how I imagine it would smell. Peaceful. Cool but warm.

Then the ache sets into my limbs and my cheeks. My pelvis throbs with a full pain spanning from hip bone to hip bone. My cheek is on fire. And my arms are a myriad of different sensations, mainly itchy.

I finally open my eyes but it takes a minute for them to adjust to the glow of the dark room to make out a thermal Henley on a hard chest, a bearded jawline, and pink lips. Finally, the realization that someone is holding me snaps into place.

Someone I don't know.

I squirm out of their hold only to land on the floor wrapped in a wool blanket that I clutch to my chest as soon as I see I'm only in my bra and underwear. The drop to the floor electrified every injury I've sustained making me whimper in agony.

"What the fuck, what the fuck, *what the fuck*!" I don't know what's going on but I need to get away, call for help, and figure out where I am.

I try to rise to my feet but the pain across my pelvis makes me wince as I stand. I don't fucking care. I have to push through the pain to save myself.

Did someone kidnap me?

I start for the door but a strong arm takes me by the waist and pulls me back until we are back to chest. I try to thrash and yell because it's my only option. I won't go down without a fight even if it's a pathetic attempt. But I'm not exactly at my strongest.

I expect my kidnapper to say something, try to calm me down or taunt me. But he remains silent as if my pain and fear hold no sway over him.

"Let me go!" I try again, even though that's never worked in the movies.

To my surprise, it does. He spins me so fast I can't see before I'm seated on the couch and the man stands before me backlit by the enormous fireplace.

This must be Hell and the Devil has come to collect.

But the face of the devil becomes clearer and it's somehow familiar. I don't recognize the beard or the broad shoulders, but the stormy eyes and dirty blond hair trigger a memory I can't pinpoint. The eyes especially, they strike a familiar chord I can't place, like a song you recall but don't know the words to. They bind me in shocked silence, I have no control over my movements when they are locked on me. I'm lost to the storm within those irises.

Then it dawns on me, and I'm one hundred percent sure I'm in Hell now.

"Jason?" I ask quietly, afraid to voice my suspicion. "Jason Alder?"

My suspicion is confirmed when Dylan Alder, who looks so much like his brother but with light brown hair and smaller set shoulders, bounds down the stairs in a pair of banana print pajama pants with his shoulder raised as though he's preparing for a fight. If I recall correctly, he's a year younger than Jason and I. But he got his GED the summer after we graduated so he didn't have to complete his senior year.

I'd heard the two brothers moved to their family cabin in the woods after that, after the death of their parents. Slowly, my surroundings filter into view. Wood floors haphazardly covered in Persian rugs. Log cabin walls of a darker stained wood bearing only a few pieces of art and two mounted deer skulls with antlers intact. And a never-ending darkness beyond the iron-paned windows that swallow the light whole.

Then there is the extra-large fireplace made of uneven stones giving it a look somewhere between woodsy and cottage-core. The fire inside was small in comparison to the size of the hearth. You could fit an entire bonfire in there, no problem.

I'm in their cabin on the mountain about forty minutes outside of town. How the hell did I get here?

"What the fuck is going on?" I blurt in a furious tone that only feels like it's skimming the surface of my rage. "Why am I here?"

"Jason found you in a car crash on the road," Dylan spoke up. I take it his brother still doesn't talk. "I wasn't there so I don't know all the details.

He brought you back in the truck. The snow is too heavy to get down the mountain now. You've got some pretty bad wounds from the accident."

That explains the pain over my pelvis, the seat belt must have done that. And the airbag must be the cause of the pain in my face and arm. It starts coming back to me, driving, music playing way too loud. A deer in the road I couldn't see because the snow was falling too heavily. Losing control of the car. *Bang. Crash.* Darkness. I must have been knocked out on impact.

It's then I realize I've been bandaged from my face to my arm. I start scanning my body, taking stock of my limbs and checking for other injuries. Did they do this?

"In case you're wondering," Dylan pulls my eyes back up, "your clothes were freezing cold and we had to check you for other injuries. Didn't need you bleeding out on us. You might have gotten hypothermia if we left you in those clothes much longer. We needed to get you warm. But we left your underwear on, we haven't seen the goods."

There's a teasing lilt to Dylan's voice so I respond with a snarky tone of my own, "Oh, well thank you for that courtesy. What a shame you didn't get to 'see the goods.'"

"Your parts don't do much for me," Dylan raises a single brow then winks.

"What a relief," I roll my eyes then turn my fury on Jason who's still standing in front of the fire glaring at me with harsh, bushy brows. "How about you? Is that why you were wrapped around me? Can't get a woman any other way so you have to hold her while she's unconscious?"

Dylan snorts by the stairs then buries his mouth in his hand. "That's funny. Jason gets more tail than most of the guys in town. Have you seen him?" Dylan gestures to his brother like he's proud of that fact.

I only allow myself a split second to look and take note of him, but I can't deny that Jason looks very different from the last time I saw him in high school. His shoulders are broader, he certainly packed on the muscles, if what I felt in the brief moments before I came back to consciousness is any indication. His hair is styled in a shaggy cut, significantly longer than his short beard that's slightly past five o'clock shadow. If I remember correctly, he had a buzz cut and no facial hair in high school.

Then again, I looked pretty different back then, too.

I can see why women would be attracted to him at first glance, but he's still the Mute. I find it hard to believe he can pick up women without speaking to them.

"Still mute, I see," I cross my arms over my chest with the blanket wrapped in each fist to keep "the goods" covered. Jason doesn't even dignify my insult with a blink or a twitch. I would have expected that name to ruffle some feathers, even years after high school.

"When can I go home?" I turn back to Dylan since he's the only other sane person in the room...I think.

"Ummm, I don't know, probably early March."

"*March?*" I burst. "No, that can't happen. I have a life I have to get back to. I can't stay here all winter. There has to be some way down."

"Sorry, cupcake, no way up, no way down. We stocked up for the winter. Jason was out hunting, that's how he passed your car in the snow. And even then, it was probably getting too dicey for the snowmobile. Can't even use that anymore."

"What are you supposed to do if one of you gets severely injured?" I'm grasping at straws, anything to find a way out of this.

"Jason knows first aid, he's the one that tended to your wounds."

"And if he gets hurt and you don't know what to do?" Another desperate straw.

"Then he dies, I guess." I'm caught off guard by how bluntly and emotionlessly Dylan speaks about his brother's hypothetical death. "I know you don't want to stay here any more than we want you here, but there's no way out of this. Whatever brought you to the mountain tonight sealed your fate, cupcake."

I'm too depressed and in denial to chastise Dylan about that degrading nickname.

Before I can say anything else, Jason storms past me toward his brother on the stairs without saying a word or even looking at me. Clearly, he's still pissed with me about how he was treated in high school.

Get over it, dude, high school sucks for everyone.

"Where's he going?"

"Probably to his room," Dylan answers. "Why don't you come on up, we have a spare room you can use while you're here."

Do I really want to accept that my fate is sealed? I hesitate a moment, staring into the orange-yellow flames in the hearth before I decide I need a decent night's sleep to clear my head and find a solution. There has to be some way off the mountain before the snow melts.

I rise and follow the men, still wrapped in the wool blanket to conceal my body, though it seems they've already seen what lies beneath so the only thing I'm really holding on to is my pride.

I follow Jason and Dylan up a set of stairs to a landing where I'm met with four identical oak doors, two on the wall opposite the stairs and the others at both ends of the landing.

With a raised hand to point at each door, Dylan directs me. "That'll be your room," pointing at one of the two doors that share a wall. "It's next to the bathroom. Mine is over here," he points to the left, "and that one is Jason's room," he points to the right. "If you need anything let us know, I'm going back to bed. I need my beauty sleep."

"Wait," I call before either of them can disappear behind their doors. "What am I supposed to wear?" I shuffle beneath the blanket drawing attention to the fact that I'm still without clothing.

Dylan exchanges a look with his brother before he answers. "I think some girls that have visited Jason have left items here over the years. Maybe he has something for you. Otherwise, your clothes will be dry and warm in the morning." He smirks in my direction, then at Jason, and I don't hide the insult in my expression. I'm not sure if he's trying to tease me, Jason, or both of us. But I'm deeply offended that he wants me to wear some skank's clothes.

My jaw drops but that's all I can get out before he walks into his room and shuts the door. I turn to Jason but he follows his brother's lead and shuts the door without giving me another glance.

I stand there wrapped in the blanket a moment longer, dumbfounded, before refusing to stand in my humiliation any longer and step into the guest room he pointed out.

It's small but nice. The room is rather cozy, actually. A full size bed with Pendleton blankets over a white quilt. No filigree such as endless throw pillows and trinkets. The solid wood dresser and matching hopechest are bare. The only sign of life in the room are the two paintings on either side of the window depicting two black and white faceless bodies leaning toward each other with foreheads bowed and hands outstretched. If the window were out of the picture, the two images would look like the people are reaching for one another.

But upon closer inspection, I see they are charcoal drawings, a mixture of harsh lines and precise blending on the paper. Simple black frames enclose the images beneath a layer of glass. Something about the pictures makes me feel sad. I can't put my finger on it but it feels like the two people are forever separated. Maybe it's the presence of the window and it would seem happier if the images were connected. But I have to imagine whoever put them there did so intentionally.

I don't know if these are the softest sheets I've ever slept in, or if I'm just exhausted and broken. I feel like I've taken a beating. Climbing the stairs was more work than I would ever let on, but it was worth it to lay down in a cloud of a bed and rest my head. I must have whiplash too considering how damaged my neck feels. The only time I've ever felt anything like that was on the fastest rollercoaster at an amusement park in Washington. As soon as we made the first big drop, the rollercoaster took off at break-neck speed around a bunch of twists and loopty-loops. My neck was sore for a week after that. I haven't been on a rollercoaster since.

I think about what led me to the mountain tonight, to that bridge that has been the cause of so much death in our town. Part of me wonders if I should have died in that car crash, maybe my body was meant to freeze in the snow and find an early grave beneath the winter until spring revealed my final resting place. Maybe Jason finding me was never supposed to happen.

I have to believe that him finding me was a mistake God didn't account for because the alternative is that I was meant to be here. And I don't want to be here. I don't want to face him. I don't want to confront my past. And I don't want to see those disappointed eyes again.

So I close my eyes and let my body drift to sleep because I know I have to face it all in the morning.

There must be a way out of this.

Chapter Four

Jason

RICHARD PETTY- BILLY STRINGS

The clock beside my bed says 6:03 am. It's still dark outside.

Of all the people that could have ended up at my doorstep, why did it have to be her? Why did I have to choose to go hunting yesterday? Why didn't the deer come out so I would have had a reason to come back sooner and maybe then I'd never be in this situation. I can't believe I have to suffer all winter with Mara fucking Meyers in my house. I like the solitude all winter, I don't like people, but I already know she's going to cause trouble. On the nights when I wish I could go find pussy, it's going to be a little too tempting to take what I want, even if I don't want it from her.

What would she think if she knew her friend from highschool gave it up so easily in a bathroom stall at The Sawmill? The same girl who always laughed at my expense in highschool didn't need much more than a head tilt before she impaled herself on my cock last year. I doubt Mara would be pleased to learn that.

It took a long time to learn, but I eventually figured out that if I wasn't going to talk, I needed to be proficient in every other aspect of my life to compensate for it. Be the biggest and strongest motherfucker so no one would mess with me. Build the best business so no one could argue with my skills—or my prices, for that matter. Be the best lay any of these girls has ever seen so they'd talk about the size of my dick, not my lack of speech.

I even became the best at pool after losing a game a few years ago. I needed to perfect every area of my life, then people would talk about everything except my silence.

Mara was living in California all this time, so I heard, so she probably didn't know any of this. Maybe that's a good thing. Let her believe she can push me around like she used to and then shock her into silence when I'm not the weak, pathetic kid she knew years ago.

Let her believe what she wants, her opinion means nothing more than my eventual entertainment when she's proven wrong.

When I finally pull my ass downstairs, I notice her clothes are still by the fireplace that's nothing more than faint embers now. I take a log off the pile stacked beside the hearth and throw it on so the house warms up a bit. Then I take Mara's clothes upstairs and drop them in a messy pile by her door. The last thing I need is her walking around in her underwear. I was too focused on my first aid training last night to really let my mind wander, but her body is beautiful. If I detach the person from the body, it might even be sexy.

Next, I start the coffee pot. Who needs pre-workout when you have coffee? As soon as it's ready, I take the cup of dark fuel to the garage where the gym is set up. It's shoulders and arms day, *thank god*, because I have some pent-up rage I need to work through. And I don't think taking it out on Mara is the right way to do it. Dylan would never allow it. He's too nice, in my opinion.

I start with some bench presses, three sets of eight reps at my current max weight of two hundred pounds. I haven't been able to surpass two hundred pounds in almost a month. I'm convinced it's mental, there's no reason my body would get stuck at one weight. I just have to work through it. But I don't want to injure anything that might prevent me from getting work done, so I start with my usual two hundred pounds and hope the tell-tale relief of being ready for another ten pounds settles in my muscles.

Sure enough, it's there, but just barely. After the first set of eight, I add a five pound plate to either side and settle back on the bench beneath the barbell. Hands braced evenly apart, I heave the bar off the supports and rest it over my chest.

I should really have Dylan out here to spot me.

With a huge intake of air and gritted teeth, I think about Mara calling me Mute last night and the fire in her eyes when she realized I'd undressed her. I feel a twinge of satisfaction at her discomfort. Using that as fuel for my energy, I force my elbows to straighten and lift the weight straight into the air parallel to my bare chest. I exhale a weighted breath of relief and lower the bar back down, careful to keep my wrists steady. I repeat the process four more times before I have to stop and rest. I'm disappointed with myself for not completing the set, but I did it, I hit a new personal record. *It's about damn time.*

I finished my last set only completing five more reps and moved on to the other exercises in my workout for the day: some lateral and front raises, upright rows, and a few others to target specific muscles. I finish with some stretches to prevent tearing and head back inside to find Dylan already seated at the table drinking his own coffee. He's still dressed in his ridiculous pajamas but now he's covered with a white shirt.

I pour myself another cup of coffee—I swear it runs through my fucking veins at this point—and start on breakfast. I have no idea when Mara will wake up but I make extra for her just in case. And if it's cold when she deigns to rise from her beauty sleep, so be it.

I'm plating the eggs and sausage onto two plates when the stairs creak alerting us to the shedevil's presence right before Mara appears at the base of the stairs in her clothes from last night.

She takes a moment to process what's before her, Dylan at the table and me cooking in the kitchen. When her eyes drift down my chest, I realize I'm still shirtless. But putting a shirt on now would feel like a retreat or submission.

I pull another plate from the cabinet and load more food onto it for her before placing all three plates and sets of forks on the table. Taking my seat, I nod my head toward the empty chair in front of the remaining plate of food indicating for Mara to sit. That's the most communication I've given her since her arrival, even if it is nonverbal. She takes the direction well and sits.

A minute into my breakfast, she says with a note of horror in her voice. "Oh my god, no one's going to take your food. Slow down."

Why can't she just say thanks for the food and leave me alone?

I narrow my eyes on her with a clear message, *don't talk to me.* Then continue eating until I'm done while everyone else is only halfway through.

"Thanks for bringing my clothes up for me," Mara says to Dylan. But Dylan looks completely clueless.

"Wasn't me," he says, darting his eyes to me. Mara's eyes follow, conveying her reluctance to thank me, and maybe a bit of surprise that I'd do something nice for her.

Without giving me the same appreciation, she lowers her eyes back to her food looking a little worse for wear. Can she really not bring herself to say something nice to me? Maybe she's ashamed. I don't know and I don't give a fuck.

"So how do I get home?" Mara speaks up again, breaking the uncomfortable silence I was thoroughly enjoying.

Dylan and I exchange looks, his worried, mine exasperated. With just my eyes I try to say *this bitch isn't getting it.*

Dylan translates more politely, "Um, there's no way to get down the mountain, Mara. I'm afraid you're stuck here."

She looks between the two of us as if the answer to all her problems rests somewhere between us.

"No." Denial. "There has to be a way."

Nope.

I stand and head for the front door covering the space between the table and the foyer in a few long strides. As soon as I pull the door open with considerable strength, the cold winter blows inside with a few flurries coating the floor and ruffling our hair. My message is clear. *If you're so desperate to leave, then go. The only way down is through the snow and you won't survive it.*

Mara meets my stare with one of her own, all hell breaking loose in her eyes. "Very funny."

I just wave a hand like a fancy butler to drive the point home. She can freeze to death for all I care.

Then why did you save her? My subconscious antagonizes me.

Her eyes only narrow in response.

I slam the door shut then take my long sleeve shirt off the back of the chair and pull it over my torso with a little more force than necessary.

"What am I supposed to do?" Mara addresses Dylan again, her only advocate. But her efforts at appealing to the sympathetic one are pointless, he can't get her home any more than I can.

"Help with day-to-day stuff around here, I guess."

When Mara drops her fork on the plate with a clang, I can't help but snicker.

"What exactly did you have in mind?" The sarcasm isn't lost on either of us. But before Dylan can answer, I stomp to the kitchen and pull out our mom's cookbook, flip to the page I have in mind, and slam it on the table beside her plate of unfinished food.

Mara scans the withered page, considers what I'm asking, then shoots those hazel eyes at me incredulously. "Bread? You want me to be your fucking cook?"

She might think it's because she's a woman, but really it's because cooking takes too much time out of our days. If she were to maintain more of the household tasks, Dylan and I would have more time to work.

After moving to the cabin, Dylan and I started a fabrication business. We mainly build custom firearms for guys with money across the country. But we also take on the occasional odd jobs such as custom parts for cars or other specific mechanic requirements. Since we don't have internet in the winter, we take all of our orders in the fall and when we run out of work to do towards the end of the season, we design new pieces to post for sale when spring rolls around.

"If I'm stuck here I'm not going to be a fucking kitchen wench for you." Even though she'd also be cooking for Dylan, Mara directs her insults at me. "Give me something else to do. I don't mind helping out around here, but I'm not going to be a slave to house chores just because I'm a woman."

That's it. I'm sick of her bullshit and disrespect. If I'd known she would be this much of a pain in the ass, I might have left her in her car in the snow bank.

Before she can protest, I hoist Mara over my shoulder fireman style and head out the back door toward the shop. She kicks and screams the whole way as if she's afraid I'm going to feed her to a bear. I don't give a fuck that my sneakers are getting wet. I don't give a fuck how cold it is. I barge my way through the ever-growing pile of snow outside until I reach the shop.

Once inside, I lower Mara back to her feet amidst her anger and protests. As soon as she's steady, she slams a fist into my chest and yells, "What the fuck was that?"

Taking her forcefully by the shoulders, I spin her around and point at the CNC machine in the shop. She looks between the stainless steel machine and me trying to decipher my meaning.

"You want me to operate it?" I nod in response. "I don't know how to use that. What does it do?"

That's what I thought.

So I point back toward the house just as Dylan catches up to us, looks like he took the time to put on his boots.

"You're saying that since I don't know how to use this I have to cook and clean? That's so misogynistic."

I'm so fed up with her and her whining. You'd think she'd be a little more grateful she's alive and we're even willing to share our precious resources with her this winter.

I take a snow shovel off the wall and shove it toward her instead. Fine, she doesn't want to cook? Then she can slave away in the freezing cold. As long as she's contributing.

To my surprise, Mara takes the shovel and storms outside even though she doesn't have boots on. She goes back up to the house, grabs a coat off the wall and her boots from the fireplace, then gets to work shoveling snow outside.

I wonder how long it will take before she realizes it's pointless. The storm is going to last all winter long.

And, as it appears, so will her temper.

Two hours later, I'm in the shop working but I can see Mara's little dark form working away through the window. The speaker on the wall is playing "Richard Petty" by Billy Strings.

I take a break from working on the Damascus steel 1911 and head inside, up the stairs, and into my room. I open the closet door and start looking on the floor where I think I threw some clothes a girl left here once. Sure enough, there's a pair of jeans and a thong down there. If I remember correctly, she wore one of my shirts home and just the shirt cause we couldn't find the clothes. Found them the next morning on the balcony. Oops.

Pausing, I consider that she's going to need more than just a pair of jeans and underwear, so I take a few long sleeved t-shirts and flannels off their hangers to add to the pile. I fold the clothes into a neat stack on the hope chest at the end of Mara's bed. Then I remember what's in the hope chest and hesitate. I haven't opened it since we first moved in. I don't want the reminder she's not here.

But...I also don't want Mara walking around in nothing but my shirts for the next four and a half months. An image pops into my head of her on my balcony wearing one of my flannels that barely covers her ass, hair spilling down her back. My stomach contracts, my dick twitches in my pants, and then I immediately push that image out of my head.

God, this is going to be a long winter.

"I don't think she'd mind." Dylan's voice sounds over my shoulder. He's been around me so much, he knows how to read my body language since it's my only form of communication.

I lift the lid on the hope chest to see the clothes our mom stored here for our visits when we were younger. There's a few tank tops and jackets, some shorts for the summer, and some undergarments. I never really wanted to think about her wearing shit like that but I guess everyone has to.

"Unless you'd rather she walk around naked all winter." I shoot Dylan a sardonic glare. That's the last thing I need, not that it would bother Dylan much.

There's not much in there, but it's better than wearing the same two outfits everyday, I guess.

I head back out to the front drive that's now only two inches of fresh snow that's fallen since Mara cleared it. She's gradually working her way down the driveway but her work is getting covered in fresh flakes. The snow is falling softly right now, but it's enough to leave its mark on the ground.

What? Does she think she can shovel her way back to town? It's a forty minute drive. It'll take her two weeks to get down there at this rate. She'll freeze to death in the process.

Fucking stubborn woman.

I walk into her peripheral vision. I know she sees me but she doesn't stop shoveling so I take the bar of the shovel in my grip to cease her pointless pursuit. Her colorful eyes turn to me looking a little weary but just as fierce as I'm used to. A jerk of my head toward the house is the only gesture I offer. She looks from me to the house, catches my meaning, then goes back to shoveling.

"You told me to shovel, so that's what I'll do."

Stubborn. Woman.

I step directly in front of her to block the trail she's making in the snow and lift my chin toward the house once more. If she refuses me again, fine, I'll leave it.

But she doesn't. She huffs an irritated breath that puffs white into the air and starts marching back to the house without waiting for me. If she would just stop assuming everything I do is out of malice, maybe this would be a little more bearable. But that would be too easy. And it's not in Mara's nature to roll over and submit, anyway.

I pass her at the front door to lead her up the stairs, her quiet footsteps so much softer than mine in my heavy boots. I'm honestly surprised she followed me without more of a fight.

I lead her into her bedroom to stand next to the open hope chest. Mara's eyes travel over the array of clothes in the hope chest and then to the clothing on the bed. The fight in her eyes disappears when she realizes it's for her, that she won't have to go all winter in the same pair of underwear.

Though she could just go commando...

No. That's a terrible idea.

Then Mara's features shift and she's angry again. What else is new?

"Are all these clothes from your one-night stands?" Of course she thinks that. I just roll my eyes in response. I'm done trying to be nice.

Then Dylan steps into the room. "So you gave them to her after all."

"Gave me his past lover's clothes? Yeah, I'm not wearing those."

"What?" The look on Dylan's face almost makes me smirk. Almost. "No. Ew. These were our mom's clothes."

The shift that takes place in Mara's expression is both priceless and heartwarming. She sees the error in her accusations but also the gesture in my actions. She locks eyes with me and I can't help the little pang in my heart at the sight. I don't want this to be anything it isn't. I'm just giving her clothes for the time she's here. I expect her to leave them behind when she goes home after the snow melts. We gave away most of our parents' things after they died, save a few of Mom's things like her sewing machine that she made so many of our clothes on, or the rocking chair she kept in her room after Dylan and I were too old to rock to sleep. That now sits in Dylan's room.

"You're letting me wear your mom's things?" She says in disbelief. "Thank you." I nod my head in response. That's the nicest she's ever been. But I know it'll be short lived.

"She left them here for family trips when we were younger. Our dad only used it as a hunting cabin the decade before he died so these are from when she was younger and a little thinner. They might still be a bit big for you but better than nothing."

I walk out of the room without warning and thankfully both Dylan and Mara follow without me having to indicate for them to. I stalk downstairs to the sewing table I moved up here when we sold the house in town and open the lid to bring the machine out of its hiding place. I nestled the table beside the front door as a place to drop shit when we walk in like keys and stuff. But maybe it can be used properly now.

When I stick my hand out toward the machine, my question is clear: do you know how to use this?

"I took home ec in school. I think I remember some of it, if you're willing to let me take in some of her things, I think I can make them fit. I won't cut anything, don't worry." She waves her hands in front of her as if that can ease my worry. But I wasn't worried about it.

The wheels are turning in her head as she stares at the machine, I swear I can almost see them work. After another glance at me, Mara walks into the kitchen and opens the refrigerator to examine what's inside. Dylan and I both watch her with curiosity. *What the hell is she doing?*

She takes some cheese out of the fridge and collects the bread from the counter before turning the oven on and moving the cast iron pan over the burner.

"I don't know how to make much," she confesses. "How does grilled cheese sound for lunch?"

Chapter Five

Mara

RIVERS AND ROADS-THE HEAD AND THE HEART
I can't believe he's letting me wear his mother's clothes. I don't know how they died, but the way Dylan talks about her is like she was an angel to them, untouchable and perfect, precious. Must be nice to have been that close to your mom. Mine has been knee-deep in disassociation methods for as long as I can remember. Operating on the conveyor belt of small town high society.

Jason pulls a jar of tomato soup they canned off the shelf and dumps it into a pot next to the pan I made the sandwiches on. I've never worked with cast iron before, but when I almost put soap on it, he grabbed the skillet from me and showed me that it just needs a good scrub under warm water. Dylan made a point to tell me they need to be cleaned while they're still hot.

That's genius, it was so easy to clean. Why don't more people use these?

We eat in silence for a bit, no one says anything about the generous gestures of the day, and no one acknowledges that Jason was nice to me or that I cooked when I said I wouldn't.

I didn't put much thought into it before I sprung into action. I just felt the weight of his kind offering and felt like I needed to return the gesture.

The first thing that came to mind was to cook for him, even if it was just grilled cheese, one of two things I know how to make.

"So they didn't teach you to cook in home ec but they taught you to sew?" Dylan finally breaks the silence, which appears to be his main job in this house.

"They certainly tried to," I answer, "but I either burnt or undercooked everything."

"Did you follow directions?"

"Ya know," I rub my finger on my chin in contemplation, "maybe that's where I went wrong."

Jason snickers to himself adjacent to me at the table before spooning another mouthful of soup to his lips. Without him saying it, I know exactly what he's thinking. *Yeah, you have a hard time following directions, don't you?*

Amazing how much I can decipher from his mind without him having to say a word.

I shoot him a glare and point with my spoon. "Don't say it." Even though he obviously won't say anything.

I'm taken aback by how natural this feels. Two hours ago I wanted to rip their heads off if it would get me the hell out of this cabin. And while I'd still like to go home to my skincare routine and clothes that fit me, I don't want to rip their heads off right now.

Then it occurs to me: I don't have any makeup. Then again, I didn't need makeup for my reason for being on the mountain last night. But still, I would like to have some in the next four months, I'm sure.

Even if I'm not going anywhere and I'm only seeing the same two men for the foreseeable future, putting on makeup always makes me feel more prepared for the day, like putting on my helmet and grabbing my shield. It wasn't about protection, it was about preparedness and self care.

"Oh no," I blurt as another realization dawns on me. "Do you have an extra toothbrush?" I absolutely cannot go the next four months without brushing my teeth.

Dylan and Jason chuckle between themselves before Dylan eases my concern. "Don't worry, I think I have extra in the bathroom upstairs. You can use my toothpaste that's in there as long as you keep the cap clean. I can't stand messy toothpaste. That's why Jason and I couldn't share one growing up."

Jason's answering smirk makes me think he might have done that on purpose. There's a devilish gleam in his eye.

"I have to go feed the animals in the barn," Dylan announces. Do you want to come with me? Meet the crew?"

I perk up. "I'd love that." I hope they have goats. I don't know why they would, but I love goats.

After stuffing my feet back into the boots I wore last night (I'm really thankful I chose to wear them, now), Dylan leads me to the ancient looking barn where they keep their animals. The wood is bleached of all color by the sun. Under the cloudy sky, the wood looks especially gray. But the barn holds a charm to it that I'd expect in a *Little House on the Prairie* episode. It even has one of those little windows on the second level. I think it's for loading or unloading hay, at least I think I saw that in a movie. Who knows.

The barn takes advantage of every inch of space it can. From tools that resemble torture devices hanging from the walls, to vertical storage solutions. I saw their canned goods in the pantry when I was looking for food to make lunch, but metal shelves lined against every open wall contain either more jars filled with food, canning jars and lids, or the tools necessary for it. When Dylan catches me taking it all in and trying to figure out what all the food is, he explains they canned it all themselves, most of it coming from their garden, and some of the jars being two years old, from the first time they took up the practice.

It seems like a good system, they can reuse the jars and supplies over and over again. Once you make the initial investment, it pays for itself.

Then we move onto the animals kept in the numerous stalls lining the center of the barn. They have one horse named Bessie (the irony of her being a horse instead of a cow is not lost on me), five chickens, two pigs named Forrest and Jenny, and to my absolute delight, one goat named Athena.

"Jason named Bessie and Athena," Dylan relayed to me. "I named Forrest and Jenny. *Forrest Gump* was my favorite movie for nearly two years. I couldn't get enough of it."

"What took its place?"

"*Breakfast Club*!" Dylan answers enthusiastically. "I'm addicted to it. Don't be surprised if you hear it in my room every once in a while. It's my comfort movie."

"Thank god you have a TV. I think I would actually go crazy if I didn't have some form of entertainment."

"Jason has a whole library in his room. Just don't take them without asking, he gets very protective of his books."

I guess I knew that Jason could read since he graduated high school and all, but I'm still confused. How does one learn to read without speaking?

I look through my lashes up to Dylan with hesitation. I've never thought to ask this before, and now that I am, it feels impolite.

"Why doesn't he talk?"

There it is. The words hang in the air while I wait for a reply and I wish I could take them back. I feel like I just asked about his dick size or something. Discomfort is definitely tangible, it feels like being stuck in jello unable to escape but you can move and try even if it won't get you anywhere.

Dylan eyes me wearily. "Have you ever asked him that?" I shake my head nervously. "I think it'd be best to let him tell you, or at least give me permission to tell you. It's personal."

"Did he ever speak? Like has he always been silent or did he stop at some point."

The debate in Dylan's head is present in his expression as well. But he decides to answer me. "He stopped talking when he was ten. I was nine."

"Why not use sign language?" It seems like the obvious answer to the communication problem.

"We all learned, except our dad. But he still doesn't use it unless he has to. Again, he should really be the one to tell you this stuff...but he doesn't like communicating with anyone. But if you live with him long enough, you learn to speak Jason. He communicates a lot whether he means to or not."

I can see that. From the way he looks at me, I know he's never forgiven me for prom night. And by the tension on his body, I know my presence bothers him. But he also lent me his mother's clothes. So maybe he doesn't entirely hate me. Maybe five percent of him likes me.

Or at the very least, tolerates me.

After the sun sets through the downfall of snow and the line between the treetops and the sky blurs into black, we all settle in the kitchen for dinner. Jason made beef stew and pointedly left a plate with one slice of bread on the table which he took before anyone else could. I guess we used most of it for the sandwiches earlier.

Point taken, he asked for me to make bread because it was needed, not because I'm a woman. I guess I'll ask one of them to show me how to make it tomorrow.

"I understand why you have chickens," I blurted to break the lack of conversation. I can't call it silence because the two men eat like they've been starved for days. There is nothing but the sound of their spoons hitting the bottom of the bowl, then scraping along the sides to scoop every scrap of food into the utensil, which is just as loud as their chewing. "But why do you have the other animals?"

Jason holds a piece of beef on his spoon letting the broth drop into the bowl. He eyes the meat and then me. Then stuffs the spoonful of beef into his mouth.

They're going to eat Bessie?

Dylan chuckles adjacent to me while giving his brother a mischievous smile that Jason meets with one of his own. These assholes have their own wordless language. I hope I'm not here long enough to learn it.

"The pigs will be bacon and pork chops soon, but the goat is for milk since we don't have fields for a cow. We have frozen milk, but you never know. We could run out or the freezer could fail, best to be safe with a backup option."

"And Bessie?" I ask. While Athena was hilarious rubbing her head on my hand and the fence, then kicking her legs up in the air before pouncing on an old tire, I felt a certain connection with Bessie. I love animals but I haven't been around them much, just at petting zoos. I mainly watched funny farm animal videos on social media. It might be my imagination, but when Bessie nudged her head into my shoulder and then her nose into my hand after feeding her a carrot, I swear I felt like she was welcoming me to the herd. Like she was happy to see me. Maybe she's like that with everyone, though.

"Transportation," Dylan answers me. "Horses will die for you if you bond with them enough. She's good to take hunting and she's always reliable."

I let out a sigh of relief hearing she won't be made into dog food any time soon.

"I'm kind of sad you don't have a barn cat."

"Oh, we do." There's a note of sarcasm in Dylan's voice. "She just lives in Jason's room." I can't help the snort of laughter that leaves me even if I tried. "When we got her, we put her in the barn the first night and she climbed her way to Jason's balcony. Hasn't left his room since."

It's kind of endearing that the cat loved Jason so much it scaled a house to get to him, though I doubt the cat wanted Jason specifically. It probably just wanted to get somewhere warm.

"Does your room smell like a barn?" I raise one eyebrow toward Jason. His only reply is to roll his eyes and take another bite of his buttered bread.

After everyone has finished their stew, Jason shoves his empty bowl and spoon towards me in a silent demand for me to clean the dishes. They don't have a dishwasher here—which is barbaric—but I take the dishes from the table reluctantly, choosing not to fight this battle. I'll bottle my rage for a cause more worthy of it.

And what do the boys do while I clean up? Lounge on the couch or in the recliner. Jason is reading a book while Dylan knits something.

Color me sexist, but I never thought I'd see Dylan Alder knitting. He was a star wrestler before he got kicked off the team. I'm not used to men who know how to do "domestic" activities like knitting. I think my dad would have a heart attack if he saw another man enjoying a so-called "feminine" hobby.

"So," I say as I flop down on the couch opposite Jason, "what do you guys do to pass the time up here?"

I bend my head at the neck to peer at the title of Jason's book. *The Shining* by Stephen King. Why am I not surprised he likes thriller novels?

"Sometimes we watch movies," Dylan pipes up to my right. "I usually download a bunch before we go into hibernation."

"Well I know what the Athlete's favorite movie is," I point my thumb over my shoulder at Dylan. "What's your favorite movie?"

Lifting his book, Jason sends his gray gaze over the top of the book to meet me then goes back to reading. Am I supposed to interpret that as *The Shining* is his favorite movie, or that he prefers reading? I guess I'll figure that out in the next four months.

But then he does something that takes me by surprise, he nods his chin at me over the top of the lowered book. *Is he asking what my favorite movie is?* Someone pinch me, I must be hallucinating.

"Me?" I place my hand on my chest dramatically. "Well...." I draw out the L sound. "I'd have to say *Hocus Pocus*."

"What?" Dylan sounds deeply offended beside me. "That's a Halloween movie."

"So?"

"So! Do you watch it all year round?"

I shrug my left shoulder. "Just whenever I'm feeling down. If people can watch *Die Hard* year round, I can watch *Hocus Pocus* year round."

"That's because *Die Hard* isn't a Christmas movie—."

"Blasphemy!" I shoot a finger toward Dylan as though it's a magic wand and I'm about to Avada Kedavra him. "It is absolutely a Christmas movie."

Dylan and I enter into a heated debate about the themes of *Die Hard* as if we are discussing a deep philosophical topic. Eventually, we don't come to a conclusion so Dylan claims he's "too exhausted by my ignorance" and retires for the night.

Being left alone with Jason feels acutely awkward. The last time he and I were alone together (excluding him saving my unconscious ass) was not a pleasant experience.

I look around the room taking in details I've already taken note of. The chip on the window frame. The uneven pattern in the deer hide rug in front of the fireplace. The evergreen design on the blanket covering the back of the couch.

The pad of a socked foot taps my thigh and I look back to Jason who is extending his book to me, is this some sort of peace offering?

I take the book in my hands and let it fall open to the bookmarked page about halfway through. By the way the spine is loose and the pages are yellowed, either this is a second hand book or Jason reads it a lot. I guess he did indicate this was his favorite. Scanning the page to recall what part of the book this is, I feel the burning weight of Jason's eyes on me from the other side of the couch. I look up and ask, "What?" Sounding an awful lot like a big sister annoyed by a younger brother. Though, I'm pretty sure his birthday was in September and mine is coming up in December, making him the older one by a couple of months.

Jason nods at the book then meets his expectant gaze with mine again. It's then I realize he wants me to read aloud.

"You want me to read you a bedtime story?" His brows manage to get even lower on his head making his brow line even more prominent. He has that whole caveman-lumberjack look going on. His facial features are so primal, nothing soft about him. But I notice his beard is cut with precision and shaped with accuracy. He's wearing a blue flannel and jeans now that he's inside, however, I saw that he was wearing snow pants earlier before dinner. Dylan said he was just working in the shop but he must have bundled up for the trek between the house and the shop.

It's an odd thing to consider, but I wonder if he'll cut his hair in the winter or if he has someone in town he sees after the snow melts. He'd look good with longer hair. Really lean into the mountain man-Viking aesthetic.

I start at the first paragraph on the page the book opened to but Jason taps me with his wooly foot again. Then he leans over to flip the pages back to chapter one and sits back to enjoy the performance.

"You've already read this part. You want to start over?" He nods, a straight answer for once.

I decide to indulge him and his demands, starting from the beginning of a story I'm sure he knows by heart.

Two hours slip by without my notice before I look from the book to the clock and realize it's past eleven. Then I gaze at Jason who is still staring with rapt attention waiting for me to continue.

"It's late," I point out. "I think I'm going to go to bed. It's been a long day. I don't think I've exhausted myself like that since I was on the volleyball team." Jason snorts a laugh at my expense. "Hey, I'm not as active as I used to be. The body needs consistency to maintain that kind of endurance." Jason raises a brow as well as the left corner of his mouth, and I know he's thinking of a dirty joke. "Watch it." I point a deliberate finger. Then I lay the book down on the couch and head toward the stairs, ready to crash on the comfortable bed and dream. And to my surprise, I do. I'm not thinking about home. I'm not thinking about when all this is over. I don't want to be here but...I'm also not as angry as I was this morning.

I'm indifferent.

Chapter Six

Mara-Senior Year

SLIPPING THROUGH MY FINGERS-ABBA

The prom is finally here. And with prom comes the promise of graduation around the corner. And after that, California. I've already been accepted to the University of Southern California with a focus on literature and a minor in communications. I want to be an English teacher, I want to read and share the best of the written word with others. What's better than reading and talking about books for a living?

It took me two hours to get ready, but most of that was spent listening to music and enjoying the solitary peace. I listened to Florence + The Machine, Hozier, and ABBA while doing my hair and makeup. The smokey eye with a nude lip paired with my smooth, loose curls is just what I envisioned. It felt all too perfect that "Slipping Through My Fingers" began to play while I was zipping up my dress.

Although Bryce isn't here yet, I head down the stairs expecting what I see in all the eighties movies, I expect my mom to have a camera out snapping photos of my Cinderella moment in the indigo blue A-line dress that perfectly flares to make me look like I have curves, and a lace off the shoulder detail to really drive the princess theme home. I expect my dad to be waiting to embrace his little girl and vet the prom date, even though he's met Bryce before.

But I should have known better. My mom isn't the sentimental type, and my dad doesn't really care for emotional exchanges. I don't even think he's home from the office yet. Probably helping someone else get a divorce when he should be focusing on his own marriage.

My mom is in the kitchen, though, seated on one of the leather bar stools at the kitchen island scrolling through details about some function she's organizing on her tablet. She doesn't even notice when I walk into the room in my flowing, poofy prom dress. She knows what day it is.

"Mom?" I grab her attention, she turns her head toward me before her eyes leave the bright screen.

"Oh, honey, you look so nice." There's a lack of sincerity to her voice, it's the same way she told Mrs. Thatcher she loved the new drapes, and how she answers my father when he confirms dinner plans with various associates. But I guess I should just be happy she isn't critiquing something about my appearance. "Though, those earrings seem a little gaudy for the occasion." There it is.

"It's prom," I try to muster up some enthusiasm, "what better occasion for full glam than that?" She doesn't agree or disagree, she nods subtly.

I pull my phone from my clutch purse and hand it to her before she can go back to her work. "Can you take a picture for me?"

"Yeah, I guess," she replies reluctantly, taking the phone from me.

"The lighting is better outside, do you mind if we go to the garden?"

"Mara, I really need to get back to work. Let's just do it here. You look fine." *You* look fine, not the *lighting* is fine. I don't know why I expected more from her. She's never been much of a mother past the point of playing the part in public. I'm convinced they had a child because they felt obligated. Because everyone else was having one. I'm no better than a Birkin bag.

I pose with one hand on my hip and the other clutching the purse at my side with a fake-ass smile plastered on my face. I move to another pose with both hands clasped in front with a slight tilt to my head in a very romantic pose, but my mom has already closed the phone screen and extends her arm to hand it back to me.

One photo, that's all I get.

I'm sure I could get Bryce to take some of me later but then he'll want to be in them, and I don't really want any photos with him, I don't want to remember prom as a night with him, just as a magical last hurrah before college. I know it's not going anywhere with him, I know that we'll break up this summer and I'll never think of him again, so I don't want him tainting these memories.

A horn honks outside just before the telltale sound of tires on the gravel half-circle driveway. My dad always parks his car in the garage so I know it's Bryce with the limo and the gang. I peep through the window to verify and see a long black limo stretched on the drive, no Bryce in sight. Apparently, it's too much to come to the door and escort me like a proper date.

"I'll be home around one, Mom," I say in farewell.

"Sounds good, honey." I'm honestly surprised she calls me honey. It's too much of a term of endearment. But she's called me that since I can remember.

Halfway to the limo, Bryce steps out of the back seat and I know before I even smell the vodka that he's drunk. The dopey smile on his face and the glazed look to his eyes gives it away before I spot the flask in his hand.

"Heyyyy, baby." What a romantic greeting. "Are you ready for a party?"

"No, I'm ready for prom," I insist. "Please tell me we will actually make it there instead of stopping off at the field to smoke behind the bleachers."

"Of course, baby," he waves a hand dismissively. "But we are totally going there after." An eye roll is all I grant him. *Why am I not surprised?*

"Oh yeah, here." Bryce hands me a plastic container bearing the corsage I asked him to get. A white rose against a bed of small fern leaves and baby's breath. The jerk didn't even have the decency to put it on me himself.

Not a battle I want to pick.

The limo is loaded with the usual suspects. Clay is in the car with his date Jasmine. Travis and Dan, two more wrestlers, are at the front with their respective dates. I recognize their faces, but I don't know their names. I don't think we share any classes since I'm the only one in the car who takes AP classes. I smile politely and compliment them.

"Hi," I wave with my free hand that's not holding the clutch. "Your dresses are beautiful." I mean it, they are beautiful, but my words still come off as insincere. It's the anxiety of being around unfamiliar people that draws that side out of me.

"Thanks," Dan's date replies for them both. "You too. I love the color." Great start to the night, awkward niceties that end in awkward silence. If this is how the night will go, I'm already dreading it.

I don't even bother to ask their names because then I'd have to admit I don't know them, and after four years at the same school—probably more, since it's a small town—I should probably know them. My mistaken identity is often that of a snobby rich girl who can't be bothered to socialize with peasants, and that's fine. I let them believe it. Because the truth is that I don't want to get attached to people I'm going to leave. I don't want ties to this town. I just want to get out of here and never look back. If the stuck-up persona keeps people from trying to be my friend, so be it. I don't care what they think because I won't be here in a few months.

To my delight, we pull up to the event center downtown where prom is hosted every year. The venue is used for everything from weddings to job fairs. There's a lush garden with sweeping wisteria crawling over the arbors and a little gazebo in the center. The entire garden is illuminated with twinkling fairy lights giving it an enchanting aura.

The theme this year is fairytale. Pretty cliche, if you ask me.

But I'll give it to the prom committee, they ran with the theme and created a little girl's fairytale dream. Hundreds of battery-powered candles lead the way to the main event space. The wall of windows opposite the entrance shines the golden hour light upon paper mache castle towers wrapped in ivy scattered around the perimeter between tables covered in lilac tablecloths. The support beams are garnished with more twinkle lights and flowers. The stage for the band is covered in more sweeping wisteria and vines that lead to a large print of a castle behind the instruments and musicians. They're playing modern music, thank goodness we don't have to listen to Disney music all night.

The sight is truly breathtaking. I've been both pessimistic and optimistic about tonight, hoping for the night of my life, but also worried it'll disappoint. But the room looks so perfect I can't help but feel a little hopeful. Maybe tonight will be as wonderful as I dreamed.

"Hey, Bryce." I turn to face my date seeing he's eyeing Chloe Taylor where she sits at her table, batting her eyelashes at *my date*. While I'm annoyed by the inconvenience, I don't really care if he is looking for someone else already. He and I will be done soon. After tonight, he will have served his purpose.

"Can you get me something to drink?"

"Sure thing, babe," he grips my ass through the layers of tulle. "Want it to be a *fun* drink?"

I don't bother to hide my eye roll. "Sure. Thanks."

He's back in a minute with a drink for each of us in silver and white paper cups. I take one sip and decide this will be the last *fun* drink I have tonight based on how strong he mixes them.

I want my wits about me tonight. No sloppy drunk girl at the prom stories. That might be ok for everyone else, but it's not who I am.

"Look who showed up," Clay says on Bryce's other side. I scan the room and find Jason Alder sitting at a table by himself. He's wearing a black sports coat and jeans but no tie, white shirt untucked. He's actually pretty good looking when he cleans himself up a bit. "Why the fuck would the Mute want to come to prom? And by himself, no doubt."

"You don't know that," I scoff at his presumption. "For all you know, his date is in the bathroom."

"Yeah. Or maybe he brought his faggot brother as his date." Bryce's comments about that are getting really old. Is he really that offended by modern relationships?

I see the mischievous gleam in his eye warning me that his twisted mind is working before he speaks. "Hey, I have an idea. Let's have a little fun tonight." A well deserved chill races down my spine when Bryce turns to me and says. "And, babe, you're going to help."

Oh no.

Chapter Seven

Jason

SKINNY LOVE-BIRDY

"I have a problem," Mara announces when she walks into the kitchen this morning. She's wearing jeans and one of my flannel shirts with a couple buttons undone at the top. Her hair is tied up in a messy bun and it looks like it hasn't been brushed in a couple days. A far cry from the sleek ponytails she used to wear.

It's been a week since she crash landed into our lives. We butt heads about as much as we get along, but that's probably because I like provoking her. She's so easy to rile up and looks kind of like a child when she does. She's stormed out of a room several times in the last week.

But she's also read aloud to me every night since that first one. Sometimes for an hour, sometimes for three. We're almost done with this book. I hope she reads the next one I have picked out, this might be a one time thing. But I like listening to her read, her disagreeable personality aside, her voice is very soothing, gentle and feminine but not too high pitched. She sounds like a woman rather than a teenage girl. Most of the girls I've slept with always wear a little girl mask. They act helpless and raise the pitch of their voice, bat their eyelashes. Who wants to fuck a little girl? I'd rather have a woman.

At her vague announcement, I turn to her waiting for an explanation. A sip of my coffee fills the time in between her speech.

"I'm due to start my period tomorrow." Oh shit. I didn't think of that. She barely has enough clothes as it is. The last thing we need is her going through them with period blood every day.

"There's a solution but I don't know if it's possible." Color me intrigued. "I have a menstrual cup in my car. I don't know if there's a way to get there, but I can use that the entire time I'm here. No need for tampons or pads." Well, that's pretty convenient. Though I'm sure the tampon companies are pissed about losing monthly profits to something that can be reused.

I nod my head in answer. I set into motion hoping she'll get the message and start shoving my legs through the snow pants by the door before stuffing my wool covered feet into boots. She follows my lead and starts bundling up as well. She was only wearing a winter coat when I found her, no snow pants. Thankfully, she can kind of fit into Dylan's. He may be nearly as tall as me, but his waist is narrower and they are only a smidge too big for Mara. Better than nothing in this weather, though.

I take a couple granola bars and toss one to Mara to put something in her belly before we set off on our mission.

After Bessie has been prepared, I boost Mara onto the chestnut budyonny horse before climbing on behind her. We ride bareback for the sake of warmth. A saddle would just be a cold piece of leather between us. Bareback, we can share heat better. Which is also why I chose to ride behind Mara and hold the reins, since she's smaller and not as heavily bundled, I try to envelop her in my warmth a little more. Last thing I need is her complaining about being cold the whole ride.

Her back pressed to my front feels like two Russian nesting dolls sliding into place. Her shoulder fit between mine. Her head sits at my chin in this position so I can see the path ahead. She smells like the winter air, crisp and refreshing.

We left a note for Dylan on the table since he was still asleep. He was planning to work in the shop most of the day, anyway.

Bessie has to walk kind of slow through the snowy terrain since it's three feet high. My feet almost touch the snow at this level. But I don't hear the crunch of ice since the snow is still so fresh, making it a little easier on the poor girl. Bessie is eight years old. She's not old but she's not young either. She's a lot more docile and spoiled than she used to be. But this is why we keep her around. Never know when we need her.

Last winter I shot a buck from my balcony and missed his heart by a couple inches. It was enough to kill him eventually but not before he wandered a couple miles. Bessie and I tracked his blood through the snow to make sure his death was not wasted. His meat kept us fed the rest of that winter.

The sound of those steady hooves is the only sound in the woods now. A gentle and familiar sound that comforts me. She's a faithful companion willing to travel through any condition for the ones she loves. It seems like Mara is becoming one of those people as well. She's taken to feeding the animals almost every day just for a chance to spend time around them. I want to make a joke about how she gets along so well with them because she *is* an animal, but that's too easy.

I'm honestly surprised Mara isn't talking my ear off yet. She and Dylan jabber like little girls any time they're in a room together. I thought the silence would kill her overactive mind and the need to fill it would overtake her. But nothing. Her head only swivels on her neck to observe the passing scenery that looks like something out of a Christmas card as we saunter through the woods.

Every puff of breath she exhales into frozen air hovers for a second in front of us before it dissipates. She breathes steadily, even inhales and exhales. It comforts me. I like the repetition of it and consistency. I focus on that instead of the sound of Bessie walking because she isn't even in her steps. When she has to step around a rock under the snow or a thicker patch where her pace slows. The variability makes my blood pulse faster through my veins. But Mara's breathing is in perfect time. In. One, two, three, four. Out. One, two, three, four. Over and over again.

"It's so beautiful here," she breaks the blissful silence twenty minutes into our journey. "It's like time stopped altogether. Kind of refreshing, actually. Maybe this time away will be good for me."

I'm used to silence, I'm used to the space between conversations that either carries a weight of tension or an air of peace. This time, Mara's silence is like an elephant in the living room, it takes up so much space you can't ignore it. But I don't ask what's wrong. Knowing her, she'll probably tell me herself in time.

"I'm sure you're wondering why I have a menstrual cup in my car." I wasn't, but I'm not about to tell her that. "I always keep an extra in my purse. My periods are so irregular that I have to be prepared for whenever Mother Nature strikes. I'm just glad she didn't make an early appearance this month." That sounds like hell.

We cross the elevated bridge spanning the distance between ledges of the ravine. Beneath us, the river has a solid layer of ice encasing the surface, but I know water still runs beneath the thick ice that's taken over. If you don't know what you're looking at, it might be easy to miss since the snowfall has created a bed of flakes below. The only disruption in the pristine white landscape is the underside of evergreen bows that peek out. Occasionally, I see various animal tracks through the snow, but most of them are hibernating for the winter or staying under cover.

It takes us forty-five minutes to reach her vehicle on horseback at that pace through the winter wonderland. The only way we found the car was because I remembered exactly where she crashed, about fifty feet past the bridge. It's been consumed and devoured by the season. Luckily, I thought ahead and brought a small shovel tucked into the loop on my pants to get to the car. It's been a week of consistent downfall, the car is sufficiently buried which will take time to uncover, but it's not impossible.

It took us another goddamn fifteen minutes to clear the way to open the door and then pry it open with brute force, but we got in. For safe measure, Mara took the entire purse in case she needed anything else out of it. Apparently, she also had a tube of mascara and a lip balm in there. She was a little too excited to retrieve them, I'll never understand women and makeup. Both were frozen, but she said they should thaw and work well once back to room temperature.

She hasn't worn makeup the entire week since she didn't have any until now. But I prefer her bare-faced instead of the dark makeup she did in high school. It always looked like she was trying to be someone she wasn't. It seemed like it was a lot of effort for everyone else's benefit, not her own. She never seemed like the glamorous makeup type.

People think that because I don't speak I don't pay attention. But it's the opposite, I see everything and everyone. I saw the parts of her she subdued for the sake of her boyfriend and the people she ran with. I saw that she loved volleyball and physical activity, she always had a serious face of dedication in weights class that told me she loved it. I saw her reading in the library during her free period on occasion, immersed in her book. But she read romances, not the thrillers and classics I read.

We're about half way back to the lodge when I decide to take a detour and show her one of the reasons I always loved this place. At home, when I was a kid, our house didn't leave much room to escape my father. But the cabin my grandpa left us had plenty of open space I could explore. Including the lake.

Well, it's more of a large pond, but I liked to call it the lake as a kid. It was a vast expanse of water that felt larger than life, bigger in perception than reality.

"Where are we going?" Mara asks when I steer Bessie away from the trail we made on our way down the mountain. We can't stay too much longer on account of needing to get Bessie back to the warm barn. But I want to see the lake. It's been a while.

When I don't respond, as she likely expected, Mara lets out a sigh of aggravation to convey her frustration without words. Clever. She's learning to communicate without words, just like me.

After another five minutes or so, she speaks again. "I'm sure you're wondering how I ended up back in town after my California adventure." I am, actually, though I feign indifference. She sighs heavily, this time with resignation, and continues without an answer.

"California ate me up and spat me back out." Her voice takes on a wistful, forlorn tone, It's like she;s being tugged into a memory. "I coasted through high school so I thought college would be a breeze. I thought I'd be a star student like I was here. But I wasn't as successful at a college in a big city versus a small town education system. I was just a name on a roster, nothing special." The top of Mara's head drops slightly like she's looking down at where my hands hold the reins in front of her, surrounding her with my arms.

"I thought I could handle morning classes, but I slept through them constantly. I thought I could handle the workload of a major and a minor. I didn't. I failed more classes than I care to admit. And after one of my tuition payments was late, they threatened to kick me out of my dorm room.

"Universities say they care about their students until they don't get their money. Then you're trash to them. I was so annoyed by how they treated me after one late payment that I just left. My dad said he wouldn't pay for an apartment in California if I wasn't going to school there. I tried working in California for a while, but it wasn't enough to fund the life I had. So I didn't have much of a choice but to come home and reevaluate. So...here I am. Pretty pathetic. The straight A student couldn't handle herself in college."

The silence hanging in the air after her explanation is as thick as the snow surrounding us. I'm honestly surprised I don't feel it as we walk through the trail leading to the lake.

"I wanted to get out of this town so badly, experience the world this town tries to ignore. And it just ruined me, instead." If I were a betting man, I'd say there's more to this story she's not sharing. The way she says ruined seems like her mind is running over something else from her time in California that she hasn't shared yet. She doesn't have to share it, but I am intrigued. And a little sorry for her. That sounds like one hell of a depressing experience. But, I suppose at the end of the day, she has no one to blame but herself.

Despite my thirst for knowledge and love of learning, I hate being in school. I hate sitting at a desk and taking notes over things that could be handed to me in a printout for me to read on my own. I hate group work and tests and pop quizzes. I hate being judged by others on ridiculous criteria. I knew college wouldn't be a good fit for me, that's why I started trade school classes my senior year of high school. By the time I graduated, I had enough training to start my business. Dylan followed my example and I was so thankful for it. He really helped me get the business off the ground. Being computer savvy, he also built the website and a social media presence to get us customers. It's grown so much in two years. I wouldn't have life any other way than building a career with my brother.

But I know he's not completely happy here.

We clear the trees and come to my favorite spot on the mountain. A crystallized lake engulfed by winter and cast in frosted ice. In the summer, it's the perfect deep dive to escape my thoughts and submerge myself in water. Water is the only place I feel fully relaxed. The shower. A bath. The lake. On the rare occasion we make the three hour drive to the beach, the ocean is an even greater security. Where others find uncertainty and fear of the unknown, I find peace.

Although I can't dive into the lake right now as I'd like to do, the sight is almost as placating. The gradient of opaque white snow piled on the shore toward the transparent center eases my mind like I imagine those adult coloring books do for some.

The entire lake is surrounded in a circle of pines securing and secluding my sacred place from the rest of the world. While it's not technically on our property, I feel possessive of it. It's as much my home as the lodge. I've never seen another soul here. Dylan will go for a swim on especially hot summer days, even though we live in Oregon and the water never really heats up past sixty degrees. As far as I know, Mara is only the third person to ever come here, to see this nirvana.

Her body went stiff as a board when we passed the tree line and she could fully see the beauty of this place. Her breathing slowed too. The puffs of air that escape her are not as steady and close together as they were before. But they return to normalcy after she speaks.

"Wow," she breathes, "this is incredible." I don't think she realizes when her body relaxes back into my chest and I brace her. The top of her head is a centimeter away from my chin. I can smell her shampoo, it smells like Dylan's, he uses something that's supposed to be better for hair health but I've never given a shit. He was generous enough to share some of his hygiene products with her since she didn't want to use my "heterosexual, ineffective man products," as she so kindly described them.

There's nothing wrong with shampoo from the dollar store. It gets the job done. If I end the shower clean, then it works. She was also repulsed by the fact that I use shampoo to clean everything.

Soap is soap! I don't know why I'm the only one who gets that.

"Thank you for showing me this," Mara sits up straighter, either because she realized she'd been leaning against my chest or because she realized she was slouching. The cold air that slips between her back and my chest where body heat kept me warm moments ago feels like ice to the balls.

I wait a moment longer before steering Bessie around back the way we came and head back to the house. Being jostled around a bit makes Mara lean back into me again and I savor the heat, the warmth, the contact I didn't think I'd enjoy as much as I do. She's silent the rest of the way back but it doesn't feel uncomfortable. It feels...natural. Like the way Dylan and I can be in the same room and he doesn't feel the need to speak to me. Maybe she's finally getting used to my silence.

It's a little scary to think Mara Meyers has spent enough time with me to get used to things. I never thought I'd see her again after graduation. And now she's living in my fucking house. God really does have a sense of humor. He enjoys forcing me to face my demons.

That's been a consistent pattern in my life.

Chapter Eight

Mara

I'LL GET BY-AVI KAPLAN

Thanksgiving is tomorrow.

My entire childhood, Thanksgiving was one of three days my dad took off every year, the other two being Christmas (even though we are technically Jewish) and Super Bowl Sunday. The holiest of all days.

Thanksgiving was always catered with normal Thanksgiving foods, and the house was decorated to the nines with pumpkins, rust tones, and the occasional turkey. My mom thought it would be a good idea to get a live turkey one year to greet guests in the front yard. But the wild beast tried to take out the food delivery boy's eye so he was shot on the spot and his body discretely disposed of.

That's something an eleven year old never forgets.

All those holidays spent in my parents house was akin to being a third wheel on a date. I was seen but not heard, present to keep up the loving family facade. Though I think I preferred that. My parents usually invited the most insipid of guests and the last thing I wanted to do was make small talk with people who didn't want to interact with me. I guess I should be thankful they didn't try to engage with me.

In college, my parents never protested that I wanted to stay in California for the holidays. I spent my first Thanksgiving away from home eating Chinese take out in my apartment with my boyfriend at the time.

The second year, I spent it in a bar trying to drink a turkey's weight in vodka sodas. I was unsuccessful. At least the bartender put me in an Uber home before I left with the guy I was making googly eyes at across the bar. And thankfully, Mr. Bad Idea didn't try to tag along. I woke up a foot away from vomit on my rug the following morning. Not my classiest moment but there were no witnesses, so no one has to know.

This year, I figured I'd be fielding questions about why I'm home from college at another awful party my parents threw. While being stuck in a cabin in the woods with tweedle-mute and tweedle-always happy isn't my first choice, I don't think it will be too bad. It might even be my best Thanksgiving ever, which is kind of sad, really.

The Thanksgiving I spent with my boyfriend eating Chinese was pretty nice, but it's now tainted by his betrayal.

A quiet holiday eating a basic meal that consists of less than twelve courses is far more appealing.

We're just having chicken since one of them started biting and Dylan said they don't tolerate biters. I can't wrap my head around having to eat an animal with a name that I helped feed everyday. But maybe if I tell myself I pulled it out of the meat section at the store, I'll be able to stomach it.

Dylan insists it'll be better than any store bought chicken. We'll see about that.

I decide to try my hand at baking and use ingredients from the pantry to make a pumpkin pie. The filling seems easy enough. Just dump and mix the ingredients, no such thing as over mixing. But the crust seems a little trickier. Anything that requires precision and worrying about consistency is a recipe for disaster in my book.

Using a marble rolling pin, I try to evenly roll the dough out over the floured kitchen island but it keeps sticking to the rolling pin. No matter how much flour I sprinkle on the dough, the sticky texture attaches to the rolling pin instead of rolling flat.

I just don't get it. I'm following the recipe exactly.

Exasperated and about ready to give up completely, I set the rolling pin down with a thud and throw my hands in the air earning the attention of the two men sitting at the table finishing breakfast.

"What's wrong with you?" Dylan oh so helpfully asks.

I shove my hands toward the mess on the island as if I'm banishing it from existence. "The dough keeps sticking and I can't get it to smooth out. It's impossible."

Much to my dismay, Jason snorts a stifled laugh I meet with a withering glare. Apparently, my agony is amusing to him.

"I'm trying here," I insist. "What do you want from me?"

Jason stands, takes his plate and fork to the kitchen sink, then comes to stand at my side. He takes the rolling pin off the counter, a pinch of flour from the jar beside the dough, and spreads it over the rolling pin without taking his eyes off me as if to say *flour the pin, not the dough. Duh.*

I meet his stare with one of my own and respond to his wordless chastisement. "Well, the instructions didn't say to flour the rolling pin, it said to put flour on the dough."

Another rub of flour into the rolling pin is Jason's only response. *Dick.*

After using the trick Jason showed me, which worked like a dream even though I almost wish he'd been wrong, the crust is flattened and fully formed in the pie dish. I pour the pumpkin pie filling into the crust after poking the holes in the bottom like the instructions dictate. As I'm sliding the pie into the oven, I peer out the window and see a large deer with swooping antlers that come to five points on either side.

"There's a deer outside," I alert Jason and Dylan.

Dylan comes to stand at my side and informs me, "That's not a deer. It's an elk."

He's magnificent. If I remember correctly, only the males have antlers. His are almost as long as his neck and head. His mahogany fur lightens to the color of coffee creamer on his legs and belly. He just stands in the snow fifty feet from the back door near the barn, tall and proud, majestic in every way. I understand now why people are so enthralled with them, he's truly a noble creature.

Click.

Boom.

I'm not even remotely prepared for the sound of the shotgun firing or the sight of the impressive elk dropping to the snow laden ground in a heartbeat. One minute he's standing tall and proud, the next he's dead as a doornail in the snow that's now stained with his blood.

"What the actual fuck?" I shout over the ringing in my ears.

What is it about Thanksgiving that makes people want to shoot things?

Jason must have crept out the front door to the porch and circled around with the shotgun while I was transfixed by the elk. He's already picking up the discarded shell from the wood porch and coming back inside to get his snow gear on.

How can he act so nonchalant about this? He just took an animal's life and he's just going about his business stuffing his legs into snow pants without a care in the world. As if this is just another Wednesday.

"Awesome, elk will be way better for Thanksgiving dinner instead of that damn chicken. We can have that Friday."

"What?" I don't even try to restrain my utter shock and horror at what I just witnessed. "You just shot that beautiful creature in cold blood." I sound like a witness on a crime drama show.

"It wasn't in cold blood," Dylan laughs like my comment is a ridiculous notion. "That beautiful creature is going to feed us all winter long. Did you see how many points he had on each antler?"

This feels like a trick question but I answer anyway. "Five."

"That's a fully grown male elk who has spread his seed all over this mountain and lived a long life. He's not a baby. He's done his service to the ecosystem and his species. And his circle of life has come to an end to keep our lives going."

Before I can argue any further, Jason holds my snow gear in front of my face silently demanding I suit up. I just stare at him, if he thinks I'm helping him butcher the elk he's got another thing coming.

At my obvious refusal, Jason shakes my coat, hardening his expression to meet my defiance.

"No," I exclaim, holding my ground with arms crossed over my chest and one hip popped, taking me back to my bitchy high school days.

But that backfired quickly. Jason swoops down bringing his shoulder to my stomach and an arm around the backs of my thighs and hoists me fireman style into the air.

Fuck. No.

"What the fuck?" Fists pounding, I protest his assault with shouts and kicks and poorly angled punches but it gets me nowhere as Jason carries me through the freezing cold to the barn and plants me beside a large butcher block table that's at least a foot thick, supported by sturdy wooden legs.

"What the hell do you think you're doing?" I shout as soon as I'm on steady ground. I feel a little ridiculous balling my fists at my side, like a child standing up to a grown up.

Jason just turns around and leaves the barn, but not before taking a fucking *saw* off the wall. Before the door swings shut I spot Dylan stepping out onto the back porch in his snow attire as well. He must be going to help Jason bring in the elk.

I could risk the cold by going back to the house, but there's at least two and a half feet of snow outside since the last time I shoveled. And my clothes would get soaked. Is it really worth it?

What the fuck is Jason's game? Why does he insist on pushing my buttons and my boundaries? I thought we were making some progress with our coexistence when he showed me the breathtaking frozen pond. And we read together almost every night. I've kept that habit up mainly because I have nothing else to do. We started Heart of Darkness two nights ago. I've never read this one before, either.

I'm stuck standing in the moderately warmer barn waiting for the two dickheads to come back and get me. I don't have a watch and there isn't a clock in the barn so I have no idea how much time passes. But it feels like a while.

As I'm taking my first step toward the door, it flies open letting a flurry of snowflakes in. I'm met with the dark eyes of a decapitated elk that are truthfully smaller than I realized. The most horrifying part—more terrifying than the bloody entrails hanging from its neck—is the fact that the mouth is hanging open. If the tongue was hanging out as well, I might have vomited right on the spot.

I jerk back at the gruesome sight as Jason stomps into the barn knocking snow off his boots in the process. He looks me dead in the eye as he steps in from the cold before gently lowering the elk head to the ground against the wall.

Dylan joins us with what looks like one fourth of the elk's body slung over his shoulders. The elk looked massive from the window. But up close, even in pieces, it's ginormous. I always pictured elk the same as deer, like Bambi. Clearly, they are substantially bigger and entirely made of muscle.

Maybe that's why everyone in Oregon goes nuts for them, the payoff of meat for one kill is exponentially higher than deer.

"Did you cut it up in the snow?" I ask with a sneer on my face. I don't even want to look in that direction when I go back to the house. It's probably a bloodbath amidst the pristine white.

"Had to," Dylan explains, "those fuckers are too heavy to carry back in one piece." Dylan swings the chunk of meat off his shoulders and onto the butcher block table with a huff of air. He certainly sounds like he exerted energy transporting it back.

Jason leaves, presumably to collect another piece of the elk carcass. But Dylan rummages through some tools laid out on a folding table instead of helping his brother. Pretty soon, he has an array of knives and tools laid out on the butcher block just as Jason returns with another hunk of elk meat.

"Why do I have to watch this?" I direct my question at Jason although I know he can't answer. But I swear the way he looks at me is almost audible. I can almost hear him say *because you need to learn.* Though, I don't know what it is I need to learn.

Dylan dons a pair of latex gloves before taking a knife in hand and starts cutting the fur away from the meat, skinning the poor beast to reveal the red meat beneath the surface. Blood is everywhere, by now, and the sound of him tearing the skin away from the body is one I'll never forget. It's akin to Velcro being ripped apart, but add a touch of slasher movie soundtrack to it.

I turn my head so I don't have to watch but remain rooted to the spot I've been in since Jason returned with my arms banded across my chest. I'm too stunned to move, at this point.

Jason heads out to collect the rest. And by the time the entire elk is in the barn in pieces, Dylan has the first part free of skin and fur and Jason aids in cutting chunks off to freeze for later.

To my utter horror, Jason strides across the barn with an outstretched bloody, gloved hand and grabs my arm, careful not to get the blood on my skin. I'm logical enough to know the blood won't hurt me, but the idea of it touching my skin still sends shivers up my spine.

With no room for argument, Jason yanks me toward the workstation and hands me a pair of gloves. I stare at the gloves then at the butchered piece of elk I saw standing in the yard not that long ago. After putting the gloves on, as directed, Jason hands me a knife and guides my hands to start cutting the meat away from the bone, pointing at fatty pieces we don't want, and expertly slicing the proper shapes.

It's disgusting. But I do it anyway. I've learned well enough that if Jason is insistent on something, there's little room for protest. So I do my part to earn my keep here and help them cut up the poor animal.

It takes nearly the entire day, but together we get the bones clear of meat and save as much as we can. Dylan explained that the liver is a great vitamin replacement, and the bones make excellent broth. No part of this sacrifice was wasted.

And by the end of the process, that's what this feels like, a sacrifice. Dylan said the elk had lived a long life, he told me that once elk reach this age, they run the risk of impregnating their own daughters and creating genetic inbreeding that's bad for the population. This is all part of the wildlife dynamic that keeps the species going.

I saw the way the elk dropped in a heartbeat, it didn't suffer, didn't even know what was happening by the time it was over. That sounds like a peaceful way to go.

After an entire day of cutting up elk meat, vacuum sealing it, and storing it in the freezer, my body felt like I'd run a marathon. Processing an elk is way more strenuous than I imagined.

And that's the reason I slept in this morning. One of the boys had to bang on my door to finally pull me from my slumber. The clock says eight in the morning when I roll over to see it. Only an hour later than I normally get up. But I've certainly started going to bed earlier with all the work I've been doing.

It's Thanksgiving, which means both Jason and Dylan are putting their work aside for a day (aside from tending to the animals) to cook for the day. Dylan was raving about Jason's grilling skills and stuffing while we butchered the elk. And he assigned me the task of making rolls today.

Seeing as it's a holiday, I decide to wear the long dress from the trunk of clothes that belonged to Mrs. Alder. It's a sage green maxi dress speckled with little white flowers. The top is smocked with long sleeves that bunch at the cuff so I can roll them to my elbows while I work. Since I don't have my usual styling products, my hair either hangs down my back or lives in a bun atop my head. Occasionally I opt for a braid like I am today. My hair isn't exceptionally long but it's long enough to hang over my shoulder, a nicer way to keep it out of my face without crinkling it into a mess.

When I land on the main level of the house, Jason is in the kitchen already at work smothering a huge chunk of elk meat in some sort of seasoning. He pauses briefly to eye my attire, I've never considered how it would make them feel to see me in their mother's clothes. Logically, I know they willingly allowed me to wear them, but it was more out of necessity than generosity.

I don't know how their parents died. Their father died during our senior year of high school. I think I heard it was an accident or maybe he drank himself to death. I don't know. I didn't really care enough to pay attention to the small town gossip. Their mother must have passed away after I'd moved to California.

The dark gray color of his eyes flashes silver before he goes back to working on our dinner. *Ignore it, he's probably just not sure how to feel about someone wearing his mom's clothes.*

Giving myself a task takes my mind off the insecurity. I start working on fried eggs for breakfast. I've come to learn that Jason prefers them medium while Dylan prefers his eggs runny. I also unwrap ground sausage from the wax paper it's stored in and pop it in the skillet with the eggs. Paired with some toast, it's a filling breakfast. Though I plan to save lots of room for dinner tonight. I've never had a home cooked Thanksgiving before.

Come to think of it, I've only had a handful of home cooked meals in my life that didn't come out of a microwave. I actually feel a little...excited, dare I say.

We each take turns in the kitchen working on our assigned dishes, since the kitchen isn't big enough for more than two people and Jason is spending most of the day working on his respective sides when he's not tending to the elk. I asked if he wanted help so he wasn't working all day but he adamantly shook his head no. I guess he really loves to cook. Fine by me since I have little to no skills. I'm a nervous wreck while the rolls are rising for fear I did something wrong. I followed the directions precisely, I measured everything with obsessive accuracy. They look normal, but that doesn't mean they will rise and bake correctly.

"Do you want to play cribbage?" Dylan draws me out of the book I'm reading on my own, not the one I read aloud nearly every night.

"Cribbage?" I dig into the recesses of my brain for more information. "That's a card game, right?" It sounds like something little old ladies get together once a week for and drink iced tea the whole time.

No wait, that's bridge.

"Yeah," Dylan replies, rising from the couch to collect something from a box beneath the coffee table, then sets it on the kitchen table. "Well, it combines cards and a board. I can explain."

Dylan goes over all the pieces, the order of operations for each phase of the game, and the point system. It seems like a gentleman's game with all the rules about the person who's not dealing being the one to cut the deck, and whatnot. But I think I've got the hang of it.

He also explains the skunk line on the board and that if you lose behind that line, it's basically humiliation. Good thing I don't care what he thinks if I get skunked.

I do have a bit of a competitive streak, sometimes, but with Dylan I'm less worried. Everything with him is so carefree and copacetic. I never feel the distinct pruning of my soul like I do around others, no worry about what he thinks. Mainly because Dylan wears his heart on his sleeve, and his opinions. He's so comfortable sharing his thoughts without oversharing. And he genuinely seems to like...well...everyone. The same can't be said for most people.

He's the opposite of his silent and mysterious brother who conceals as much of himself as he can.

By the hair of my chinny chin chin, I don't get skunked. I make it two points over the line when Dylan wins my first game of cribbage. I didn't expect to win my first game, but it helps that Dylan is a gracious winner and I'm not a sore loser.

Maybe that's why I was subpar at volleyball, I didn't have the drive the coach was always preaching about. I didn't feel that competitive fire in my belly or the need to prove myself. I was just existing and surviving, successful without being extraordinary. I was a good teammate and volleyball player, but I never made any game changing plays.

Cribbage was fun, though, and I'd definitely enjoy playing again.

"That was fun," I say as I stand to pop my rolls in the oven. "We should play again sometime."

Thankfully, the rolls look like they inflated the proper amount which gives me hope I made them right. Now, all I have to do is bake them at the perfect temperature for the correct amount of time.

You can do this.

"Is the oven free?" I point to the appliance in question while looking to Jason for an answer, since I know it's a visual, not an audible, reply.

He nods his head and I slide the rolls in, setting the already warm oven to the correct temperature and starting the timer.

I scan over the various pots and pans Jason has laid across the counter or stovetop. Yams topped with some sort of brown sugar crumble, green beans cooked with bacon, stuffing (or as my mom calls it, dressing). Everything smells incredible.

Dylan prepared the cranberry sauce and mashed potatoes with gravy. It's a traditional Thanksgiving feast. The only traditional part of Thanksgiving dinner at my parents house was the turkey. The other courses were things like a pear and blue cheese salad or shrimp cocktail. I don't think I'd even had pumpkin pie in that house. It never occurred to me how depressing the customs of my childhood home were until I was out of it.

I wonder what my parents are doing today. Do they miss me? Did they look for me?

Did anyone look for me?

I can't believe I almost wasn't here for this holiday.

Thanksgiving is about gratitude, and I guess I'm glad to be alive, even if this isn't an ideal situation. I'm grateful Jason didn't leave me to die in the snow, even if he did make me butcher an elk yesterday.

It makes me uneasy that he can hold the whole *saving my life* thing over my head the rest of my life, but I guess the alternative isn't as ideal.

I'm glad I'm here. I'm glad I'm alive.

I have to be.

Chapter Nine

Jason

RIVER-LEON BRIDGES

When I saw Mara in that dress my brain went on the fritz. She wore tight skirts and sparkly shit in high school but nothing as homely as the dress she came down the stairs in this morning. Feminine, simple, beautiful. I know it's my mom's dress and it shouldn't have had that effect on me, but I couldn't help it. The way she looked with the braid over her shoulder and the top of the dress tight to her chest caused me to forget how to think for a moment.

I'm glad I got to spend the whole day cooking, it was a nice change from all the work I have in the shop for me. I know I have all winter to finish the orders but I have a tendency to get as much done at the start of the season as I can, which gives me the rest of winter to work on projects *I* want to work on. I don't think I have a lazy bone in my body.

Cooking has always been something I enjoy, much like metal work and crafting firearms, it calms my mind and gives the anxious energy something to focus on. Gives my restless hands something to do.

My mother saw this side of me very early in my childhood, she said "idle hands are the devil's handiwork" so she asked me to help her in the kitchen. She was always baking or cooking something. Muffins, scones, stew, pot roast. She taught me everything that she learned from her mother. She's also the one who taught me how to can and preserve food, even though we didn't grow the food we preserved. We didn't have room for a garden at that house.

In turn, I taught Dylan when we moved up here.

It was kind of strange sharing the kitchen with Mara, today. She didn't force conversation, but she didn't seem repulsed by me as usual, so I hindered my resentment as well. For today, we can be civil, for the holiday, maybe we can be friendly.

If she'd been different in high school, if she's been more like she is now, maybe this whole situation would be different. Maybe we would've even been friends in high school.

I know her boyfriend, *Bryce,* was the culprit behind most of my adolescent torment. But she was a pawn he used to play the game and she willingly went along with it. Besides, he never coached her on what to say. Every jab at me or my brother was entirely her own creative, spiteful mind at work. She can't blame her own maliciousness on another person.

Hours of cooking between the three of us paid off because Thanksgiving dinner is excellent, if I do say so myself. Even the rolls and the pie Mara made turned out well, though I would have done the pie crust a little differently. Though, I'll admit, watching her struggle with rolling it out was kind of entertaining. And cute.

In honor of the holiday, we break out a bottle of Merlot to go with the elk. I wouldn't say I'm a wine snob, but I'm a quality food snob. So I wouldn't have wasted the bottle on fucking chicken.

When I took a bite of the pumpkin pie Mara made, I held up the OK symbol to congratulate her on a pie well done. Like I said, I would have done the crust differently, but for her first attempt she did a damn good job. My mom would be proud.

"Ok, ok, I have a question for you," Mara directs at Dylan. She's only had a glass and a half of wine but it seems to be hitting her now. I guess her little body doesn't need much alcohol to feel the effects. "Why stay in this town as the only openly gay person here?"

I have to restrain my eyebrows from shooting up to my hairline. That's a pretty bold question.

And also a little silly. Dylan might be the only *openly* gay guy in town, but he's not the only man who prefers male company in our neck of the woods.

"Oh Mara," Dylan chides. "How's that wine treating you?"

She blushes a little, probably realizing how brazen her words were after they skipped past her tongue.

"But to answer your question, I like it here. I like the life Jason and I have for the time being. Maybe one day I'll move away, but not far. I like big cities for a weekend, not forever.

"That being said, I don't want to live with my big brother forever. And I can still get my dick wet in this po-dunk town, so what's the rush?"

"What?" Mara's jaw drops, she's back in high school feeding off the gossip. "Who else is gay?"

Dylan lifts his wine glass to his smile and takes a sip, keeping Mara on the edge of her seat.

"Well, you want to know the real reason I was kicked off the wrestling team?" I can feel Mara's anticipation in a wave of heat. "Coach Garner was my first. And apparently I was his too, in a sense."

I snort a small laugh, I knew that already but Mara's slack-jawed expression is priceless.

No one would expect the burley wrestling coach to be into men, and especially not young men since it's a bit of power play. But I know Dylan was the one that pursued him so I don't give a fuck.

"You're kidding," she says on a disbelieving breath. "I don't believe it."

"There have been a couple others, a couple regulars I can call when the need strikes, but no one serious. No one willing to come out and make it official."

"Oh, Dylan," Mara extends her hand across the table but stops short before taking his hand, second guessing herself.

"Don't feel sorry for me," Dylan says with all seriousness. "I don't want someone who only wants a secret. Feel sorry for them, they're the ones living a lie."

"Wise words. I wouldn't be so ok with it in your situation."

Dylan lifts his nose in the air like an aristocrat. "You just aren't as evolved as me." Mara holds her hand to her chest in mock offense. But when I chuckle behind my glass, she turns beady eyes toward me.

"What about you?" She redirects the conversation so I'm in the hot seat. "Any women you want to settle down and have twenty kids with?"

Twenty? That's a stretch.

I roll my eyes because that's a ridiculous notion. First, that I'd want to settle down. And second, that any girl in our town would want to live away from civilization in our secluded cabin. Not that I'd want any of them anyway. The girls in our town tend to be—how can I put this nicely—lacking in complexity. They're simple creatures with simple desires and simple minds. There's nothing intriguing about them and nothing remarkably interesting to discuss.

I shake my head no in case she didn't get the meaning of the eye roll.

"So you've just hid on the mountain jerking off alone all this time?" Wow, she really is getting bold. Good thing the wine is gone.

"Who said he's been alone," Dylan remarks. "I mean, where do you think he got the clothes that weren't our mom's?"

Mara scrunches her nose and shuts her eyes at the reminder, as if she can make that fact untrue with sheer will power.

"Well, good to know you're not a monk."

Dylan laughs at her expense. "Now who's being a prude."

But I don't laugh. I'm not happy she's wearing past fling's clothes either. I prefer not to have the same girl here more than once, but sometimes a girl will make her way back late at night and, because I'm a gentleman, I don't turn them away.

I don't want anyone getting the idea it's more than it is. It's just sex. No relationships. No feelings. No commitment. I like my sanctuary free of other people (aside from my brother) and I like my isolation. But because I'm a straight man, I crave the occasional warm body.

That's why I don't like having Mara here. She's a reminder that during the four months I'm locked up here, I can't indulge from time to time. I'm not going to lie, there have been a couple nights it's tempting to think I could go to her and get rid of the need to fuck someone. She's beautiful. She's got a great body, from what I can tell, if she didn't spar with me the whole time, it would be a tempting thought. But I know it would be a disaster and she'd probably tell me I'm doing it wrong.

But the more civil we get, the more I wonder if maybe she'd be open to a mutually beneficial arrangement.

Then I remember prom night and that goes out the window.

Not long after, Dylan heads to bed to sleep off his little buzz while Mara cuts another slice of pie to "soak up the alcohol." I let her stick to that story.

After a minute of watching her eat pie in silence, which is actually awkward for me, and not much makes me feel awkward, I walk to the living room to grab the cribbage board and cards. I set them in the middle of the cleared dining table and start shuffling. Mara watches me while she slowly chews a bite at slug speed, eyes on a pendulum back and forth between the cards and me. I set the deck in front of her to cut. She looks at it for a moment, considering my request, then takes half the deck and sets it beside the bottom half without taking her eyes off me.

And the game begins.

"River" by Leon Bridges plays softly from the speaker as we near the end of the game. I'm in the lead with six points to go, but only four points separate us. For this being only her second game, she's picked up the tricks and patterns quite well. Cribbage is a game of skill, not just luck. You can't predict what cards you'll be dealt, but it's about how you use those cards.

I'll be honest, I thought this game would be a cakewalk but she's kept me on my toes, even passed me at one point. But a lucky twenty point hand put me ahead of her again on a hand I dealt. This round I'll have to focus on pegging, so I set up my hand for just that.

"Close game," she comments. "I guess it will all be decided before we even reach counting our hands." Clever girl. She's a fast learner.

I dealt so she has to start the round.

She lays down a seven and announces her card.

I lay down a four. I'm supposed to announce my card like a gentleman, it is a respectful game, after all. But there's no way I'm breaking my silence for that. It's going to take a lot for me to ever consider speaking.

Mara sets a six of hearts on her pile.

I lay down a five nonchalantly and take my three points for the run without even a smile. I catch Mara's nose twitch out of the corner of my eye, the only tell that she's frustrated. The gears are turning in her head to figure out how to use her last two cards to win this.

She plays an eight, adding up to twenty-eight. I can see she thinks she's gotten me, but I lay down an ace and take the two points for reaching thirty-one.

The realization she's lost makes her facial features tighten, but at least she's not a sore loser. She lays down her last card, a three, and I lay down mine, another eight. I get the Go and take my final point for the win.

"Good game," she says politely, though I can tell losing bothers her. Or maybe it's just losing to me. "Thought I'd pass you, for a minute. Oh well."

I offer a half smile and dip my head to thank her for the game as I start to shuffle the cards for the next time we play and Mara stores the pegs in the little compartment beneath the board.

Using her hand flat against the tabletop, Mara presses herself up into a standing position then stretches her arms out. The top of her dress flattens tighter to her chest with the motion. With the gathered material I can't tell if she's wearing a bra or not.

She yawns. "I think I'm going to go to bed." She turns and heads for the stairs. With one hand on the banister, she turns around to face me again with her eyes downcast to the floor boards.

In a soft voice I barely register, she speaks. "In the spirit of Thanksgiving, thank you for saving me, Jason." I stop at those words, at the emotion lacing her voice with sincerity. "And...I don't think I've ever said this, but I'm sorry for the way I treated you in high school. I made mistakes, a lot of them. And I'm sorry for the way I acted. For what I took part in."

Silence. I hope she wasn't expecting me to forgive her or wash her of her sins.

But she apologized. She said what no one else has. She dropped herself down a level and willingly offered her shame on a silver platter. I don't know how I feel about it. I'm not angry, I never forgave her, but I also forgot about it long before she came back into the picture. Her spitefulness wasn't worth any more consideration.

God, it would have been so much easier if she'd never driven headfirst back into my life.

After a long pause following her apology and gratitude, she drops her head and walks upstairs with a heavy weight in her posture. And I'm left to think about shit I don't want to cross my mind.

Chapter Ten

Jason-Senior Year

Mr Brightside-The Killers

Prom wouldn't have been my first choice on a Saturday night. But Mom insisted I attend at least one normal school function before I graduate. I never went to football games, never attended Dylan's wrestling matches before he was kicked off the team. And I sure as hell never went to any school dances.

It's as tortuous as I expected.

Lots of flowers, twinkling lights, a dorky theme that was designed by little girls to live out their childhood fantasies. We even have the cliche trifecta: jocks spiking the punch bowl, a girl crying with her friends over something stupid, and a power couple suffocating whatever space they occupy.

People like Mara Meyers and Bryce Quinn are infuriating. They're both good looking and they know it, which leads to stuck up personalities wrapped in an egoistic bow. How stereotypical can you get? The good girl who's perfect at everything she sets her mind to and the dumb, asshole jock who doesn't have two brain cells to rub together.

I was in the same SAT testing room he was assigned to and the guy who answered for Bryce when the monitor took attendance was not Bryce Quinn. But I'll bet his test scores were good enough to get him into college.

I don't even know why I took the SATs since I don't want to go to college. I've been taking courses for metal work and fabrication. Trade jobs are going to become the more lucrative career path, mark my words. And I want to be a well established business by the time that comes around. You don't need good SAT scores to operate a leith.

I don't exactly have *friends* at this school, but I have people I tolerate and in turn tolerate me. I sit with a couple of them at a table in the back of the large event room drinking the punch from little plastic cups.

Even though spiking the punch is a cliche, I'm not complaining.

People dance in a provocative manner on the dance floor to the mainstream covers the band plays on stage, I think it's called "Mr. Brightside".

Dancing isn't really the right word for what they're doing. The girls without dates jump up and down with their dateless cohorts while the couples leave absolutely no room for Jesus between their bodies. There's a couple of chaperones around the room, but none of them care enough to interrupt. Or maybe they're afraid they'll accidentally be incinerated by the heat from the friction the *dancing* is giving off.

Bored of the people I'm with and trying to pass the one hour I told my mom I'd stay for, I head to the buffet table to scrounge up some edible food. Whoever was in charge of the catering menu ordered more accommodations for the vegans and gluten free weirdos than for those of us who eat normal food.

But every party has some form of pigs in a blanket and this one is no exception. Little cocktail sausages and cheese wrapped in a flakey croissant. Paired with some vegetables from the colorful spread with various dips makes for a lackluster meal, but sustaining, nonetheless.

Standing at the end of the buffet table watching the pornographic display on the dance floor, my left side ignites with awareness of someone else standing oddly close. Oddly because very few people risk getting this close to me. I see vibrant blue out of the corner of my eye, then platinum blonde hair.

Mara Meyers? What the fuck is she doing? Maybe she doesn't see me or mistakes me for someone else.

"It's overwhelming isn't it?" She says to me without taking her eyes off the mass of bodies on the dance floor.

I finally turn my head to look at her. She's stunning. Her dress hugs all the right places without trying too hard. She used the fairytale theme perfectly without taking on a full cartoon princess vibe. The neckline of her dress draws attention to her chest that's expertly lifted but not completely spilling out, the swell of her breasts shine with some glow she must have applied herself.

Captivating.

She meets my gaze then looks back to the dance floor. "I'm kind of surprised you're here," She admits. "I didn't think this would be your scene. But I guess you're full of surprises. Keep them guessing, right?"

That's one way to look at it.

Then she fully turns her body to face me, direct and powerful. She carries herself with the confidence of someone who's never been bullied a day in her life.

"Do you want to go somewhere with me?" She asks with so much conviction it's scary. "We don't have to leave the building. Let's just...not be around all this."

I'd normally say no. If anyone else had asked I'd just walk away from them in silent rejection. I'm tempted to turn her down.

But the look in her eyes draws me in. Since I communicate with body language instead of words I pay more attention to people's eyes and faces than anything else. And her eyes have a plea in them, desperation I wouldn't have expected in someone so sure of herself all the time.

The spell she casts on me takes instant effect and I nod.

Lead the way.

Mara grabs my hand and pulls me toward a side door that leads into the hallway. She clasps my hand with our palms locked, thumbs intertwined as she picks up her pace to a speed walk toward the bathrooms but stops outside and sinks to the floor against the wall. The weightless fabric of her dress fans around her like a magical blue pool of water. I just stare at her with my hands tucked in my pants pockets for a second.

"Are you afraid I have cooties?" She teases, then pats the space beside her. Reluctantly, I sit on the floor that looks like it hasn't been swept in a week. I'm kind of surprised she'd let a dress that costs a car payment touch the dirty floor, she'll have stray hairs and food crumbs stuck to the back of her dress when she stands.

Of course, if she needs someone to brush it off I'll happily oblige.

"You look nice, by the way. I don't think I've ever seen you in anything besides jeans and a t-shirt. Although, you pull those off pretty well too." Mara angles her head a little more toward me but I keep staring ahead. "I'm a little surprised you haven't dated anyone, or hooked up with someone. You're a good looking guy. I'm sure there's gotta be some girl who isn't concerned about talking because what she has in mind doesn't require words."

She'd be wrong. Her boyfriend made damn sure people saw me as a pariah and no one wanted to get too close. He's made life hell. I don't know if my school life would've been easier without his torment and bullying, and I never will. No one wants to go near the Mute or risk social suicide by associating with me.

So why does she?

I'll never admit it, but I've never kissed a girl, never had sex, none of it. And it never bothered me until now. I don't know why but I care what she thinks. And although I don't care what her boyfriend thinks, I care about how this stunning creature beside me views me. I can't help but think she isn't as mean or distant as the person she is around her peers. But she's a great actress.

Before I register what's happening, I feel soft lips on my cheekbone and a gentle hand on my jaw holding me in place as she kisses my cheek. Her touch is warm, a fire ignites where her lips meet my skin and travels to my belly where it cools with nerves.

Why did she do that? Why *would* she do that?

We've barely interacted in the twelve years we've been in school together. Our parents aren't friends. We don't have any mutual friends. Sure I've noticed her from afar, who wouldn't? She's beautiful. Her personality is captivating. But that's it. So why is she initiating communication now?

The second she pulls away I turn my head quickly to make out what just happened in her eyes. I see hesitation, I see nerves, I see fear of rejection. Does she really think I'd be upset? I'm not upset, I'm fucking confused, but I'm not upset.

Actually, it was nice. Her touch sparked a chemical reaction like a base and an acid mixing to create something new. I'm not foolish enough to think anything like *she was made for me,* or some bullshit. But I can't help the gnawing in my gut that tells me I want more.

I want more.

Turning my torso to mirror her angle, I take her hand in mine and run my thumb over the lines of her palm, tracing what others think can determine their future, define their lives. And I understand for a split second why they might feel that way. It's not my lines that mean anything, it's hers. Her pulse in my hand, her skin beneath mine. Such a light touch and it feels so heavy.

I'm not the kind to romanticize the meaningless, but part of me sees the sweet karma in my bully's girlfriend being my first kiss. How I'd like to run my hands and lips over the same skin he thought he'd claimed.

"It's a good thing you never dated anyone," she validates my choices. "It's easier to outgrow this town when you're not tied to it. Bryce is...a dick. But at least he's not a long term commitment kind of guy otherwise I might never be able to leave." *Leave?* "I don't want to be stuck here forever and pick up right where my parents left off. I don't want their life. I want to see more of the world. I want something more meaningful than just another cog in the system."

That I do understand. I have no desire to live in a big, busy city with people who can't function without validation from others. But I don't want to stay in town either. I want a life of my choosing, designed by me for me. One that simplifies what others strive for. Stability. Purpose. Happiness. I think people assume they can only find that when they feel special or unique. I disagree. I think it can be found when we humble ourselves back to our roots.

But my line of thinking isn't for everyone.

Mara looks at the bathroom door beside us then back at me. "Come on," she says with a sly grin that brightens the world. Rising to her feet, she doesn't let go of my hand, just takes me along with her until I'm standing over her as she pushes into the men's bathroom.

It's empty. I go to lock the door but she stops me, "What? Are you afraid I'll escape?" I catch the meaning behind her words. *Don't cage me in.* Okay, I won't give the impression she's trapped, but if someone interrupts us, I'm not stopping.

I press her back to the wall by walking her back, chest to chest, hands still locked. Leaning my forehead against hers, I inhale her lavender scent like I'm hotboxing a car, taking every intoxicating fume into my core.

She slides her hands up my chest to the first button that closes my shirt. She unhooks it and continues her way down until my shirt is open in front but hanging on my shoulders.

I wrap my still covered arms around her waist to her back to feel for the zipper to her dress. Much to my frustration, I find a long row of tiny buttons. *Great.*

But she claps my forearms before I can get to work. "Wait," there's panic in her voice, a little fear. *Is this her first time too?* "I'm...I'm not ready yet. You first?" It's not a demand but the nervousness in her voice makes me think she'd be more comfortable if she's not the first one to get naked.

I don't really want to be the only one naked either, but if someone has to go first, might as well be the gentleman.

Although a men's bathroom isn't really ideal. If things were different, I'd have taken her to my lake on the mountain and laid a bunch of blankets in the bed of my truck. I hear girls like things like that, but I also like the idea of the seclusion, just her and I and no interference. Forget the world around us and the past and fall into the relief of our bodies.

But if this is what she wants, who am I to deny her?

So I let the shirt fall from my arms to the floor. Nimble fingers loosen the belt at my waist before sliding my pants down my legs. I slip off my shoes but leave my black socks on, no way I'm touching this nasty floor. No way she is either, when she's ready, I'll hold her up between my chest and the wall so she doesn't have to get dirty.

Shit, I don't think I have a condom. I guess she'll get a *little* dirty, after all.

Last but not least, I slip my boxers down my legs then rise to stand fully bared before her, vulnerable and faking confidence. Something about being naked in front of her makes me feel like I might not be enough. I crave her acceptance.

I get just that when her eyes fix on my cock and her lips part in surprise. I guess I'm impressive enough.

With that little boost of confidence, I step forward to meet her nose to nose, breath to breath. I plant my hands on the curve of her dress where it flares at her hips and breathe her in again, marking her scent in my mind so I never forget. I never want to forget the feel of her tight body in my grasp, or the way she's looking at me with so much anticipation.

"Jason," she sighs breathily. I can feel her heartbeat since her chest is molded to mine. Is she excited? Nervous? Flustered? Maybe all of it.

I'm trying so hard to keep my eyes locked on hers, as close as we are, and not let them wander south to her breasts that lift with every shallow breath she takes.

But I'm breathing just as hard. I'm a little nervous since I haven't done this before, but I have this distinct feeling that when I'm inside her, it will all come to me, that I'll know what she needs on pure instinct.

Bang.

Before I get the chance to find out if that's true, the door is thrown open and hands are on me before I can react. One person puts me in a choke hold while two others grab my arms and lock me in their will. I'm dragged off of Mara watching her sorrow filled eyes as they follow me out the door.

I don't have to guess who has me, I'm not surprised they planned something to humiliate me, but I am gutted that Mara would do something so cruel.

This isn't just poking fun or belittling me. This is evil, public humiliation, harassment. This is so far beneath her.

Or at least I thought it was.

Goes to show you that people are capable of savage things. Some people excel at fooling the world as much as themselves.

I guess she is as shallow as she seems.

Bryce and his thugs drag me back into the main event space hollering all the while.

"Look what we caught," Bryce announces to the gathered students on the dance floor. "A mute fish caught with his pants down."

"Looks more like an eel to me," someone shouts from the crowd, earning laughter.

The two holding my arms back release me and Bryce shoves me from behind so my side lands on the wood paneled dance floor.

Where the fuck are the chaperones?

The laughter rings in my ears, it's barbaric and cruel. It's the sound of people who don't care what sort of humiliation they've faced in their lives. As long as it's not happening to them, it's hilarious. I'm the butt of their joke, I'm their source of amusement. I'm the joker. The clown. The fool who meets pain and embarrassment as a source of entertainment for the masses.

I'm nothing to them. Maybe one day that won't matter. But today, it hurts.

I scramble to my feet and back away from the crowd before turning to face my tormentors. Bryce is bent over laughing with his friends at my expense.

Then Mara runs into the room carrying my clothes. The fucking bitch has the gall to look ashamed. *Yeah right*, if she was really ashamed, she wouldn't have participated in the game.

I storm past her pathetic boyfriend who will never be bigger than he is now and snatch my clothes out of her hands.

"Jason," she says timidly. I don't think she has anything else to follow it up. I stare at her for a second, imprinting the pitiful expression on her face in my mind.

I don't need to speak to convey my message. I just stare at her with all my fury until her parted lips close and she sucks them between her teeth.

Fuck you.

Chapter Eleven

Jason

BURNING HOUSE-CAM

I don't know why I dreamed about prom last night. What the fuck is this girl doing to me? Why did she have to bring up prom on Thanksgiving?

It took me way too long to get over that night. To live down being the naked kid from prom. Eventually, people forgot about me in place of the next short lived, news-worthy story.

Guess I should thank them, though, plenty of girls saw the "eel" between my legs and didn't care if I was the mute kid anymore, not when my body was better than expected and girls started wondering what that eel could do.

Turns out, my first time would be in a bathroom after all. And just the way I'd planned to touch Mara, I fucked her friend instead.

Apparently, it was good enough that word spread and I didn't have to work hard to get laid after that.

God, I need to get laid if I'm dreaming about Mara in the bathroom at prom. Or, more accurately, I need to jerk off.

I roll over in bed to grab a dirty t-shirt off the floor then roll onto my back, slipping my cock free of the sweatpants I slept in. No matter how cold it gets, I never wear a shirt to bed, it makes me feel like I'm suffocating, choking, like a noose. But it's been fucking cold lately so I've been wearing thick sweatpants to bed.

I fist my hand around my dick at the base of the shaft and start stroking upward to the head. Every so often, I swirl my thumb over the tip eliciting small shockwaves up my spine. Normally, I think of faceless women with perfect tits and curves for days, with thighs wrapped around my waist as I fuck them senseless.

An image pops into my head, smooth skin with a layer of water coating her as I hold her tight in my lake. A firm ass in my hands to keep her afloat and her core positioned with my cock. I never picture a specific woman and I never kiss them in my fantasies. She's just a nameless, faceless warm body to achieve release. After all, we all have urges, don't we? And we all need to feel satisfied.

My pace quickens with each thrust when another image comes to mind, Mara backed against a bathroom wall in a stunning blue dress with come-fuck-me eyes batting long lashes in my direction. No timidness, no hesitation, just the desperate desire for me.

Fuck, no. Not what I want to think about right now. It's just cause I had a dream about it. That's all.

I go back to my lake and imagine what the cool water feels like in the heat of summer with the body heat of a girl in my arms. Her body is wrapped around every inch of mine while I'm buried deep in her, hearing pants and moans of pleasure the more I drive into her. The imaginary girl likes it rough, hard, vicious. She can take every ounce of bitterness I'm fucking out of my body.

Then she breathes my name and her voice sounds familiar. *"Jason."* I know that voice. I know because I heard her say it just like that. It was about as real as this vision is.

Suddenly the woman in my arms in the lake takes a little more shape. Her hazel eyes clarify and the pink lips she spills so much hate from takes form, smiling at me with a seductive tilt. The rest of her is a little fuzzy, but I imagine full breasts and a narrow waist. I can practically feel her bending beneath my touch, warm amidst the cool water where our bodies join.

I keep fisting my dick through the image trying to force the memory away with my masturbation.

Fuck.

Fuck.

"Jason."

I can't get her face out of my mind or her voice, but I don't soften either. However, her face is not what I want to come to. Anything but her.

Damnit, why did she have to get in my head like that? Apologizing for prom and thanking me for saving her life. Is she on some apology tour trying to find redemption in her adult life? Who says her words were genuine, anyway? For all I know that was a bunch of bullshit.

But why would she lie about it? She has no reason to.

This fucking girl. She's getting in my head and I don't like it. It was easier when we hated each other. It was easier just to acknowledge her when absolutely necessary and subtly piss her off the rest of the time. Being nice to her or tolerating her presence is so much more complicated.

No matter how hard I try, I can't make myself come so I toss the shirt in the hamper across the room and roll out of bed to get dressed.

Fuck it, I'll try again tonight.

I can't go one more day without an orgasm.

After I'm dressed I head downstairs, the first one up, as per usual. The smell of the coffee awakens my soul as soon as the machine starts to brew. I used to live on coffee alone in the morning, but since Mara has been staying here we've fallen into a routine. She makes breakfast, Dylan makes lunch, and I make dinner. It's a good system. And it hasn't escaped my notice that Mara does most of the dishes and the laundry in the house, either. She's gotten good at finding things to help with instead of waiting for us to assign tasks. She'll work inside on things that need to get done or go out and shovel snow, feed the animals, anything she can find to keep herself busy. She's even taken to organizing the shop for us. If I didn't know better, I'd think she likes this life, an honest living with simple needs and routine. Mara always seemed like she longed for the excitement of city life. She certainly didn't waste time getting out of town after graduation. Hell, she left the entire state.

My heart does a weird little flip when I think about how vulnerable she got with me on the horse ride to her car. I don't know if she actually wanted to tell me all of that or if she just needed to get it off her chest and I was there. I suppose she knows her secrets are safe with me.

"Morning," her voice greets me from behind. "Is the coffee ready?" She reaches around me for a mug in the cupboard, taking the pot and pouring her half a cup before adding milk and swishing them together. If I didn't know any better, I'd think her actions were a little more choppy than usual.

Then she gathers ingredients for breakfast, based on what she grabs, I assume she's making pancakes. She's getting better with her cooking and baking. Even her bread making skills have vastly improved.

She throws the fridge open and stares inside for a minute before closing the door and stuffing her feet into her boots by the door and throwing on a sweatshirt.

"No eggs," Mara says dryly. She opens the door then shuts it with a little extra force and heads to the barn. She shoveled a path to the barn yesterday but it already has six inches of snow again. I watch her walk into the barn with heavy footsteps like she's purposely trying to smush the snow beneath her boots.

What crawled up her ass?

Dylan saunters down the stairs next still wearing his pajama pants but he threw on a thermal shirt first. Shortly after, Mara stomps back inside, kicking the snow off her boots on the door frame. She extracts five eggs from the front pocket of the sweatshirt and sets to work making breakfast. It's then I notice the baseball hat she's wearing is mine. It's an olive green *Orvis* fly fishing hat, and it looks like she even adjusted the strap at the back to fit her head.

Where did I leave that hat?

Oh well, not a battle I want to fight. I've got plenty of other hats. And if I'm honest, it looks better on her. Come to think of it, the sweatshirt she threw on is also mine. I don't know why but I get a sick sense of pride seeing her in my clothes.

No, no you don't. It's annoying as fuck and she doesn't look good in them.

My thoughts from this morning pop back into my head. That's the last thing I need right now.

After a very quiet breakfast I head to the barn to kill one of the chickens. We have some eggs incubating for chicks to replace the ones we eat this winter. Dylan hates this part of farm life so I do it without asking. Shooting a deer forty yards away is fine by him, but butchering the animals we raise makes him squeamish. It's not like it's a fun task, but it has to be done.

I think Dylan named all the chickens at one point, but I can't keep track of them. All I know is the ones with yellow ribbons around their feet are the oldest which means they are the first to go.

I pick one up and take her over to the stump we use for splitting wood and grab the hatchet beside it. Holding the chicken against the flat surface of the stump, I position the blade of the hatchet above her neck to take aim.

Just as I raise the hatchet, I hear a voice over my shoulder. "Hey Jason, Dylan wants to know where—."

Whack.

I bring the hatchet down smack dab in the middle of the chicken's neck, severing its head from its body in the middle of her sentence. The body still fights me for a moment even after the head has fallen to the ground.

"*Oh my god,*" she cries behind me. When the chicken's body goes limp I finally turn around to face her horrified expression. She looks from the dead chicken to me and back again. "That's barbaric."

It's survival. But I don't have the desire to persuade someone who will always be set in their ways.

"You couldn't have waited until I was done asking you a question? God, what a shitty way to go."

It's quick and painless. What's so shitty about that? Besides, it's just a fucking chicken.

Maybe it's the sad way she's looking at the chicken carcass, but I take pity on her and lead her to the incubator in the chicken pen. We keep the barn pretty warm for the animals so the hens continue to lay eggs in the winter. I point to the incubator and dots start to connect in her clever mind.

"These eggs are going to hatch?" She asks while inspecting the machine and the eggs it contains. I nod. "That's pretty cool. It'll be fun seeing baby chicks. How soon do you think they'll hatch?"

I hold up one then two fingers.

One to two days.

She nods her understanding before looking at the eggs again. The child-like excitement on her face is pretty cute. I've grown so numb to what others consider out of the ordinary. Most people take their kids to a farm for a couple hours to pet and feed the animals. They don't talk about what happens to the animals when they get old or how they come to be in the first place.

The little joy Mara found thinking about the chicks close to hatching was short lived when she realized she had to eat the hen I butchered for dinner. And even less thrilled when I sat her down to teach her how to pluck and clean a chicken. I don't really give a fuck if she thinks it's gross or depressing. But watching her face morph into pure anguish at the task of plucking feathers was pretty amusing.

At least she's good entertainment.

Mara stomps around the rest of the day in a mood. She's acting like a petulant teenager who didn't get her way. I don't know what's different about today to put her in such a foul mood, but eating the hen for dinner didn't help either.

Stubborn. Arrogant. Prissy princess.

She's dancing on my last nerve with her sour attitude so I head back out to the shop after dinner to decompress with some metal work. When I'm not working on firearms, I still enjoy crafting and creating. Lately, I've been working on making light fixtures from whatever I have. Antlers are pretty popular and I know I can sell those in the spring after the snow melts. After a lot of shed hunting in the spring, I have quite a collection for chandeliers.

It's a precise skill to wire the antlers and create pathways for the wires without compromising the structure. That's the part that keeps my brain working. The creative part is designing the look of the chandeliers.

Dylan won't let me hang one above the dining table because he thinks it will be too "straight white redneck" for him. I'll oblige him for now, but I know my brother. He won't be here forever. He may not want to live somewhere like Portland, but he likes people too much to stay on the mountain.

Eventually, it'll be just me and the animals to inhabit the mountain. Part of me is looking forward to having things just the way I want them. I'm looking forward to not tip-toeing around anyone else's feelings. It's exhausting considering other people's feelings.

But a part of me knows I'll miss him. A part of me fears what my mind will do with too much silence and no human contact.

Besides, we built this business together. I'm not delusional, I know he doesn't want to do this forever, but I also don't feel right continuing it without him.

I'm bent over my work station when a light catches my eye out the window at eye level. I look up with a sharp snap of my head, concerned about what it could be. But a wave of relief washes over me when I see Mara head toward the barn with a lantern in hand, bundled in a thick blanket.

That relief is quickly replaced by curiosity.

What is she doing out here?

No way I'm just going back to work with the unknown nagging at me. So I set my work aside for the night, turn off the light before closing the door, and head for the barn.

I slowly creep inside, shutting the barn door as silently as possible. I shouldn't be so suspicious but it is pretty unusual for her to be out here this late.

Passing each stall, I find Mara in the chicken pen seated on a little stool we use to milk the goats. She's staring at the incubator. I notice one of the egg shells is peeled off in a couple spots which means the chick is close to hatching.

She's just staring at them. She's so still and...pitiful. Not in a pathetic kind of way, but my chest tightens at the sight of her looking so down and out. Something is going on with her and she isn't talking about it. And I've learned Mara is the kind of person who needs to talk through everything.

And I mean everything. When she was on her period she scarred Dylan and I with a graphic description of blood clots and period cramps. It sounded like she was describing a fatal injury from battle. Not a monthly cycle.

I step forward with purposeful steps to announce my presence but Mara doesn't turn around. She's staring intently at the little chick poking through the thin layer of membrane beneath the shell and coming into the world.

What an easy way to bring life into the world. Chickens lay an egg, and the baby does all the work. Seems like a better plan than the torture humans go through.

A little gasp escapes Mara's mouth when the chick emerges from the shell it called home until now. She lays a hand on the lid of the incubator The little thing starts chirping away causing Mara to laugh a little.

"Hey, little thing," she says to the bird. It's too small to know the gender. "Welcome to the world. Do you want to know a secret?" She sniffs. Is she crying? "We share a birthday."

What?

Shit. It's her birthday today? That explains the mood she's been in. And, honestly, I don't blame her. What a shitty birthday.

"Thanks for making your grand entrance into the world today. You kind of saved a crappy day with a good ending."

"It's also been a month of living here," Mara tells me without looking away from the new addition to the chicken family. "And if you think about it, I wasn't supposed to be here for this birthday. But I am. I don't know if that's a blessing or not."

Wow. I actually feel bad for her. I don't really celebrate my birthday but at least I'm not questioning my existence. A magnetic pull forms between me and Mara, something urging me to comfort her the way I know women like to be soothed. I want to put an arm around her shoulders, I want to tell her it'll all be ok.

I want to tell her she's here for a reason, even if it's not clear why, yet.

But that's not me. And that's not us. I'm not her BFF or her mom.

I'm not exactly her friend either, but we've become reluctant acquaintances.

"I wonder if my parents are thinking about me today. They don't know I'm alive. For all they know I've been kidnapped or murdered or drove off a bridge into a river. Then again, I doubt they'd think to look for my car in a snowbank on the mountain." Her voice softens just a hair. "I bet they're going about their lives as if I never existed today. As if my mom didn't give birth to me twenty-two years ago today." They aren't really the sentimental type, anyway."

My father wasn't exactly my hero, he made sure I felt unwanted most of my life. But I always had Mom, and she made every birthday special. She always baked birthday cakes for Dylan and I that could beat the local bakery in a contest any day. My father didn't let us have friends over (when we did have friends) for birthday parties, but Mom would make sure we celebrated in style.

I always had her, and Dylan. But it sounds like Mara has never had someone who loves her the way my mom loved me. I actually pity her. She's never had to save for a shiny new toy, never had to wonder if she'd get what she wanted for Christmas. I'm sure she had birthday parties with lots of people in attendance. But she's always had to wonder if the people around her really cared.

Whereas I never had much in the way of physical gifts, but I always knew where I stood with my parents. And I knew one of them loved me more than life, she loved her kids more than anything.

If I'd known it was Mara's birthday today, I wouldn't have made a big deal about it, that's just not who I am. But I might have made her breakfast so she could sleep in. Or maybe made a cake for dinner and called it good. Something. Cause that's how Mom raised us.

Instead, she got to spend her birthday doing chores in a place she doesn't want to be with people she doesn't even like. And all the while, she's stuck on what other people who don't matter think. Yeah, your parents should matter, but if they don't care about you, they don't deserve half a thought. So no, they don't matter.

I don't know what possesses me to do it, but I head over to a box of random shit that doesn't have a place to go and find a box of matches.

When I go back to where Mara is standing in the chicken pen, I strike the match against the box to ignite the flame and hold the small, lit stick in the space between us. Her eyes dance back and forth between the match and me, taking in my neutral expression.

I'm not going to sing for her if that's what she's expecting.

Mara closes her eyes for a moment, taking in a deep inhale of breath that seems far more labored than it should. Her brows pinch together. Then all her features soften on an exhale as she puckers her lips and blows the match out, casting her birthday wish into the universe. She stares momentarily at the thin stream of smoke billowing from the extinguished match before locking eyes with me again, hazel peering up between thick lashes. The muscles around her eyes tighten for a moment, almost as though she's pleading for something. A flash of desperation and then her face softens again.

"I'm going to bed," she announces before walking out the barn door to the lodge.

It's about an hour later when I finish my work and head inside. I'm an idiot for staying up this late when I have to wake up again in six hours to start my day. May seem crazy to get up that early to work out in my isolated lodge in the woods, but I don't like getting lazy. I don't like being idle, either. So I keep my routine consistent.

The minute I walk through the back door into the kitchen, I freeze. I shouldn't care, I shouldn't even be tempted. But when I see Mara standing in one of *my* thermal shirts and a pair of underwear at the kitchen island, my whole body quivers with need. It's been over a month since I last fucked someone and a half naked, gorgeous woman standing in my kitchen at midnight isn't helping.

At the sight of her bare legs and the lower half of her curved ass, my cock does a little twitch like a dog catching the scent of its prey. With that, the air in my lungs hardens for a minute before I can breathe again.

"I…" her voice trails off when the weight of my attention falls on her. "I found your liquor cabinet, I was just making a drink." Then I notice the bottles of whiskey and bitters on the countertop beside a glass of ice. Looks like she's already poured a bit of sugar in the glass.

"Want one?" The nervousness in her voice draws my attention back up to her eyes that carry more emotion than they should. Self doubt. Arousal. Hesitation. Curiosity. Longing.

Does she want me to make a move?

Would we be able to coexist as roommates with benefits?

I'll give her credit, she's not crumpling into a ball of humiliation for the state I caught her in.

I don't know if this is a good idea. I'll be a man and admit I'm attracted to Mara, her curvy body turns me on, but then I look at her face and remember who she is. What she's done. The person she was in high school.

But I'm not the kid I was then. I know she's not the girl from the bathroom anymore, but maybe a part of her is—or was. I don't know, this is all confusing and I can't concentrate on anything when she bears part of her ass as she leans over the counter to stretch for the jar of cherries. She has to know what she's doing, right? She has to know her round ass hangs beneath the shirt a bit and I can see the curve of her cheeks. She has to know that when she lifts on her toes and bends over the farmhouse sink to wash the spoon she used to stir that I can see where her underwear disappears between her ass cheeks. There's no way she's that oblivious.

I can't take it anymore. I don't care if this little show is an invitation or not. Without a second thought, I plant my hands on her solid hips and breathe in her scent at the nape of her neck all at once. My touch makes her jerk in surprise which only backs her into my chest so I have a tighter hold on her.

And even better, it presses her round ass into my hardening cock. She's extremely aware of how turned on I am.

The sound of my heavy inhale and her stuttering breaths mingles in the air, the only sounds I register at all. When I graze my teeth over her throat I feel the quick pulse beneath, I feel it all the way from my lips to my dick.

Fuck. She smells insanely good. It's warm and comforting like a wool blanket in bed on a snowy day, laced with something floral. And her skin is pure silk. Every sensation is clouding my judgment and my thoughts, I can't think clearly with her captured between the side of the sink and my hard body. The last time I felt her this close, she was unnaturally thin and pliable in my grasp. Now, she's a handful, a woman with the body of one. A narrow waist that I easily snake one arm around beneath the shirt as my teeth take a quick pull of her earlobe eliciting a soft moan from her.

She's divine.

When she doesn't protest my hold or try to free herself, I take it as silent permission for me to go further. The arm around her waist lifts so her heavy breasts are supported by my forearm while my free hand splays over the expanse of her stomach in a slow dip toward her panty line.

She has limited pairs of underwear and of course tonight is the night she decides to sleep in them. No matter. It's like unwrapping a present.

I slip one finger beneath the flexible fabric, then another, and another until my entire hand is beneath the flimsy barrier and I can feel the little tuft of hair at the apex of her thighs. I usually prefer a woman bare, but seeing as she doesn't have a razor, I can understand.

Just makes the mission to the center that much more rewarding.

When my hand dives between her legs in one long, languid slide to her center, she drops her head back to my shoulder. At the feel of her soaking wet pussy, a low growl hums through my chest and up my throat. Mara's body tenses at the sound and the feel of me, but that's no detriment to me. It only eggs me on. I lick from her earlobe to the top around the entire shell of her ear and one finger dips into her wet cunt and pulls out again. I wish I could see her glistening on me, but I'm not about to break this powerful hold I have on her. So instead, I slip a second finger in. When her gasp turns into a moan, I know she's in agony under my slow torture. That's exactly what she deserves, to writhe with need, to need me as much as I needed her. To *want* me as much as I wanted her.

The only problem is I still want her.

I want her badly. I want to bend her over the sink and fuck her until she's screaming. I want to feel her come around my cock. I want to come *in* her.

But I'm not about to give her that. It's too easy, too generous to a woman who crushed my spirit and humiliated me. Too nice for the girl who was so mean and made me believe she wanted me.

Well, she wants me now. So I'll show her the beast she's cursed.

I pump my fingers in and out a few times before spreading her arousal all over her hard clit. I drop the arm looping her rib cage so my hand spreads over her lower abdomen and press, opening her ever so slightly for me so her clit peeks out even more. The breath in her throat hitches and stutters, her body goes rigid before melting into my hold. Her head lolls to one side exposing her slender neck to me again and I hover my mouth over her skin, letting my breath dance over the sensitive skin.

She's so pliable, so willing, so desperate. It gives me a sick satisfaction that the woman who made my life hell is now under my control. As long as my fingers keep circling her clit at this smooth, leisurely pace, she's completely at my mercy.

"Jason," she sighs. And it draws me back. I was so lost in the lust I forgot where I was, too fixated on how tight her pussy felt and how warm she is in my hands, back to my chest.

Jolted out of my trance, I pull away suddenly. Let her feel the mind altering desperation and disappointment I felt on prom night.

She spins on me with a look so cold and ferocious a weaker man might have been terrified. But I'm not weak. And I'm not afraid of her. I match her look of rage with an amused one of my own as I dip my wet fingers in my mouth and suck her off me. The act makes her nostrils flare.

"No, fuck no. You're not getting off that easy." She declares as though she can stop me. Like I owe her an orgasm or something.

I head for the stairs but she stops me in my tracks with a line I can't resist, one I can't back down from.

"Finish what you started," she demands. Then the pitch of her voice drops deathly low as she finishes, "or I will finish it myself."

Challenge accepted.

I turn on her so fast she doesn't have a second to prepare before I have her pinned against the wall with a hand at her throat. Her pupils dilate and I know she likes that.

Interesting. I wouldn't have guessed Mara would be into that. But there's no mistaking the eager excitement in her gaze when my fingers flex on her throat.

Before she even knows what's happening, I'm on my knees in front of her with my head buried between her legs and her underwear pulled to one side, driving my tongue into that tight pussy.

"Oh god," she sighs at my explorative touch. I taste every inch of her inside and out. Committing her flavor to memory and trying not to notice the way my body reacts to hers. I've eaten plenty of girls out but I don't usually feel this crazy hunger when I do. Usually, I want to make them see stars so my reputation improves. But I'm starving for her. Starving to taste her come on my tongue.

With one hand on her thigh, I prop her leg on my shoulder to grant me more access to what I want, to what I need. Mara braces her hands flat against the wall down by her hips for balance.

"Fuck," she hisses.

If she wants to challenge me then fine, I'll exceed expectations and make her beg for release, leave her so satisfied she'll be begging for more. But that won't happen. I'll give her a taste of what she threw away and leave her wishing she could have it all.

But greed is a sin, so I'm told. And sinners deserve to be punished.

My arm loops over her raised thigh so my thumb reaches her clit and presses down. Hard. Tight circles on the bud of nerves drives her wild and she starts panting harder and harder, body unable to stay still as my tongue and thumb work together to drive her to the edge of madness.

It's when her fingers lace through my hair that I know she's close. Just where I want her.

That's the moment I choose to slip my tongue out and bite her clit tenderly while plunging three fingers into her cunt and go to town.

"Jason. Oh god. Jason, don't stop. You're going to make me—" Her cries muffle when she bites her lip to stifle the sounds of her orgasm as they echo in the quiet kitchen. According to previous lays, most men don't do what I do. They stop as soon as it sounds like a girl has come. I, on the other hand, increase the pressure when I hear that tell tale cry. I bury my face deeper as her body vibrates with tension and stiffens at my touch.

I lick her through the orgasm until her breathing grows heavy and her weight deepens against my shoulder. Then I release her and let her slide to the floor.

She thinks she's done, she thinks this was a one sided encounter and now she can go to bed satisfied by me.

Think again, prom queen.

I rise from the floor so my pelvis is in line with her face and start to unzip my pants, pulling my rock hard cock from its prison. It almost hurts how hard I am, I so badly need to come. And she's going to do it for me.

I point my cock directly at Mara's mouth earning me a death glare. I watch carefully as the resentment turns into a fire meeting my challenge as she grabs my cock with a pull that shouldn't be as sexy as it is. She's a little rough but that's ok. I like it rough.

She shoves my dick in her mouth without further instruction and starts licking, sucking, humming. Up and down. Root to tip. Driving me wild. There's no gentle ease into the act. There's no tenderness or teasing touches. It's all fire and burning hatred sprinkled with lust. She wants this even if she doesn't want to admit she likes it.

But that rage softens to desire as her eyes roll back in her head and she gives into this. If I didn't know better, I'd say she enjoys sucking my cock.

But fuck, I certainly enjoy it. She's taking me like I was made for her, I fit so perfectly inside her mouth and it makes me wonder if I'd fit perfectly inside her cunt too.

Such vigor, such ferocity. She's an animal starving for it. And her mouth works so well that I'm ready to come way sooner than I'd like. I want to draw this out as long as possible and make her take my dick as long as I can.

But she's too good. She's too sexy. Heat blooms at the base of my spine, my balls tighten but the agony of that is quickly washed away when I can't hold back any longer so I jerk my hips back releasing my dick from her mouth, the pop of her lips over my head lingers between us before I give myself one tug to explode come all over her pretty face. White beads of it drip from her forehead to her cheeks to her chin. The fiery resentment on her face is almost as satisfying as my orgasm.

But what she does next kills me. She swipes a finger through the come on her face and sucks it into her mouth like a fine delicacy before standing to meet my glare. A foot shorter than me and she has more balls than most of the men I've met in my life.

In all honesty, I'm impressed and quite amused by the way she holds her shoulders back and head high. Nothing can destroy this woman, nothing can break her. She continues to surpass my low expectations and rise above the standard. Even her blow job is probably the best one I've ever had.

Oh fuck.

This isn't the last time we do something like this. It can't be. We still have four more months in this house together and it's going to be damn near impossible to resist her now that I know how good her mouth feels. How tight her body is. And how primal sex with Mara Meyers can be.

She swipes a rag from the counter to cleanse her face, takes the untouched drink from the counter where it leaves a ring of condensation, shoots me a seductive, malicious glare, then heads up stairs, ass bouncing with each step.

Fuck! I'm screwed.

Chapter Twelve

Mara-Senior Year

D REAM **G**IRL **E**VIL-**F**LORENCE **+ the Machine**

It's graduation day. I can't believe I made it to this day. Today marks the start of the rest of my life. Everyone has acted like high school is the peak of their life, the greatest experiences they will ever have will be during these four formative years.

I was not under the same delusion.

How could high school be the best years of my life when there is so much more to do? There's an entire world outside these halls that calls to me. The best years are ahead of me.

I'm not an emotional person, but the weight being lifted off my shoulders today has me feeling sentimental and excited for the future. It felt like the end would never arrive.

With classes finished for the seniors, I have the first half of the day to myself. So I decide to go for a run. Just because all of the sports teams I was involved in are over doesn't mean I should let myself go. Besides, I have nothing better to do all summer.

My house is a mile away from anything else and a few miles outside of town. I typically run to the gas station three miles away and back. Our driveway is half a mile long and downhill so that propels me forward for a good start before evening out to a steady rhythm. And then an intense uphill burn at the end. Perfect for my body type and my needs.

"Dream Girl Evil" by Florence + the Machine is playing in my earbuds as I near the gas station and prepare to turn around but I catch myself with a sharp intake of breath. Jason's car is parked beside one of the gas pumps and he's walking out of the station with an energy drink in hand. He stops dead in his tracks the second we lock eyes and I can feel the rage radiating off him. The hurt. The anger.

I never had his number but I wanted to call him and apologize after prom. He's narrowly avoided me since then. Convenient since we don't have any classes together and he's been eating his lunch elsewhere. I saw him once in the halls after school but he was walking away from me. And I didn't want to approach him with so many people around.

What would I even say? *Sorry my boyfriend is such a dick and I helped him humiliate you in front of our entire graduating class.*

That wouldn't go over well. I ease the sting of guilt by telling myself we're graduating and then we will never see each other again. That night is in the past. He will forget about it as well and live the rest of his life. And prom will be nothing but a fading memory like a bad dream that you eventually can't remember.

The spell holding us grounded in place breaks and Jason darts for his car, shutting his door with a slam and driving away without any more interaction.

Even though I've stopped moving, my heart rate is still high. Once the shock wears off, I start my ascent back to my house, savoring the burn and pain of a long run that is well deserved.

For more reasons than one.

I spend the afternoon getting ready for graduation. Deciding on natural glam makeup and soft big waves in my hair so the graduation cap sits nicely on my head. Our school colors are baby blue and scarlet red. This year's class has to wear the blue robes with a red tassel on the hats. It alternates every year. Good thing I look best in blue.

We got to pick our seating at rehearsal and of course I'm seated next to Bryce and his friends. Who else would I sit with? But tomorrow I'm ending things with him. Sure I could wait until the end of summer but what's the point? He's a dick and selfish in bed. So he has no further use to me.

Absent-mindedly, I look around the crowd of students that I've attended school with for twelve years. And I could probably only name twenty of them.

It's never bothered me before how little I interacted with my peers. But it hits me that I've spent twelve years with the same group of people I know so few of. What if I'd reached out and become best friends with someone? What if the love of my life is in this class and I never met him because I was so secluded and stuck in what was easy?

Maybe it's because I'll never see them again that I'm feeling this remorse. Like a kid who isn't interested in a toy until someone else wants it.

But it's too late for what ifs and what could have been. This is it for me. After today, I start a whole new life that doesn't involve the small town restraints that I've known here.

California awaits!

Suddenly it dawns on me, I don't see Jason. He's an intelligent kid, I know he passed all his classes so he's graduating. But he's not here. Is he late? The ceremony is about to start since we've already walked in.

As the principal takes the podium on stage, I come to the gut-wrenching conclusion that he's not coming. Sure they can just mail him his diploma, but doesn't he want the satisfaction of walking across the stage and bidding everyone farewell?

I guess the things that matter to us don't matter to everyone. And just as I'm ready to be done with this town and these people, he's long past that point.

But a contrite and guilty part of me knows there's probably one big reason he isn't here. And I'll beat myself up over the fact I played a part in taking this defining moment from him. For ruining what must have been a hard twelve years for him.

But I'll have to feel guilty later, cause I've waited too long to let anything sour this success.

Try as I might, the gnawing pit in my gut doesn't go away as my name is called and I cross the stage. I take my diploma in its shiny case, shake the principal's hand, and switch the tassel on my hat to the opposite side. What an anticlimactic, ceremonious end to this chapter of my life.

Chapter Thirteen

Mara

TWISTER-DELTA RAE

Oh my god.

That's my first thought when I wake up. I don't have any other words to describe how I'm feeling about last night. What does it mean? Is that going to be a regular encounter? Does Jason want me? The spitfire in his eyes tells me he does but he doesn't want to want me. He hates me but he craves me. The way he touched me...the way he made me come harder than even I can make myself come.

The way he demanded what he wanted from me without a single word after driving me to combustion. I shouldn't have liked being so degraded but...I think I did. I've only been with beta males, weak men who hardly contribute to sexual interactions. They never had the same passion Jason showed last night. He just took what he wanted.

I've come to realize passion is not only a romantic thing. There's passion in romance, passion in anger, passion in achieving a goal.

Passion is a powerful motivator.

The clock beside the bed says it's 6:30 am. Which means Jason is already awake and working out in the garage. I shouldn't feel like I need to avoid him but I do. How do I even interact with him now? He didn't kiss me last night so I'm assuming it's just casual. Just sex. But we also only did oral stuff. I don't know. I guess I'll just take his lead.

I fling the covers off me and walk to the closet to get dressed. I pull on one of the leggings that were left here by some skank who slept with Jason, and one of his flannels. No bra. Buttoned just high enough to cover my boobs. I've noticed the way he eyes his clothes on me. Before, I wasn't sure if he was upset about it or turned on. Now, I'm starting to think it's both.

After brushing my teeth and tying my hair into a single braid over my shoulder, I head downstairs. Just as I'm pouring myself a cup of coffee, Jason comes back inside from the garage glistening in a sheen of sweat that coats his bare chest, broad shoulders, and muscular arms.

God, why does he have to be so hot? It's like the revenge body concept. He was made fun of in high school so he got hotter after graduation to get back at everyone who ever teased him. From what it sounds like, several women changed their opinions about him after seeing the weapon he was concealing in his pants.

He doesn't even hesitate when he sees me, he lets his eyes roam over my clothed body as he passes me to pour himself another cup of coffee. The only sign that anything happened between us is the way his eyes darkened for a second, like the shadow of the memory passed over him. He's equally insufferable and attractive. I don't know whether to shun him or beg for more.

"Not going to acknowledge it?" I ask nonchalantly, or at least trying to sound like I don't care.

Jason doesn't even look at me. He pulls the carton of eggs out of the fridge and slides them across the clean counter top to land in front of me.

Message received.

Prick.

The only reason I even bother to make eggs is because I'm hungry. Not because he told me to.

"You could be a little nicer," I remind him. I don't exactly know how he feels. Does he like me? Does he hate me? Was that a hate fuck or something?

Again, not an actual fuck. But he doesn't have to be so curt with me.

Jason's only response is his usual eye roll that feels more like a challenge than a snarky reply.

"I'm starting to think eye rolls are your main form of communication." Although his coffee cup is in the way, I catch the way his cheeks dimple a bit as the corners of his mouth turn up. Finally, a smile. I knew he had a sense of humor somewhere beneath all that apathy and muscle.

Heavy footfalls on the stairs alert us to Dylan's presence before he's even visible. As soon as he lands on the main level, he rubs his eyes and groans.

"Ugh, I slept horrible." He announces before pouring himself the last of the coffee and stirring in the milk. "I knew you guys would fuck eventually but do you think you could keep it down next time?"

Choking. I'm choking on my coffee and trying to cough it out of my burning lungs. Apparently I forget how to drink coffee and swallow properly when I'm startled. That's the last thing I expected him to say and the last thing I want to talk about with him.

"What? We—I—you must have—nothing happened." *Real smooth, Mara.*

"So someone else was shouting *'Oh god, Jason. Don't stop'*?" His impersonation of me is a little offensive but I can't deny it.

Jason just walks past us toward the stairs. As he crosses my path I glare and tell Dylan, "Don't worry, I don't think it'll be a problem again."

Jason's eyes dart to me without turning his head then back to the stairs. What does that mean? Does he want it to happen again? Or is he just offended?

Fuck. Why does he have to be so confusing and annoying and...and...*sexy?*

December passes with the most snow I've ever seen in my life. Piled on every surface and obscuring the rest of the world behind a curtain of falling snow storming around us. It's like living in a snowglobe that's being shaken vigorously by a child. I can hardly see the barn through the haze from my place on the couch where I'm drinking my morning coffee. It's Christmas morning. Similarly to Thanksgiving, we decided to shirk our responsibilities for a day of relaxation and Christmas traditions. A week ago, all three of us traipsed through the woods to find a Douglas fir to cut down for a Christmas tree. After shaking the snow off the tree on the front porch, we brought it inside where it fit perfectly in the corner of the living room with just enough room to top with an angel. Dylan told me the decorations are from their childhood. Their mom loved Christmas.

Dylan doesn't talk about their dad much. And I don't ask. But their mom sounds like she was a lovely woman.

Jason is already awake and in the garage working out. Dylan is still asleep. I used to sleep until the afternoon but over a month of getting up early has changed my internal clock. Most mornings I hate being awake this early. But this morning, it's peaceful, serene, and fitting for the holiday season. I even seasoned my makeshift latte with cinnamon and nutmeg to add a little extra Christmas spirit to the morning.

For the sake of the holiday, I also grabbed *A Christmas Carol* from the shelf when I found it this morning while looking for a new book. There's something so picturesque and timeless about sitting on the couch snuggled under a blanket while reading and sipping coffee. Like something the female main character of a Hallmark movie would do on Christmas Eve right before the love of her life knocks on her door for a passionate kiss that solidifies their relationship.

Not that I'm into any of that cheesy stuff.

Classic Christmas tales are way more my speed.

To my surprise, Dylan jaunts down the stairs not long after I've settled into the couch where I intend to spend my morning in such a chipper mood. He's acting like a kid on Christmas morning, which kind of suits his golden retriever personality. I didn't expect him to be up until one in the afternoon since we don't have any work to do today.

"Gooooood morning," his chipper voice gnaws at my pessimistic disposition.

"Merry Christmas," I reply. "You're in an awfully good mood."

"Of course!" His exuberance is infectious. "It's freaking Christmas! Best day of the year."

I can't help myself, I laugh at the joyful man before me in on-theme pajamas sporting candy canes of every size in red and green variations.

After Dylan pours his coffee and stirs it with a candy cane (very on brand for Dylan) he announces it's time to break out his moms Christmas vinyl records. The first one he plays is none other than a Bing Crosby Christmas album. His deep voice and lyrical music fills the space in no time with a full orchestra and tinkling bells.

"Was Christmas big in your house growing up?" I ask just as the door to the garage opens and Jason steps in. No matter how many times I see this sequence of events, I can never get over the sight of him shirtless, sweaty, and radiating testosterone as he wipes himself down and pours his second cup of coffee for the day.

"Oh yeah," Dylan continues on as if the most delicious man I've ever seen didn't just walk into the room. A man who made me come so hard a couple weeks ago and hasn't touched me since. "Our mom decorated every square inch of our house just like this with homemade garlands and dried orange slices and ribbon. Anything she could make or already had. She'd cook all day but loved it cause we'd help her. And play these exact records the whole time. When we were little she'd get us to dance with her."

"You didn't dance with your mother as teenagers?" I ask as though it's a personal offense with a hand clutching my nonexistent pearls.

"Of course we would," Dylan said matter-of-factly. "She's our mom. She just had to convince us with pumpkin pie."

Dylan talks about their mom with such affection it's adorable. Someone else in my position might feel envious of all the love he and Jason got from their mother, but I'm just in awe. I'm more jealous I never got to meet her.

"I one-hundred percent believe you dance, Dylan, but there's no way you can convince me the grinch over there dances willingly. Let alone dances well."

"Only for our mom," Dylan answers for his brother with a wink toward Jason, the playfulness the two brothers share on occasion takes me so off guard. If it weren't for the similar resemblance, you'd think they were only roommates sharing bills and a business.

I didn't realize a challenge had been thrown down, but when the song changes to "Rockin Around the Christmas Tree", Jason approaches me, sweaty bare chest and all, and yanks me off the couch where I was cocooning for the day. Before I have a chance to gain my footing, one of his large hands presses to my lower back, sealing our bodies together while the other takes my left hand and holds it out like we are about to waltz. But this isn't a waltzing song. This tune requires frivolity, light-heartedness, and lots of movement. Jason sweeps me into a twirl around the room while I struggle to keep up with his pace. We're making a circle around the couch as he corrals my two left feet into something that resembles a dance. If I didn't know any better, you'd think I was dancing. I'm good with my feet when I'm playing sports, but anything faster than a gentle sway on the dance floor is out of my comfort zone.

Yet here I am, rocking around the proverbial Christmas tree with Jason Alder on Christmas morning. I never would have guessed this would be in my future. I shouldn't even be here for this Christmas. It's like Jason intervened with the universe's plans and now I'm smiling and laughing at how silly I feel dancing around the living room with him. Even he starts to smile a bit. Try as he might to hide it, the left corner of Jason's mouth pulls up ever so slightly to reveal a hint of a dimple. There have been very rare occasions where he graces us with a smile. It blinds me every time to see the contrast of his hardened features softening to a smile with something that one might call happiness.

It dawns on me that maybe he always looks unhappy because he is. Even in high school. All the years we've orbited around each other in our respective circles and somehow I've never seen him smile or look remotely entertained until I started living here.

Even prom night in the bathroom. He wasn't happy, per se, he was determined. Horny, maybe. No smiling was involved.

I can't help but wonder what his smile would look like at full force.

Jason releases me half way through the song by twirling me under his arm so I come face to face with Dylan who takes Jason's position and we start to dance with the same gaiety. I can't contain my laughter. This is just too wild. It feels so *normal* but also completely new and enthralling.

I've never had a Christmas with so much joy and it's only eight in the morning.

When the song ends I curtsy to both the boys and return to my spot on the couch where my book is waiting on the last page I read and my coffee is cold. But I don't care.

After a while I decide to dress for the day, one of the other items from their mother is a quilt pattern maxi skirt that I pair with a long sleeve top also given to me. And, for once, I opt to go barefoot, blank toenails and all. I don't think my feet are very pretty so I always hide them. But at this point, I don't care. I should just be happy I'm alive.

I feel good today. I don't know if it's because of the holiday, but I'll soak up that feeling as much as possible.

We cook. We listen to music. We eat more food than we can contain and share a couple bottles of wine. It's a perfect leisurely holiday.

Then it's present time. I wasn't sure if the two even exchanged presents but I pulled a couple things together for them anyway. Obviously, I didn't have the means to order last minute gifts on Amazon for Dylan and Jason, so I had to get crafty which is wildly outside of my comfort zone.

I don't expect anything in return, I'm sure they prepare for Christmas while they can still get to and from town. But it feels wrong not to attempt gifts even if they will probably throw them away right after opening.

Dylan opens his present from Jason first, a vintage hat that looks like it time traveled straight from the 1940s. It looks like it was made for Dylan, suiting his features and style so well. Almost like he was missing the hat this whole time.

Jason opens his gift from Dylan next, a new pair of work boots. So practical. But also so on brand for Jason. Dylan explains that Jason only ever wants practical gifts for birthdays and holidays. He's too frugal to spend money on himself and too selfless to ask for anything frivolous.

"Then you're going to hate my gift to you," I tell him. "It's not practical at all."

Out of deep curiosity, he takes the poorly wrapped present from under the tree addressed to him. Brows dropping to shield his eyes, he unwraps the box I found in their overflowing recycling bin since the trash service hasn't been here in almost two months. I reconstructed it and put the hand drawn portrait of him atop a layer of crumpled tissue paper. I drew it from memory, but it was the moment he shot the elk the day before

Thanksgiving. I tried to capture the intensity and lethal focus in his gaze. My style isn't very precise, but I like to think it holds emotion. At least, that's what I try to depict in my drawings.

Eager to see if he received a similar gift, Dylan rips into his gift to find similar packaging of his portrait. I drew an image of him bent over a lieth working on a part for one of their orders. He's so serious when he works, which doesn't match the playfulness of his personality.

I make a mental note to draw us dancing around the living room this morning, something to commemorate the life he injects in this house. Without him, it would be a dull place to live. He's definitely the heart of this place. He's the Yin to his brother's Yang. And I believe everyone needs that balance.

"Mara," he gapes at the drawing, "these are incredible. I didn't know you could draw."

"Kind of," I confess. "I've never had any formal training. I just do it to calm my mind. I normally draw on a tablet but it was nice to get back to my roots with good old paper and pencil.

"Sorry I don't have anything more for you, considering all you've done for me. But since I didn't know I'd be spending Christmas with you, I didn't exactly pack gifts in my car when I went for my drive all those weeks ago."

"These are more than enough," he breathes.

I turn my hesitation and insecurity to Jason. "I know it's not practical but do you like it?"

Without taking his hardened eyes off the drawing, he nods slowly. I don't know what he sees in the drawing, but that's the beauty of art, it looks different to every person. I hope he sees the strong, confident man determined to survive. When he shot that elk, I saw a killer. But after a lot of consideration, I saw so much more.

I'm not sure I want to watch all my meals die right before my eyes, but I'm starting to understand their way of life a bit more. I'm starting to see the beauty and purity of providing for yourself as opposed to constant reliance.

Dylan and Jason don't strike me as doomsday preppers, but if the day ever comes that the world crashes down around us, they can still survive. They don't rely on grocery stores to provide all their food. They don't rely on a million different tradesmen to keep their home operating. Even though they pay for electricity, I fully believe they'd figure out how to generate electricity on their own.

There's one present left under the tree with my name on it. I stare at it for a split second wondering if they wrapped up a random household item for me just so I'd have something to open this morning. They didn't exactly plan for me either.

Taking it in my hands, the weight has me suspicious. It feels like an L shaped block of steel, which isn't far off from the truth. As soon as I clear the red and black checkered wrapping paper my eyes fix on a beautifully engraved pistol. I should be terrified to be holding a gun, I should be worried that their idea of a good gift is a gun.

But I'm not.

I'm floored by the intricate paisley detail of the engravings carefully etched into the metal. And I'm even more touched knowing they probably spent hours making this for me. *Me!* I know how much they charge rich guys online for one of their handcrafted firearms and here they are just handing one over to me as a Christmas present.

I lift disbelieving eyes to Jason first, seeing the glimmer of hope there, hope that I'll appreciate the gesture. Then turn my gaze to Dylan who's bright smile brings mist to my dry eyes.

"You made this for me?" I ask dubiously. A steady nod comes from Jason to confirm what I already know. "But this must have taken you both hours?"

"Well, we wanted to do something special for you. Besides, it's not like we have a bunch of gifts for women lying around." Dylan laughs.

"But you've already done so much for me." I remind them. "My crappy drawings pale in comparison to this."

"They aren't crappy," Dylan insists while Jason conveys the same sentiment with a shake of his head. "In fact, they're on the same level. They're both from the heart and hard work."

There's a keen crumpling in my heart I haven't felt before. I should have felt this before. I've received some beautiful gifts from my parents before. Designer bags, the latest phone, anything I ask them for. But nothing has ever held so much sentiment as this. No one has ever made me anything, not even a handmade valentine in grade school. This is the most selfless gift I've ever received. And it is a gift, a gift of unconditional friendship. I don't know how they can see me that way when I've been such a burden, but I'm so honored.

I'm not an emotional person but I feel emotion swelling in my throat. Choking it down is no easy feat but I manage as we move on with the rest of our day.

Smoked ham serves as our main course for dinner, accompanied by a variety of delicious, festive side dishes. And red wine, of course.

After the dishes have been washed and Christmas is coming to a close, Dylan puts on an instrumental Christmas record while I read *A Christmas Carol* aloud, lounging against the arm of the couch with my knees bent in the air, covered by a thick blanket. All of this is far too wholesome and pure to feel real. We actually feel like a family. I don't think I've ever relaxed in my parents' presence. If I'm around them, there's a purpose for it, meals, schedule coordinations, social events. We never watched a movie together or listened to music. I don't think my parents ever read me a bedtime story. I didn't realize that bothered me until now. I feel cheated out of a loving relationship with them. But the sting is softened by the warmth of this moment.

This is the first time I don't want to leave when the snow melts. For a split second, I entertain the thought of what it would be like if I stayed here.

But that's impossible. I'm not related to them. And even though we are friends—for lack of a better word—that doesn't mean we can all live together and resume normal life with that major change come march.

So I smush that flicker of hope beneath reality and close the book after reading the final line. I peek over the top of the closed book to see Jason watching me. He stares so unabashedly, which is normal for him, but with how I'm already feeling, his stare feels heavier.

I replace the book to the shelf where I found it and wave with a two finger salute before carrying my sullen body upstairs to bed.

This has been the best Christmas I've ever had. And that thought makes me feel a combination of guilt and remorse.

After I've showered and changed into one of Jason's t-shirts, I lay in bed restless with energy and a mind that won't shut off.

Jason.

Stay.

Go.

The gift.

The want.

The need.

God, I'm so agitated. I tried masturbating after the night of my birthday but every orgasm felt like something my body was supposed to do but didn't really want to do. A basic action like eating or walking. They didn't have the same ecstasy that Jason gave me. His tongue, his fingers, they were unlike any fuck I've ever had, sending me down a spiral of pleasure I didn't realize I was capable of. I've given myself some intense orgasms before with vibrators, and I've had some entertaining fucks but the two men I've slept with never made me come that hard. I always had to focus, concentrate, and work hard to achieve orgasms that seemed extreme at the time but could never hold a candle to that night.

If it's that intense with just his tongue and fingers, what would his cock feel like?

Fuck this. We're grown adults who can have casual sex. It doesn't have to be more than that. And I know he's just as desperate as me. So I decide I'll be the bigger person and initiate what we both want.

I throw the covers off me, throw the door open before shutting it softly behind me, and stride over to Jason's door on gentle feet. I can hear soft music from inside his room before I open the door and sneak in as quickly as possible, irrationally afraid Dylan will catch me.

As soon as I close the door and lock it, I turn around and back myself against the hard door, mildly taken aback by what I see.

Chapter Fourteen

Mara

YOUR NEEDS, MY NEEDS-NOAH Kahan

Jason. Naked. Lying flat on his back with his hard cock clutched in his strong hand while the other arm is bent behind his head accentuating the contours of his biceps and abs. He's a Greek god. A statue sculpted by Michaelangelo himself. Perfect in every physical feature on display. And though it's only been a couple weeks, I forgot how impressive his dick is. A thick vein running up the underside like an arrow to the proud head that's glistening with a bit of precome. Utter perfection.

I only get to ogle him and the collage of tattoos decorating his pec and shoulder for a second before his eyes snap open to lock on mine. There's no shock or shame. There's only desire there.

He doesn't miss a beat, hesitation is thrown out the window when he leaps off the bed to close the distance between us in half a second. Aggressive hands grip the hem of *his* shirt ripping it up and over my head, my body following along silently to make undressing me easier.

I need this. I *need* it. And so does he. We crave each other way too much for two people who can't stand one another half the time.

Without an ounce of tenderness, Jason backs me against a wall before he pins my hands above my head with an iron grip. I'm at his mercy when his mouth dips to my pebbled nipple, sucking it into his mouth until it's painfully peaked. Desperate for friction between my legs, I rub my thighs together to soothe the ache but it only makes the angst worse. Noticing my actions, Jason slides his hand at rapid speed down my body and darts between my pressed thighs to run skillful fingers through my soaked lips.

Ughhh. It feels incredible. But it's not enough. The slight moan that escapes me eggs Jason on, so he plunges two fingers into me without even bothering to ease in slowly. There's nothing gentle about any of this. It's animalistic and primal and *rough.* Which is just what we need. We're not pure and delicate. We're volatile and explosive. We're passionate in all the most damning ways.

And that's just how it feels when Jason finger fucks me while holding me captive against the wall, circling my nipples with his pointed tongue, back and forth between the two.

He transfers his attention from my nipples to my heavy lidded eyes. His eyes bear down on me with an emotion I can't place. It's so intense I don't know if he's angry or excited.

Maybe all of the above.

But one thing I'm irrevocably certain of is he is getting off watching me come undone at his touch. Flared nostrils, dilated pupils, a broad chest that vibrates with bated breath as he enjoys the symphony he's composing.

I'm used to guys closing their eyes in the darkness as they utter phrases like "oh yeah baby. You feel so good." Or "just like that." The silence hanging between us in this moment speaks greater volume than anything a man has ever said in bed with me. It's raw. It's untamed. I don't know how to remain confident and composed under such a heavy gaze.

"*Fuck,*" I hiss as the orgasm builds and builds.

How the fuck does he know exactly what to do with my body when he's so inexperienced with it? Obviously he's not inexperienced overall, but this is only our second time together in a sexual capacity. He shouldn't be this in sync with me.

Just when I think the climax is about to explode, Jason unsheathes his fingers causing me to grunt in frustration. I pull my hands from his grip with one sharp jerk then shove at his chest with both hands until he's backed up to the bed. With one push on his shoulders, Jason is sitting on the edge of the bed so I can straddle him with both legs squeezing him between me. One hand behind me to guide him, I lower my body onto his hard girth to revel in the blissful stretch of my flesh around his. I was honestly worried he wouldn't fit. But I'm a masochist and I enjoy the sting, the stretch, the fulfillment. All of it elicits a cry muffled by his hand clamped over my mouth so we don't alert Dylan of our rendezvous.

"Fuck," I repeat my sentiment after Jason moves his hand from my mouth to my ribcage and starts guiding my frenzied bouncing. Using my quad strength, I rise and fall over and over on his solid cock. Jason's sturdy hands that craft such beautiful works of art hold me steady at the waist as my back arches in ecstasy.

Clit thrashing against the place our bodies join, I climb higher and higher to that peak of destruction. "How did you—*ahh.*" Just before I fall over, Jason latches onto my nipple with his teeth, drawing a shocked cry from my core as I tumble over the edge into a free fall. It's the same feeling I get on roller coasters, a gut-wrenching, tummy-twisting, mind-blowing plummet that rocks my entire body.

But refusing to let me fully revel in the sensation, Jason has us in the air again and he backs me into the wall once more without ever letting our bodies part. One hand cupping my ass for support, one hand pressed against the wall. My legs circle his waist landing on his hip bones for leverage.

I won't lie, the steady strength he displays in flawlessly transferring us from the bed to a standing position does something to me. It's unfair how the basic features of this man can make me feel hot and bothered.

Trapped between Jason and the cabin style wall, he doesn't miss a beat and starts pounding into me repeatedly wringing the last orgasm out of me as the next one collects low in my belly.

He's relentless in his ministrations, forceful, and—dare I say—possessive. I had a feeling he'd be aggressive in bed but I didn't expect this kind of cataclysmic reception. I didn't even know if he would want to fuck me. For all I knew, the night of my birthday was a one time thing.

Clearly, he has a lot of sexual frustration he needs to release and if this is to be the outcome, I'll happily be the recipient.

In and out. The liquified sound of my orgasm and the heavy breaths Jason exhales through his nostrils are driving me insane to the point that I don't know if I'll be able to walk when he sets me down.

I'm so close, *so close*, I can't take the agony of the moments before the orgasm hits and I'm praying that it's as powerful as I think it will be.

When Jason removes one hand from the wall while the other remains on my ass, he encases my throat in his free hand with just enough pressure to drive me over the edge. It won't leave a mark. It doesn't cut off my breath entirely. But damn does it make my pulse skyrocket and my body convulse with shockwave after shockwave of pleasure. I bite my lower lip to keep from screaming and all that accomplishes is stifling the groan/cry that fights for release in my throat.

In a series of perfectly executed moves, Jason unclasps my legs from around his waist, drops me to the floor so I'm standing in front of him, pulls out of me, and pumps his erection so ribbons of come paint my stomach. The only sound he makes is a guttural groan that resonates in his chest like a bee trapped in a glass jar, buzzing in a deep baritone. I've often wondered what his voice sounds like. In moments like this, I can't help but imagine it's close to Henry Cavill's sexy voice.

The degradation of his come dripping down my body in little trails equally offends and turns me on. I know his reasons were twofold. First, because we didn't use a condom. And second, because he will find any chance to belittle me, to remind me that the tables have turned and I am not on top anymore.

But I...kind of like that. I like this dominant side of Jason Alder. I like the way he consumes me and makes me feel like I'm under his power. I like the possessive look in his eye and the control in his actions. He's too sexy for his own good.

After Jason recovers from his own release, he stalks over to a chest of drawers and pulls a t-shirt from the second drawer to the right to wipe his dick clean. When he's finished, he throws it in my direction so the wadded material almost strikes my face. I catch it before his discarded come can land on my skin and start to wipe myself up.

No after care from you, I guess. I shouldn't have expected much to begin with. He's not the doting type.

I head for the t-shirt I wore in here which sits on the floor by the door but Jason snatches it before I can reach it and smirks. He fucking smirks knowing I'll have to walk back to my room naked.

What an asshole.

But I already knew that.

Thinking on my feet, I bolt for the same drawer he retrieved the shirt to clean his junk and grab one before he can stop me, slipping it on as quickly as possible. I shoot back my own triumphant grin before saying, "Thanks for the fuck, asshole," and exit the room.

But what a fuck it was. I sincerely hope that's not the last time. If Jason fucks as hard as he hates, this could be an eventful rest of the winter.

Chapter Fifteen

Jason

POWER OVER ME- DERMOT Kennedy

"I've never done this before," Mara says in the cold morning air on the front porch. "It feels weird."

I'm sure it does, if it's her first time.

The snow has stopped momentarily which gives us a clear view of the targets I set up down the driveway for Mara to aim at.

When she admitted this morning that she'd never shot a gun before, Dylan and I jumped on the chance to teach her how to use her Christmas gift. A stainless steel 1911 with an engraved relief designed with a feminine paisley pattern. Some of my most intricate work. Dylan helped with the main structure of the firearm but he's not as skilled with engravings as I am. I lost myself in the process, letting my subconscious take over to create something beautiful for her.

Yeah, we put a lot of time and resources into making her Christmas gift, but it was worth it to see the look on her face.

I don't like admitting it, but she's become one of us. Not like a sibling, that would be weird. But part of our misfit family. Having her around feels way too natural. But I won't complain as long as we keep fucking like we do. We've hooked up every night since Christmas. The night after she came into my room, I went into hers and flipped her onto her stomach in another one of my t-shirts—and only the t-shirt—before lifting her hips and plowing into her. We've used a condom since then, as well. It was reckless of me not to use one the first night. Sometimes we have sex in my room, sometimes hers, but we never fall asleep together. That's too much intimacy for me. I'm sure some would say fucking is more intimate than sharing a bed, but it's easy for me to detach emotions from sex.

Mara is the one who taught me that emotions have no place in sex. They just complicate shit.

"Am I holding this right?" She asks, pointing the gun toward the target with poor posture. She's arching her back with her shoulders back and her arms stick straight. Not to mention her finger is on the trigger and the safety is still on.

Dylan already explained how to load the clip and empty the chamber.

I chuckle to myself at the amateur sight. I move closer so I can guide her finger to release the safety. Then I model the correct posture. One foot back, one forward to steady. Torso leaning forward so I pivot at the hips, shoulders are forward. Right arm bent at the allow and left arm straight for stability.

Mara almost mirrors my posture perfectly, but not exactly. I guide her trigger finger to the side of the chamber and nudge her back so her front folds forward from the upright position she's in. If she'd fired the gun as she was before, she probably wouldn't have fallen on her ass.

Which, in hindsight, would have been fucking hilarious.

"Keep your finger off the trigger until you're ready to shoot," Dylan instructs, "that's gun safety 101."

Mara nods in understanding.

We're all wearing hearing protection. Mara looks particularly funny in her giant headphones and safety glasses. Out of place.

I give her the thumbs up once she's in position. A deep breath, and then she pulls the trigger. The gun performs perfectly propelling the bullet forward while spitting the case to the side. Even though a 1911 is fairly user friendly, and nothing compared to some of the shotguns I own, the recoil shocks Mara so much she stumbles back and lets a little yelp leave her. A beat of silence lingers in the cold air while her astonished face takes in what just happened before she laughs uncomfortably. I can't help it, I chuckle a little too. It's just too funny. Any time I'm ever sad, I'll just think about how her little body jolted and the horrified expression her face contorted into beneath the dorky glasses. That should cheer me up.

"Try again," Dylan says between snickers. "You didn't even hit the target."

Mara takes position again, catching on quickly to all the minute details of her posture that help her maintain balance. Moving her finger to the trigger when she's ready to fire, she pulls it back releasing another round that strikes a hole in the bottom left corner of the target. Not actually in the red rings on the target, but at least she was closer this time.

"I did it!" She shouts with pride. "I mean. I know it's not a bullseye but I hit it!"

I smile, her joy is infectious. It's cute how proud of herself she is over something so little. If I'd taken a shot like that, I'd beat myself up over a lousy shot. But for someone who's just learning, she should be proud of any improvement. Especially for her second time firing a gun, that's not half bad.

Mara catches me smiling and stares like I'm a fucking pink unicorn in the wild. Eyes wide and breath hitching. She only pauses to stare for a second before taking aim once again.

Mara empties her clip making subtle changes each time to improve her aim. By the time it's empty, her last bullet grazed the outer ring of the target. Linear improvement. That's something to rejoice.

Dylan praises her, "Well, hey, if you ever have to shoot an intruder, at least you can do some damage. Just aim for the chest."

"Let's hope that never happens," she frowns. "Are you guys prepping for a zombie apocalypse or something?"

I shake my head.

Dylan replies, "No. But it's good to know how to defend yourself. Especially as a woman, you should always protect yourself. There will always be men who want to hurt you no matter how much equality between genders has changed."

"Can't argue there."

I'm working in the shop when Mara enters bundled in her snow gear. She discards the thick coat in the heat of the shop but leaves the snow pants and boots on. As she's looking around at the tools and materials.

Wordlessly, she runs her hands over the leith and scans the machinery we use to craft our products while The Steeldrivers plays on my phone. A leith is considered a primitive way of crafting metal, these days, a CNC machine is the most widely used, now. But when we started our business, this was all we could afford and it still nearly cleared out our bank accounts. Now, I like the simplicity and familiarity of it. Some of our customers even prefer we use a leith so they can brag about how much work went into their handmade firearms.

I'm currently engraving a special order a woman placed for a Damascus GMX with her husband's name engraved on the side. She even sent an example of the font she wanted. It all has a very cowboy western vibe to it. Not my personal style, but we have had a lot of customers who like the style, especially from Texas.

I want to ask Mara what she's doing here since she hasn't said a word while she peruses the shop. But I keep my mouth shut and my head down.

Until I see her frame stop near the tarp covered vehicle I keep in the back. I haven't given myself much time to work on it this winter.

"What's this?" Mara asks with a brief glance in my direction. "Can I take the tarp off?"

She doesn't even wait for confirmation before walking it back over the hood of the car and tugging it over the roof to reveal the 1965 Chevrolet C10 truck beneath the warn tarp. It needs a paint job and lots of other updates. But it runs and drives.

I just haven't touched it because it belonged to *him* and it's hard to work on it without thinking about him.

An audible gasp leaves Mara's mouth when she sees the faded rust colored truck in all its run-down glory. I haven't started it up since last spring. It's like it's cursed and every time I get near the damn thing, I can't unsee his face. I can't unsee how his life ended. I wouldn't say I feel remorse for his death. But...sometimes guilt seeps in. It was my fault, after all, even if Mom and Dylan insist it wasn't.

Sometimes I don't even feel right being in this house. The cabin was his place. As much as the rest of us loved it, he loved it more. And he had it long before he met Mom. It was his sanctuary yet here we are, the two people he hated most in the world, occupying it like squatters. He's probably rolling over in his grave considering how much of his life we've taken. The fact that we are still thriving in his absence.

"Jason," Mara breathes, "this is incredible. I mean, I don't know much about classic cars, but it looks like it's in great condition. Did you fix it or find it like this?"

A little bit of both. The interior was new when we moved up here. And the engine was halfway restored. Dylan and I finished the rest but cars really aren't Dylan's thing, so I've been slowly replacing parts that are too old or worn out to operate. As well as updating a couple things to make it safer to drive. Right now, it's somewhere between "original and unrestored" and a resto-mod. Not sure how much more I want to do with it.

"We should really figure out some way for you to answer questions if you're not going to talk."

It's called sign language, and I don't do it on purpose.

"Blink once for no, and twice for yes. Did you find it in this condition?"

I just stare at her. I'm not playing this game.

"Ugh, you're impossible," she gripes. "I don't know why you still refuse to speak, but sometimes I wish you'd get over whatever is holding you back cause I have so much I want to ask you."

Interesting. This is a rare sight of vulnerability from Mara I don't see very often. *What kind of stuff does she want to know?*

Knowing Mara, it's probably all trivial like my favorite movie or if I was hugged enough as a child.

"Give me something, Jason," she leans her pert ass against the hood of the truck. "Where did you get this car? I don't want to play guessing games with you. I do that enough as it is."

She was already nosy before we started sleeping together, but apparently fucking for a week has made her even bolder.

I roll my eyes. Grabbing a piece of scrap wood and a marker I use for drawing guiding marks on projects, I scribble a single word on the board.

DAD

Mara's hazel eyes scan the board earnestly. I know it didn't take her longer than a second to read the word but she stares at it longer. Then her eyes meet mine.

God, they're beautiful. The mirage of colors in her irises is easy to get lost in. But the pity they hold morphs into curiosity.

"Dylan wouldn't tell me what happened to your dad," she announces. *Good, it's none of her business.* "He said it's not his story to tell. But I suppose you won't tell me either." I shake my head slowly. No way in hell am I reliving it. I already have to see it in my sleep on a regular basis.

"Fine," she concedes.

Planting both hands on the hood, she lifts herself so her ass and thighs sit on the flat metal while everything below the knee dangles over the edge. Keeping her hands flat against the hood, she hunches her shoulders forward.

"Tonight's New Year's Eve. Do you usually stay up until midnight?"

My shoulders rise and fall in a silent chuckle. I haven't stayed up on New Year's since I was a kid. Dylan and Mom tried to get me to in high school but I didn't care to stay in my father's presence any longer than I had to.

"Will you stay up tonight?"

Why the hell does it matter?

"Come on! It could be fun. We can have some drinks, play games. Dylan even made snacks. We'll have our own little party."

At first thought, a party with my brother and the stray I'm fucking doesn't sound like much fun. But maybe afterward it'll turn into a party of two.

I stalk toward her with devilish intent, darkening my gaze so she knows what's coming.

Seeing her perched on the hood of my truck makes me all kinds of hard and crazy. Especially while she's wearing one of my flannels, and the top few buttons are undone so I can see down to her bra while she's hunched over. Her fading blonde hair is brushed over one shoulder in loose waves from sleeping with it in a braid.

She's sexy as hell. Always has been. She could be wrapped in a carpet and still turn me on. Maybe that's why it makes me nervous, because I don't like someone having that much power over me.

I walk toward her grabbing my cordless jigsaw and set it on the hood of the truck beside her. I grip her knees to spread her legs apart which she does so easily like a good little girl. Her need for me turns me on just as much as her rosebud lips. She's willingly giving me the power in this situation.

One hand smooths the flannel fabric over my chest while the other supports her against the car as she leans her torso back a bit, arching her back so her tits are in the air.

The music changes to the next song as it shuffles through all the music downloaded on my phone. The heavy sounds of "Power Over Me" by Dermot Kennedy fills the space as I give the buttons on the front of the snow pants a sharp jerk, the snaps break contact and I'm pleasantly surprised to see she's going commando.

As soon as I slide my fingers between her legs, she's wet for me. A sick satisfaction takes over me. I lower my face closer to hers and deeply inhale her feminine scent before flicking her clit with my index finger. The quick pressure makes her body jerk so I wrap my free arm around the small of her back, tugging her closer. Her breathing becomes erratic, nothing consistent about it aside from the way her breathy moans consistently make my cock stand at attention.

Then I shove two fingers directly into her tight pussy without warning. *God, she's tight.* I knew she wasn't a virgin and I thought maybe she'd be a little...worn out, for lack of a better description. But just like the rest of her, her vagina is just to my liking.

I start pumping my fingers in and out of her, curling them against her inner walls in the process to work her like an instrument. And I'm proficient at playing Mara.

The higher she climbs into the sky, the more flushed she grows. Her cheeks turn pink, her chest reddens a bit, and her lids grow heavy. Reaching out for support, she wraps a shaking hand around my neck as my pace quickens until she's panting and proactively gyrating in my arms.

Nervous about the intimacy of that gesture, I remove her hand from my neck and flatten her suddenly against the hood of the truck. Her body meets the truck with a bit of a *thwack* but it doesn't seem to bother Mara. In fact, it seems like she likes it. I've noticed how her eyes darken with need when I'm rough with her, how they practically scream for more.

So I grab the jigsaw, flick the switch to turn it on, and press the butt of the tool (not the sharp end) against her clit so the vibration ripples through her from the center out. All while furiously finger fucking her into oblivion. This, to my surprise and delight, makes her go wild. She lets out a moan of "oh god" and laces her fingers through the roots of her hair.

I know when her breath hitches and her eyes shut that she's about to come so I press the active jigsaw body harder into her clit right before she erupts. Her body clamps and pulsates around my fingers. A cry that could be mistaken for painful bounces off the walls of the shop in a key that ignites me. When her eyes open they meet my fierce stare. I hold her gaze for a minute and give myself permission to lose myself in her endless hazel abyss. She hesitates before taking another breath like it might kill her.

But my actions might.

I remove my fingers from her pussy and suck them between my lips, cleaning my fingers of her, swallowing her down. Releasing her, she's star-struck where she sits on the hood. I wave my hand in the air in the universal sign for "wrap it up" so she knows to replace the tarp before she heads back inside. And I go back to my work, pretty proud of myself for the look plastered on her face.

Chapter Sixteen

Jason

Don't Come Home A-Drinkin'

Panic sets in. I see the pure terror in Dylan's eyes, hear Mom plead for our father to stop, crying in between sucking in lungfuls of air she can't hold onto. And my chest caves with the weight of it all. I can't see them hurting. He can hurt me all he wants, but not them.

So I do the only thing I can think of.

I can't believe he's dead. I watched it happen and it still seems impossible. The monster that's been slowly killing us seemed infinite. Yet there he is, laying in a growing puddle of blood on the flagstone pathway to the street from our front porch.

He's dead.

I look from his lifeless body to Mom and then Dylan. We all share the same shock, fear, and a glimmer of relief. We shouldn't be relieved he's dead, it sounds cynical and morbid. But we've all been through so much with him.

And so much transpired in the last five minutes. If I'm struggling to process all of it, they must be, too.

My mother's watery stare lifts from her dead husband to me. On a hushed breath she utters my name.

"Jason?"

Music is blaring from downstairs. Not much rouses me from sleep aside from my nightmares, but whatever they're playing is obnoxiously loud.

Frustrated and curious, I whip the covers off me and tug on some sweatpants before heading down the stairs to make a point of turning the music down.

"Don't Come Home A-Drinkin'" by Loretta Lynn is playing when I enter the living room to find Dylan wearing a crown of fake flowers and Mara dancing around in short cotton shorts that allow her ass to hang out. They're barely hanging onto her hips with the drawstring pulled tight. I know my brother has no interest in her, but still the thought of her showing those round cheeks off for anyone else pisses me off.

"Jason!" Mara exclaims when she finally notices me on the bottom step. "Look! I made shorts! I mean they aren't perfect, a little short, but good enough to sleep in."

It's then I notice the sewing machine we showed her two months ago is out and an old sheet has been cut into scraps. *Not too shabby.* But I still don't like the jealous green monster that rouses in my chest.

I make a point of scanning her up and down.

"Sorry, is the music too loud?" *No shit.* "I'll turn it down."

"Don't you dare," Dylan points at her from across the room. He looks fucking ridiculous with that flower crown on. Where did he even find those flowers? I guess our mom had more craft supplies here than I remembered.

"Come dance with us," Mara pulls where her hand meets my bicep. *No fucking way.*

I notice two empty bottles of wine on the counter. *Of course.* I should have known these lushes would get into the wine for their little celebration.

The clock on the stove says 11:50. Hopefully their festivities die down after midnight. After all, once midnight strikes, it's just another day. Nothing special about it.

I resist Mara's sloppy attempt at pulling me into their drunk orbit. She pouts puffy lips that only make me think of how they looked around my dick.

Damn, it seems like I can't get my mind off sex around this girl.

Dylan is still dancing in his own oblivious little world.

Sidling up to me so our chests meet, Mara lowers her voice so only I can hear.

"Ya know, I don't know what happened in your past. I don't know why you don't speak. I don't know why you're always so angry. But that's a choice. I know better than most you can't just wish away your feelings and your demons. But you can *choose* to make a better future. You don't have to live an unhappy life."

Unhappy? What about my life makes her think I'm unhappy? I have a house most would dream of. I work for myself on my own terms. I don't have to answer to anyone, not even my brother.

And as my dream just reminded me, I'm free of *him.*

I am happy.

I'm happy!

And maybe if I say it enough I'll convince myself.

Mara remains planted in front of me a second longer before accepting defeat with a wounded puppy look on her face and stalks away. The song changes to some fifties song (quite a sporadic playlist) with a mild tempo. Fast enough to dance to but not too fast, either.

Fine. I'm not choosing happiness. I'm choosing to extend an olive branch.

My arm shoots out without a second thought, I'm not even sure I consciously made the decision. It's like my body rejected the idea of dampening Mara's spirits on its own. Leaving my brain a split second to catch up, I spin Mara back to me and keep our hands clamped while the other hand moves to the small of her back. I muster everything my mom taught me and start twirling her around the living room with a lack of precision. I'm not the most graceful person, but I can keep up with the beat.

The shock on Mara's face morphs into pure joy as we jive to the music. Fifties jazz really isn't my style, but it'll have to do. And I have to admit, I like the smile that stretches from ear to ear on her face. She lights up when she smiles. And fuck if that doesn't make me want to break my bitter facade to mirror the action. To fuel her glow.

Cause for the first time since she's been here, Mara looks like she's glowing. She looks truly happy.

Maybe it's just the alcohol, but I swear she looks brighter.

"My turn," Dylan cuts in. I think he's going to grab Mara but instead he takes her place and the fucker tries to dance with me. I give him a little slap upside the head and step away before he winks at me and grabs Mara to spin her around the living room again.

I've done more dancing in the last week with these two than I have in the last decade.

It's ridiculous.

Dylan certainly shows more talent for dancing than I do, and he's far more skilled than I am. Although Mara is giggling with the music, I swear she was brighter when I was her dance partner instead.

"You're insane," she tells Dylan teasingly.

"Maybe, but mostly just drunk." He counters. I can't argue with him there.

Dylan twirls Mara under his arm so she spins clumsily into me. I catch her in my arms to steady her but she just leans against me. This feels way too intimate for comfort.

"Heyyy," he draws out the word with a gleam in his eye. "I have an idea. Have you ever smoked pot?" He asks Mara.

Miss goody-two-shoes? I'd be shocked.

"I ate a brownie on accident, one time," she admits with a shrug of her shoulders.

Figures.

"Then I think it's time we properly corrupt you."

Mara lifts her gaze over her shoulder to me as if to say *you've already corrupted me enough.* I return it with a blank stare. She hasn't even begun to pry open the dark recesses of my brain.

Mara agrees. So we file out to the back porch furniture wrapped in thick coats and blankets. Mara sits on the bench beside me which isn't ideal. So I stand and take the rocking chair instead. I need to make it clear we aren't a couple. Just because we fuck doesn't mean we're a couple or something. I still despise her.

That's my story and I'm sticking to it.

Though her warmth would have been appreciated because it's fucking freezing out.

Disappointment marks her face as Dylan joins her on the bench, none the wiser to the hard line I just drew. He dug the box of materials out of the pantry and starts rolling a joint from the flower we keep sealed in a mason jar with an airtight lid.

"So you've never smoked anything before?" He clarifies with her. She nods to confirm his suspicions.

He begins to instruct her while grinding the flower and packing it into the roller. "Alright. Well here's a little run down. Common smoking circle etiquette is puff, puff, pass. Take two hits then pass it to the next person. Curl your lips in so you don't get the tip too moist. Suck in air like you're sucking dick and hold the smoke in your cheeks to cool it off before inhaling it in. Then blow it out like you're—"

"Blowing a guy?" She supplies for him.

"See, I knew you'd pick it up quickly." Mara and I both roll our eyes at that.

Dylan starts the joint by lighting the end and inhaling to draw the burn from top to bottom at a leisurely pace. After his comparisons, I can't help but think that he's actually sucking on that joint like a dick and I could have gone my whole life without that fucking image in my head.

Jackass.

He demonstrates twice before handing the joint off to Mara. She pulls one arm out from under the blanket before taking the joint and eyeing it like a snake preparing to bite her.

Hesitantly, she follows Dylan's instructions by curling her lips under her teeth so she doesn't lip it. The cherry glows bright orange as she inhales. And just like every first time smoker, she coughs out the smoke instead of steadily exhaling.

Rookie.

Mara laughs and coughs at the same time, holding a fist up to her mouth in the pointless socially acceptable gesture everyone does when they cough. Doesn't matter it does nothing to stop the coughing or to prevent the spread of germs. People are mindless rule followers when it comes to shit like that. Always doing what the herd is doing.

I get the joint next. It's been a while since I partook in this form of debauchery. As soon as the bitter smoke hits my lungs, I feel the instant calm and loss of tension. Another puff and I relax even more.

"So," Dylan breaks the silence, "who's going to fess-up first?"

Mara and I look from Dylan to each other and back again, confused by whatever the fuck he's talking about. He already knows we're sleeping together. I mean, we haven't confirmed it, but how can he not know?

"What's going on between you two?" Dylan waved a finger from Mara to me and back again. "We don't have Facebook to make things official, up here."

Great. Leave it to Dylan to make an uncomfortable situation even more uncomfortable.

"We're not in a relationship," Mara explains on our behalf. Then she lifts heavy eyes to me as if it's painful to look at me. "We're just fucking. No need to make it a bigger deal than it is."

Well, at least she doesn't want more than I can give her.

Maybe if I was the kind of guy who wanted a relationship, the kind of guy who could love a woman. Maybe I could give her more. There was a time I wanted to give her more and I wanted more for myself. But those days have long since passed. I'm not the same boy I was in high school. I don't think I'll ever find that piece of myself again.

Not sure I want to, either. That boy felt too much. Too much pain. Too much humiliation. Too much. Too much too much. It's easier to be blissfully numb than it is to let emotions alter my life.

"Well fuck," Dylan coughs after taking a hit off the joint. "Aren't you two straight people lucky. Why couldn't you have found a hot gay guy for me to fuck all winter?"

I just shrugged my shoulders. But the weed must be kicking in for Mara cause she bursts into a fit of giggles that infects Dylan as well. Their little laugh fest earns an eye roll from me.

"Ugh," Mara sighs, "I'm so tired and I know this one will be busting down my door at six in the morning for chores." One pointy nailed finger is thrust in my direction. "I'm going to bed. Happy new year, guys. Oh wait—" she stops suddenly. "We missed the countdown to midnight."

"Sorry, toots," Dylan says with a smirk, "guess you'll have to come back next year and try again." I don't know why, but that comment makes her look sad, especially when she raises her gaze to me.

Mara bounds back to Dylan, grabs his chin, and plants a kiss on his cheek with more force than she probably intended.

"Night, guys."

Seeing her stumble to the door, I figured I should help her get upstairs. I can almost hear my mother screaming at me from beyond the grave to be a gentleman.

I catch up to Mara inside and place a steadying hand on her waist before she shrugs me off.

"I don't need help. I'm fine," she insists.

Hoping she might eat her words and trip, I let go of her as she starts up the stairs. But that part of me that wanted her to admit I was right is overpowered by the part that doesn't want her to get hurt when she actually does trip and fall to her knees with a smack that sounds painful.

I scoop her up in my arms like a sack of potatoes and head up the stairs.

"Why aren't you more clumsy?" She asks.

Because I have a higher tolerance. And I haven't been drinking all night.

I lay her down on her bed still burritoed in her blanket. She rolls over on her side, face smashed into the pillow.

"Night." She says curtly, my queue to leave.

Guess we won't be fucking tonight.

Chapter Seventeen

Mara

HIGH-STEPHEN SANCHEZ

He made his point perfectly clear. And although I'm not look-ing for anything serious with Jason, I don't like being treated like trash and then used for my body. I've already done that. I don't need to repeat that toxic dynamic again.

I'm trying to right the wrongs of my past. I'm trying to make amends with him. I understand holding a grudge all this time, but I did apologize and I've been trying to be cordial. The least he can do is treat me with a little more respect.

Isolated in a cabin in the woods, it's not like I can publicly apologize or make any grand gestures.

But despite my actions in the past, two wrongs don't make a right. Maybe I deserved the degradation at first. Actually, I definitely deserved it. But I'm not the one who dragged him naked into a room full of people.

Who am I kidding? I'm just as bad. Bryce humiliated Jason. But I toyed with his emotions and gave false hope to a kid who suffered his whole life at the hands of his peers. I was a bully, no different than Bryce. And I've paid for it ever since between the shit treatment I got from Bryce and the crappy relationship I had with my ex—if it can even be called a relationship.

Tanner, my ex, was a real piece of shit. I didn't want a purely physical relationship so I told him I wanted to wait a bit to have sex. He pressured me into intimacy of other forms until I finally gave in. And then I was never good enough.

When my body started changing because I wasn't working out as much, he made comments about it. He complained I wasn't as active in the bedroom as he was, insinuating that he did all the work while I just layed there. And if I gave him a blowjob every day, it still wouldn't be enough and he'd tell me I didn't make enough of an effort.

His comments live rent free in my head at all times.

"Do you really need dessert?"

"Why is it always me who has to do the work? Sometimes I'd like to lay there and get fucked instead."

"Your blowjobs could use some work, babe."

"Maybe if you did some of the work, I'd be more turned on by you."

I really shouldn't have been surprised when I found out he was cheating on me. I don't think he ever called me his girlfriend until I was breaking up with him. That was also the first time he told me he loved me.

Apparently, my services in the bedroom and my body weren't so bad that he wanted to live without them.

Good thing he had his piece on the side to ease the pain of my absence.

Fuck, he is the last person I want to be thinking about right now.

Another day of repetition. Make coffee. Make breakfast. Feed the animals. The only addition I'm making to my daily routine is to ignore Jason. The silent treatment is petty in my opinion, not my style. But in this case, it seems like the right course of action.

Jason saunters in from the garage like every morning while I have sausage patties and eggs going on the stove. He pours himself a cup of coffee as usual but deviates from his normal routine of waiting for breakfast by setting the table for all three of us.

Odd.

He doesn't normally help me with breakfast. Is he trying to be *nice?* Jason doesn't do *nice.*

Dylan joins us just as I scoop the last of the scrambled eggs from the skillet onto his plate. We eat in silence for the first few minutes before Dylan—in true Dylan fashion—breaks the silence but not the tension.

"Happy New Year, love birds."

Jason stops mid chew and I drop my fork to the plate. Two sets of eyes pin Dylan to the chair. Clearly, he was trying to make a joke, but he quickly realizes his mistake when the awkwardness draws even more taut.

"Too soon to make jokes?" He tilts his head toward a shrugged shoulder like a kid trying to get out of trouble. Paired with the puppy dog eyes he's mastered, I'd guess he got out of a lot of trouble with that look when he was a kid.

"Yes," I answer curtly.

I take my plate and fork to the sink before taking my coffee and bounding up the stairs to get dressed for morning chores.

It's been a while since I looked at myself in the mirror, I try to avoid looking at how much my body has changed since I was eighteen. I know we live in the world of body positivity and shaming those who shame others for their body. But I still find it hard to love the way I look when I used to look so much better.

This morning, I take a second to look at myself in the mirror before pulling my snow pants on.

I see more muscle definition than I had before I came here. All these farm chores and plowing snow has helped me regain some of my muscle mass that I used to have. And my love handles that I got freshman year have all but disappeared. Most women would kill for the body I had two months ago, even if it wasn't perfect. Yet my ungrateful self couldn't be happy with the image in the mirror because it wasn't love handles I was seeing, it was weakness. It wasn't cellulite I saw, it was depression.

Even though those traits are less visible than two months ago, I still see a depressed waste of space, unworthy of positive attention.

The animals are great company today.

A few weeks ago, Jason taught me how to clean and shoe Bessie which has to be done more frequently in the snow. He or Dylan take her for rides as much as they can so she can stretch her legs. That's what I'm doing when Jason approaches. He looks too damn sexy resting one hand on the beam over his head, leaning into the stretch so all his muscles are flexed.

Why does he have to look so good?

He's temptation incarnate.

I continue to ignore him as I finish the last shoe on Bessie and start to clean up the remnants. I walk past him narrowly avoiding contact by ducking under his arm. It's when I'm putting the tools away on the shelf that a calloused hand scales my body from my lower back to my abdomen. Still irritated, and not caring if I seem petty, I shake his touch away before storming back toward the barn door to go inside.

That same muscular hand grabs my arm and spins me back so I'm face to face with Jason, inches apart. His body heat envelopes me making me feel trapped even though it's only his hand holding me hostage.

Why does his presence make me forget how to walk, how to breathe?

"Jason, let me go," I demand. I'm gearing up to rip my arm out of his grasp, but the pleading look in his eyes deters me. I don't know how he does it, but Jason's body language conveys more than words. The way he's earnestly leaning over me with questioning eyes says it all.

Talk to me.

A request. Not a demand.

A heavy sigh leaves my chest before I make my confession.

"I don't want a relationship from you," I admit. "I'm not looking for pretty words and romantic gestures. But I'm not just a warm body for you to stick your cock in, either." My words taste like venom, not because they're spoken with the intention to hurt, but because they're derived from a deep place of insecurity.

"I deserve a little more respect than cold shoulders and the expectation we're going to fuck whenever you want."

The pain I've been fighting so hard to bury must be detectable in my voice because Jason releases my arm and steps back. The space between us finally allows me room to breathe, to think. The fog his closeness creates dissipates.

Brushing past me, Jason retrieves my coat from the hook by the barn door and hands it to me. The gesture is rather gentle compared to his usual gruffness. But those pleading eyes beg me to comply with his request. So I slip the coat on and zip it up while Jason saddles Bessie and his intention becomes clear.

In a matter of minutes, Bessie is saddled and I'm nestled between Jason's strong thighs atop the horse, my back pressed to his chest so our body heat merges into one. Although he hasn't said where we're going, I have a pretty good idea.

Not long after leaving the barn, we pass beneath the towering pines that border the frozen pond Jason brought me to weeks ago.

It doesn't take a genius to realize how special this place is to him. I told him I don't need romantic gestures because this isn't anything serious. But maybe this is a gesture of friendship instead. Cooperation. Comradery.

Maybe bringing me somewhere he holds so sacred is his way of telling me he accepts and respects me.

Jason dismounts Bessie first then guides me off with hands around my rib cage, lowering me to the ground before him. A look passes between us for half a heartbeat before I walk toward the crystallized frozen edge of the pond.

"I know I already apologized," I speak up, wrapping my arms around myself. "But I really am sorry, Jason. I was weak and too easily influenced by others. I've felt guilty for the part I played in prom night ever since. And I've been paying for it at the hands of karma everyday."

He doesn't say anything, I didn't expect him to. I don't even look back. I just start walking toward the center of the pond. One foot at a time. The solid ice beneath my feet crunches with the fresh snow beneath each foot step. Since the snow isn't falling right now, visibility is clear. Everything is white. The clouds in the sky, the tree tops, the hardened ice over the water's surface.

I finally turn around to see Jason standing beside Bessie watching me closely. He looks stuck, unsure...I don't know. I can't really place what's on his face. As much as he can express with just his body language, he can also mask it.

We lock eyes for a long moment before I turn and walk toward the other side of the pond. I don't know what I'm walking toward, but it feels good to get out of the cabin for a minute and explore somewhere unknown.

A sharp crack is the only warning I have before the ice at the center of the pond shatters beneath my weight and I plummet into the freezing water.

The rush of water in my ears sounds like voices, whispers, calling my name in panic.

"Mara!"

Chapter Eighteen

Jason

EXHALE-TAYLOR SWIFT FT. BON Iver

I've only experienced panic like this one other time in my life. Heart-stopping. Breath-hitching. Paralyzing fear where your brain can't comprehend what it just saw, but your body jumps into action without a second thought.

I spoke. *I spoke!*

Without thinking, my mouth moved and a garbled version of her name came booming out. I wasn't thinking. I was just acting. And apparently my panic seeing her fall through the ice overpowered my fear of talking.

I burst into action bolting for the center of the lake where I saw Mara sink into the frozen water without caring if the ice might break under my own weight. As soon as I reached the gaping hole in the ice, I slide to my knees and rip off my coat. Trying to anchor myself in place so I can take stock of my surroundings. I have to act quickly but jumping into action without a plan could be just as catastrophic.

Testing the stability of the ice, I could get within eight inches of the hole. The water is a dark abyss beneath the ice. I can't see much. But I have to do something so I lay flat against the ice and plunge my arm into the ice-cold water that makes just my arm feel numb. I can't imagine how Mara must be feeling right now.

Swishing my hand around in the water, little by little, I pray I don't have to dive in after her.

But I would. I don't know how I know this but when the thought crosses my mind I don't even hesitate to accept that fate. I'll submit myself to the same torture if it means I can save her.

By some miracle, my hand brushes something soft when I'm nearly shoulder deep. So I lower myself even lower at the risk of the ice giving out and feel soft fabric, tendrils of wet hair, and a hard, round shape. A shoulder!

I grab the fabric in my firm grip and start to lift until a mop of wet blonde hair breaches the surface of the icy water. Using both hands now, I twist Mara's body so her coat acts as a barrier between her body and the jagged edges of the shattered ice.

She's weighed down by the drenched clothes that are more like a sponge than insulation. But I manage to get her on the ice. Unconscious, her lips are already turning a bit blue and her skin is so, so pale. She looks like a fucking corpse. But upon checking her pulse, I'm reassured she's alive.

I release a long breath I didn't realize I'd been holding in. *Thank God she's alive.*

I carry Mara back in my arms to Bessie before stripping off her coat and bundling her in mine. I have to get her warm. Fuck this snow, though, cause it's slowing me down. Bessie can only go so fast with this much snow in her way. I don't even know how long it takes us to get back to the cabin, I just count her breaths, every time her chest rises shallowly against mine where I have her cradled in my arms, trying to raise her body temperature.

As soon as we're back at the lodge I don't even bother locking Bessie in her stall, I just shut her into the barn and run to the house. Slamming the door is my way of alerting Dylan something is wrong. Thankfully he was already on the couch.

"Hey where'd you crazy kids g—." His voice stops abruptly when he sees me carrying an unconscious and frozen Mara in. She has flecks of snow and frozen tips of her hair from the journey that felt like it would never end.

"What the fuck? Hypothermia?" I nod. Then I'm bounding up the stairs and into the bathroom to start the bath water. All my earlier jealousy about Dylan seeing the round bottom of Mara's ass cheeks dissipates in the need to heal her, save her. So I start stripping her drenched clothes from her body, peeling them away like a second layer of skin.

Dylan pops his head in, keeping his eyes fixed on me out of respect for Mara. I pause my work long enough to sign *fire* to him and he jumps into action, understanding my needs from a simple word.

I hope he knows how much I appreciate him and the way he understands me.

She's practically translucent, I can see every blue and green vein criss-crossing her body through her ghostly-white skin.

As soon as the water is at its highest temperature, I lower the temp a bit to avoid sending her body into shock with the rapid change of temperature and lift the lever that switches the flow of water to the shower head. If she were awake, I know the warm water would sting like hell.

Not giving a shit about my own clothes, I step into the bathtub with Mara in my arms, holding her beneath the stream of warm water so it cascades over her smooth, frozen flesh. Water seeps into my own clothes but I don't give a fuck. My body temperature is fine and clothes can be dried.

She's what matters.

Mara isn't exactly heavy, but she is dead weight while unconscious. So I lower us to the bathtub floor, bending one leg so my knee is raised like the back of a throne for Mara's body to rest against. Cradling her head to my chest isn't necessary, but it feels right to support her head like this.

Gradually, her skin starts to warm beneath the water, beneath my touch. My thumb makes anxious circles over her shoulder, my other hand on her thigh rubs up and down trying to use friction to warm her. And the action does something to calm my nerves. Adrenaline pumping, heart pounding, mind racing. My body is singing with nervous energy so I continue to make repetitive motions that ease my worry and slow my pulse.

She's alive, I remind myself. *She's here. She will be fine.*

I have to tell myself over and over because she's just so unnaturally cold. I feel like I'm holding a corpse and that is a feeling I want to forget. I hate this feeling. The unknown. A sickening twist to my gut makes me question if she will be ok, even though I know logically she will be fine. Hypothermia is deadly but it is often overcome more than it isn't.

She's alive. She will be fine.

Dylan pokes his head in again, in this position my body shields Mara's from his line of sight.

"Fires going in your room," he lets me know.

But he doesn't leave. Dylan takes another step into the bathroom that I catch out of the corner of my eye. I turn my gaze to his then back to Mara when I see the worry in his eyes. Only, his worry isn't for Mara.

"You know, it's ok to like her." That's the last thing I want to talk about right now. "I know what she did. I know you hated her for a long time. But clearly, she's not the person she used to be. Neither are you." He knows better than anyone.

I release a steady, laden breath.

"For someone who wants to make it clear there's nothing but sex between you two, you certainly act like it's more. Just wanted you to know your principles aren't lost if you change your mind about her."

With that parting thought for me to marinate in, he leaves us alone.

After her body rises to a slightly less concerning temperature, I shut off the water and carry Mara into my bedroom where a glowing fire roars in the hearth. Dylan, the thoughtful guy he is, laid out layers and layers of blankets on the floor five feet in front of the fire.

I lay Mara on the makeshift mattress Dylan constructed then quickly cover her with two heavy quilts. Then I strip my own wet clothes and climb under the blankets with Mara. Pulling her close to my chest feels so natural, as if I've done it a million times before.

Maybe our souls knew each other in another life. Her body calls to mine, her scent feels like it was made for me. Even the way she nestles into the crook of my neck and shoulder, legs intertwining with mine, bears a resemblance that I can't place.

The heat of the fire starts to filter through the quilts warming our bodies, warming her. Her breathing is so much more peaceful, now, it's resumed a steady rhythm I could compose a symphony to. My body heat seeps into hers and I'm unbelievably relieved to feel how warm her body is now, in retrospect to what it was thirty minutes ago.

I thought I knew cold after several years of living in this cabin, but I've never known the kind of chill that her body carried after her frozen plunge. Maybe it's exaggerated in my head but I can't shake the shiver running up and down my spine like a current of electricity at the thought.

Before dozing off to sleep, I'm left with the compromising ideas Dylan planted in my head.

Mara *is* different. And so am I. We've both experienced a lot in the time since we last saw one another. We've both grown into different people for better or for worse. But the essence of our core makeup still exists. She was never a spiteful person at heart, she was just too eager to please the wrong people.

I tug Mara closer to me, relieved when she lets out a soft sigh and buries her face into my chest even more.

She's alive. She's fine.

But me? I've always been bitter. I've always been different, angry, resentful for the cards I was dealt. The root of my problems was only amplified by time and experience. That can't be what she wants.

But is she what I want?

Chapter Nineteen

Mara

I **G**OT **Y**OU—THE **W**HITE **B**uffalo

I was falling.

It was cold.

So cold.

And that was all I could remember. The cold was so all-consuming that it's all my body could register. Dark, cold, wet, and devoid of life. That's what I felt until the warmth spread from my center to my extremities.

I become vaguely aware of the solid body beside me and the warm scent of him surrounding me. It took a moment to realize the steadiness I felt was from arms holding me so close so I didn't slip away again.

Blinking once, my memories of the ice cracking under my weight and plummeting into the frozen pond rush back like a tidal wave. I don't know what happened after that but I'm somewhere warm now, so either I'm dead...

Or I'm safe.

And there's only one logical explanation for that.

He saved me. He saved me? I thought he hated me. But maybe not as much as I thought if he was willing to risk his own safety for my life.

Another blink and the blurry orange-red glow of the room solidifies a bit more so I can make out the shadowed contours of the man holding me.

The *naked* man holding me.

That doesn't turn me on simply because he's naked, but because I can only assume he was trying to share his body heat and raise my own.

There's something so intimate about it. Dare I say...romantic. Neither one of my exes ever cuddled me unless I asked for it. And even then I would lay on Bryce's chest while he scrolled Instagram on his phone. I always had this feeling that my relationships were one sided without fully acknowledging them.

Until I did. And it broke me how used I was.

It doesn't take a doctorate to realize that my insecurities with Jason stem from my past experiences. The hurt I felt had little to do with him and more to do with unresolved feelings.

I never got the closure I needed. I never got to tell either of them how emotionally abusive they were, how much their actions hurt me. Not that they would care. But I was too weak to speak up and say anything besides "you're a piece of shit." In hindsight, that really didn't pack the punch I wanted it to.

Then there's Jason.

Jason, who pulled me out of my car on the side of the road in a snow storm.

Jason, who saved me from a frozen death.

Jason, who has made it very clear I'm just a good fuck, yet he's still holding me in such a possessive manner that I can physically feel his concern for my life. I don't know if he has some sense of duty over me or something. Should I be grateful or suspicious that he keeps saving my life?

I open my eyes fully and try to tilt my head so I can see Jason. But he moves his strong hand to the back of my head and holds me in place. I don't know if he's awake or subconsciously tucking me into him. But I comply.

The scratchy length of his beard rubs against my smooth hair. My bare breasts press against his hard pecs and every inch beneath that is in contact with the other. Flat palms against my back. His stomach against mine. My legs layered with his. His erection is stiff between us.

Yet...he isn't acting on it. He's just holding me to him and keeping me as warm as possible. I finally realize we aren't in the bed but laying on a pile of blankets on the floor, bundled in quilts beside the fireplace I didn't realize was in his room. I noticed the house had two chimneys outside but never asked where the other fireplace was. Here's my answer.

It's unbelievably warm. The light sheen of sweat over Jason's body melts us together so our skin feels like one. But my body is still recovering from the accident so the heat is a welcome relief. The only thing still tinglingly cold is my toes.

Which seem to have a weight on them. When I wiggle my foot I hear a soft *meow* and assume it's the infamous barn cat I heard about, resting on my foot.

Finally, I notice that one arm is looped under Jason's so the hand can rest on his tricep while my other hand is flat against his pecs. My face is buried in the area where his neck meets his shoulder so his scent is overpowering.

It's like a drug. I'm addicted to his scent. To him.

Closing my eyes, I speak into his chest, "You saved me." No answer. "Again."

Callused hands sweep up and down my spine from the nape of my neck to the top of my ass. On the last pass, his hand lands on my ass cheek and stays there like a home base.

"Thank you," I whisper into him.

Jason shifts his head so his mouth and nose are against the crown of my head. He doesn't kiss my hair like I thought he might, but it's still a sentimental gesture.

Rest. I can practically hear him telling me.

So I do.

The next time I wake up, we're spooning. I must have shifted in my sleep to face the hearth, and a sleeping Jason didn't lock me into place like before. Every curve of me fits all his curves, every bend in our bodies nestled together like puzzle pieces. His arm loosely bands around my waist. But not too tight.

The weight of the cat is gone so I slip out of his hold and lift the covers to rise. Thankfully Jason doesn't stir. Seeing he's still fast asleep, I move to the dresser I got a shirt from last time and pull out a long sleeve black Carhartt shirt before slipping it over my torso.

I've been in this room a handful of times but I was...preoccupied every time so I haven't gotten a good look at the room.

It's so *cozy.* I expected a bleak room. But the flames flicker light over beautiful wood panels on the floor, a large wood frame bed covered in a beige comforter, and a rust red Pendleton patterned rug on the floor. A set of French doors leads to a small balcony with a light dusting of snow.

But what really catches my eye is the rows and rows of floating shelves on either side of the fireplace neatly lined with books. Upon closer inspection, I notice they're arranged alphabetically. I had a feeling Jason was anal-retentive and this solidifies my suspicions.

I have no idea what time it is but it's still dark outside. The juxtaposition of the cold winter night outside and the homey, ember coated interior of the room separated by glass doors does something to me. Some feelings can only be described by a scene, a smell, there's no word for how you're feeling. That's Jason's room. Moody, cozy, it makes me want to curl up in front of the fire with a book for hours.

Shuffling behind me alerts me to Jason waking. Spinning around, I see the panic on his face melt into relief when he sees me standing in front of the book shelf.

This might be the first time I've seen his hair pulled into a manbun at the back of his head. Sweeping his hair away from his face reveals just how jagged his features are, how masculine and chiseled. All of this to say he looks like a Viking ready to pillage a town for treasure. Fierce, deadly in his own way.

"Sorry if I woke you," I say. Though I wasn't making any noise. It wouldn't surprise me if Jason has Spidey-senses that know when something is amiss.

Taking my hand, Jason pulls me down to the floor on my knees between his spread thighs. A less than graceful hand runs up the length of my stomach beneath the shirt, lifting the fabric with it until his hand meets my breast. Adjusting the shirt, Jason lifts it so he can access my nipples, wrapping soft lips around one while his beard scratches the sensitive skin around it. All the while, my hands weave through his hair, longer than when I arrived. I can practically feel the shivers run down his spine from my touch, just like he's doing to me.

We fuck, I sit on his lap and ride him like I can clear my mind of all the chaos if I grind hard enough. And just before he comes, Jason lays me on my back, shirt still lifted, so he can paint my skin with his release.

It wasn't as rough as usual, probably trying to be careful with me after today (or yesterday, not sure). But it was...different. I don't know how to describe it but the way Jason handles me, the way he looked at me, felt different than our usual rutting.

And different isn't alway good. It plants a seed of doubt and I worry that's not what he wanted.

As I wipe the come from my body, I ask, "Is our sex what you want?" The question slips out before I can stop myself. Then immediately regret it but the words are already there, hanging like a noose between us. "I mean...do I do enough of the work. Do I do what you like? I'm completely satisfied, don't worry, but I want to make sure I do what you want too. Pulling my own weight in our situation."

Oh my god, Mara, stop rambling.

Jason stares at me without a nod or a shake of the head or anything. So, naturally, I assume I've made things awkward.

As usual.

"Do you want me to be on top more? I mean, my ex said I never did enough of the work in our sex life and I'd expect him to do everything. So I'm consciously trying to be an active participant in this arrangement. Soooo, is it ok? Do you want to change anything about our sex life?"

After another endless moment of silence, Jason shakes his head firmly, putting my rapid heart rate at ease.

As long as he's happy, I'm happy.

"Ok. Good." I still sound like a blubbering idiot. "I'm gonna go get a little more sleep before the sun rises." I point toward the door and by extension my room before lifting off the ground, and lowering his shirt to cover the important parts and head for my room.

A part of me expected him to take me back to the pile of blankets and quilts on a wordless request for me to stay.

That same part of me wanted him to.

But he doesn't move to stop me so I leave his room and enter my own with a mix of emotions I can't place. A sickening pit in my stomach that keeps me awake until the sun peeks through the curtains of my room. It's a new day. But I feel like something changed. Like the rest of my time here will be different.

Chapter Twenty

Mara

Us-James Bay

"So I hear you had quite an adventure," Dylan greets me when he enters the kitchen for breakfast. It's that moment that Jason comes in from the garage gym.

With my back to him, I don't have to make awkward eye contact. I can't believe I basically asked him "was it good for you?" last night. I sound like an insecure virgin.

Well, half of that is true.

After I put the English muffin breakfast sandwiches on the table, we all take a seat in our usual spots.

It's such a mundane and ordinary morning considering what occurred less than twenty-four hours ago.

"How are you feeling today?" Dylan asks me.

"Tired," I answer truthfully. "I feel like I haven't slept in a week and ran marathons the whole time. But other than that, nothing wrong."

Dylan scoffs, "Pft. Sounds kinda harsh. You should relax today and let your body recover."

"No, it's ok. I want to help. I'll go feed the animals," I start to rise but Jason's motions catch my eye.

He pats his chest and makes a swiping motion as of to say *done*.

Looking from him to the barn through the window, I ask, "You already fed them?"

He nods.

That's an uncharacteristically nice gesture.

I wonder if he woke up earlier than me to do the chores and workout on purpose, or if he never went back to sleep after I left.

The feeling of his body wrapped around mine is tattooed on my skin. Not because it was arousing but because of the gentle touches and intimate way he held me. It seemed like something a boyfriend and girlfriend might do. But that might be taking it a little too far.

It didn't occur to me until I went back to my room that I've never been held like that before. Neither of my exes would hold me after sex. I've never had a man in my life who did things for me just to make me happy. My father gave me attention and presents because it was expected of him. My exes gave me flowers and chocolates when they fucked up and wanted to win my good graces back. I've never had a man who cooked for me just because, or held me without the expectation of more.

While I should be thrilled I experienced that with Jason, even if it was under odd circumstances, it makes me jealous. I feel cheated out of those experiences with the men who were *supposed* to give me that kind of unconditional affection.

"Thank you," I tell Jason. Then I scoop up our plates and begin washing them.

There's nothing dire that has to be done today. Nothing that can't wait until tomorrow. And my body does feel like it needs more rest. I guess it wouldn't hurt to take today off and read for a while. Maybe I can do some chores in the afternoon.

That was my plan, anyway. But I must have fallen asleep while reading. I woke with a start when a heavy weight shifted the couch at my feet, startling me out of my slumber.

Jason sits at the end of the couch where my body stretched in my sleep. One arm leaning on my bent legs, the other hand holds the book I was reading. *Wuthering Heights.* I've noticed the collection of books in his library tend to lean more toward the classics.

I read a lot of smut before, but beggars can't be choosers.

Besides, reading classic literature without the expectation of writing papers and giving PowerPoint presentations in class makes them far more enjoyable.

"Sorry." I prop myself up on my elbow. "Didn't mean to fall asleep. What time is it?"

Knowing he won't answer, I look to the large clock on the wall. Two o'clock in the afternoon. I don't even know what time I feel asleep, let alone how long I've been out.

Jason hands the book back to me, open to the page I must have left off on.

"Have you read this before?" He nods.

"Did you bring all these books up here?" He shakes his head.

"Did your mom?" Another nod.

"Did she read to you often?" Jason sways his head from side to side as if to say *sometimes.*

"I hated this book the first time I read it," I confess. "Must have been junior year of high school. I thought it was so slow. And then I had to write a one thousand word essay on it. To this day, I couldn't tell you what the essay covered. I barely remembered the plot until I picked it up again. It's like I'm reading it for the first time. Makes me want to read books like *The Great Gatsby* and *Grapes of Wrath* again."

Jason's tall form rises from the couch and goes to the bookshelf where he extracts a gray fabric bound hardcover from the middle shelf and hands it to me.

Pride and Prejudice

"I've read this three times," I tell him. "By the time I had to read it for school and write a paper on it, I practically had it memorized. It's a right of passage for a book girl." I laugh.

Instead of taking it back, Jason lifts my legs beneath the blanket he must have thrown over me while I slept, slides his lower body beneath my legs, then lays them on his lap.

Staring expectantly, I get his message to commence reading *Pride and Prejudice* aloud. All the while, Jason stares directly at me with such an intensity it's tangible. I can feel the weight of his gaze and the severe shift in it. He used to fire daggers at me from his eyes. Now, it feels more like he is assessing me. It's no longer a glower but a pensive, considering gaze.

After dinner, Jason hands the book back to me to continue reading so we reoccupy our positions on the couch and resume the text.

I have no idea how long we sit there. Even Dylan listens for a while before heading up stairs for the night.

At the end of the current chapter, Jason leans over me to place the ribbon I used as a bookmark between the pages and shuts the book gently. After placing the book on the end table beside the arm of the couch, he slides out from beneath my legs and scoops me into his arms so I'm forced to cling to him for stability. He lets his eyes rest on my face, my eyes, my lips, before watching his steps as he climbs the stairs.

This is so uncharacteristic of him. I don't really know what to make of him carrying me in such a romantic gesture. But there's not much time to consider it before he lays me gingerly on the bed so I lie side to side, not end or end. I become acutely aware of the fact that I haven't changed out of the shirt I took from him last night and the shorts I made all day. They must smell like sleep sweat. But it becomes less of an issue as Jason slides them down my quads, over me knees and ankles, and slips them off my legs. He starts kissing his way up my right leg, switching between leaving achingly soft fires with his lips and burning desire with the scratch of his beard against my soft skin. When he gets to my hip bone, Jason leaves a little bite and adds his hands to the mix as they apply firm pressure on my sides, scaling up my body, taking his shirt with them until he pulls it over my head and up-stretched arms. At the sight of my naked body, nipples hard with nervous anticipation, his eyes visibly darken as though shadows fall over his eye sockets. Lust, pure lust. He looks like he needs to own me.

I feel his leering just as much as his hands as he scans every curve of my body, every contour, every line. The pent up energy fizzling beneath my skin makes me want to squirm under his touch but I fight to stay still, to not back down from whatever this is.

And whatever this is, it's different. So different. We've fucked, before, we bang and bone. This feels like...more.

As his stormy stare lands on the apex of my thighs, Jason lowers his head so the point of his tongue can flick my clit, sending a jolt of electricity up my spine. He follows that with a long, languid trail of his tongue pressed flat against my flesh from bottom to top. I can't help it, my body arches into him as it silently begs for more.

The first time he ate me out, it was feverish. This time feels lazy in the best way, as though he has nothing better to do than bury his face in me for the rest of the night. As if there's nowhere else he'd rather be.

Every stroke of his tongue drives me closer to explosion. Every flick and lapping motion makes it harder and harder to keep quiet. He's meticulous with every touch knowing just how to drive me fucking crazy. Knowing the right moves to fill my orgasm without letting it spill over yet. I'm completely at his mercy. This feels more vulnerable than confessing my darkest secrets. I'm entrusting so much to a man who has notoriously hated me.

It's too intense, now, it feels like my orgasm has been walking a tightrope for so long it'll fall any moment. I'll fall. I can't handle the edge of pain and pleasure from balancing so long. But he gives me my relief with a hard suck of my clit, sucking me into his cheeks to detonate me. I explode. I don't know up from down, left from right, where I end and he begins. My body just quakes under him until Jason releases me so he can scale up my body until we're face to face. The sight of me glistening on his lips does something riveting in my soul.

I'm his. I want to be his and I want him to be mine even knowing that's not his style, not what he wants. But I know at this moment that's what I am, under his spell.

Thinking I need to return the favor, I try to reach my hand down between us so I can grip him, but Jason grabs my wrist before I can wrap my fingers around his dick and lifts my arm above my head, pinning it in place with his strong clutch. The fire in his eyes tells me he's in charge, just the way he wants it.

Suddenly it occurs to me. Last night I told him about my insecurities, I told him about how my exes were and he's proving that a healthy sexual relationship doesn't always have to be a 50/50 exchange of effort in every encounter. It's a balance over all.

He wants me to enjoy every second of this without overthinking it, without trying to figure out if he's enjoying himself.

He is. I don't know how I know that but I can feel it right down to my curling toes.

Positioning himself with his free hand, Jason lines his cock up with me and slides in so seamlessly, so torturously slow. Despite having an orgasm already, I need more. I want to feel the complete fullness of him inside me, consuming every inch of me that he can take. His girth stretches me to a point of *almost* pain that I love.

Once he's seated inside of me, Jason takes his sweet time pulling out inch by inch, then back in at that slow pace, letting my body recover from the firm mind-blowing orgasm. Gradually, he picks up speed, but it's still not enough.

It'll never be enough.

With so much time between orgasms, I feel every muscle relax and tense again. I feel where the last climax ended and this new one starts to rise. My heaving breaths beg for more. Pulled taut like a bow string.

And my eyes tell him what I need. Because our eyes haven't broken contact since he entered me. Jason has kept me in his sights as long as he's held himself above me. Both wrists in one of his hands, now, the other holds my rib cage as each pump of his pelvis increases in intensity. By the time he's up to speed I can't deny the one word to describe his body. Power. He is power incarnate. His movements are powerful. His body is brimming with power. He makes me feel so energized with it I don't have any way to release that bottled energy under his pleasurable torment.

"Oh god," I break the silence because I can't hold my mouth shut anymore. "Jason, I—" I don't know what I want to say. I'm just trying to release some of the crippling buzz inside me that he's rattling, stirring. "I need to—"

He knows exactly what I need and shifts higher up the bed so his pelvic bone grinds against my clit while his dick creates beautiful friction inside me until I'm ready to explode again.

"Jason," I cry out and he silences it with his mouth.

Jason Alder is kissing me.

Jason Alder is kissing me.

And all the while my body convulses beneath his. Nipples vibrating against his chest. Thighs clenching to him for dear life. Arms straining against his hold begging to feel him.

Jason kisses me passionately through my rupture until I'm a puddle of weak limbs and blissful sweat beneath him.

Chapter Twenty-One

Jason

E VERYWHERE, EVERYDAY-NOAH KAHAN

I kissed her. I've never kissed anyone before. But I kissed Mara. And it felt so *right*. I thought my first kiss would feel foreign and weird because I've never done it before but not with her. I don't know what came over me but I wanted to swallow the cry of ecstasy she made so I could possess it. I don't know what she saw in me earlier but the way I felt staring at her naked, perfect body was possessive. She's mine. I don't want anyone to touch her, look at her, think about her. I want to own every inch of her and that's what I plan to do.

I started this rendezvous because I wanted to show her that she doesn't always have to worry about me enjoying myself. I enjoy every fucking second I'm inside her, touching her, breathing her in. But now, I want to devour her whole so she can never leave me.

So I seared her with my kiss. And that kiss lit a fire in me I intend to let burn us both to ashes.

My movements become so manic that my body controls the quick pace without my brain telling it what to do. I just need to make her come again. I need to see the way she comes again and again and again. I need to feel her vibrate like that again. So I thrust into her so violently it shakes the bed from side to side. Fuck it, if Dylan hears. I don't care if the entire mountain topples with the way we rock the house I just need to fuck her so hard our bodies become one.

So that's what I do. I shove in and out of her with such force our bodies send a smack through the air that mingles with her whimpers of pure pleasure. The friction her tight pussy creates around my cock sends heavy shockwaves through my entire body until all that pressure builds at the base of my spine, in my balls, and I know I'm about to come any second.

But not without one more orgasm for her. So I pull out painfully sudden and shove three fingers into her cunt and finger her into oblivion. Without my mouth above hers to swallow her cries, she cries out as clear liquid gushes over my fingers in a hot wave that makes my alpha male pride shake with satisfaction. I don't even need to touch myself to come but I do anyway, laying my balls on her hot sex and pumping my come onto her beautiful abdomen so she's marked by me, branded with my seed so she knows who she belongs to.

I gaze down into her hazel eyes to relish the affection in them. Affection, something I never thought I'd see from anyone let alone Mara Meyers. She looks at me like I'm the whole world, like she needs me to breathe.

When the spell breaks just enough for me to realize we're naked and soaked, I lift myself off the bed and grab a clean shirt to wipe the come from her stomach before poking my head out to make sure Dylan's door is closed. I run to the bathroom, turn the shower on, and come back for Mara to find her in the same position on the bed. It's like she's so thoroughly exhausted she can't move. So I lift her once again and carry her to the bathroom. She stands on her own two feet, albeit, a little unsteady, when I set her down.

Chest to chest, face to face, we stand under the burning stream of water letting it envelope us in a cloud of steam and tension. There's a lot to unpack, a lot that isn't being said.

A lot I won't say because I can't.

But I'll keep trying to convey it without words as long as she'll listen.

I take the shampoo off the shelf of the shower and squirt a dollop into my hand, lathering it between my palms before working the suds into her silk hair. I massage Mara's scalp as her head tips back into my hold, exposing her slender neck.

It occurs to me how vulnerable that is. I could end her in a split second with one swift movement but she trusts me not to.

She trusts me. She *trusts* me.

And I don't know what to do with that.

So I keep washing her. And much to my surprise, she finds enough energy to return the favor. Running her fingers through my hair and over my arms, cleansing me of every horrible thought I've had. Washing away all the resentment I've felt toward her for so long. It's like a security blanket I can't let go of. But her gentle touch replaces it with a feeling of worth.

Her eyes tell me I mean something to her as easily as mine speak to her.

After we're good and clean and warm, I hand her a towel to dry off and go to the bedroom to change the comforter for a heavy Pendleton wool blanket I have for the especially cold nights. With a fire going in the hearth, it will be more than enough for tonight.

When I go back to the bathroom, I take her delicate hand in mine and lead her back to the bedroom.

I hope she doesn't plan on wearing another one of my shirts to bed cause I want to feel every inch of her against me tonight. I want the constant reminder that it's *her* beside me, wrapped around me, it's her I'm holding.

So I pull back the covers and slide into bed, bringing her with me so she's cradled against my chest. We're propped against the pillows which isn't conducive for sleeping but I don't think either one of us is ready for bed yet.

Mara tugs the blankets over her chest, flattening them against her by laying her arms over the material.

"You want me to sleep here tonight?" She asks, her voice laced with hesitation.

I just tighten my hold on her in response, bracing the arm that's already wrapped around her and laying my free hand on her thigh.

We can't look one another in the face very well from this position.

"I've never done that before," Mara admits to me, which only inflates my ego further.

"What does this mean?"

I don't know. I don't know how to convey what I'm feeling, and I'm not sure I know how to describe it, either.

"You don't have to put a label on it," she says soothingly. I won't deny the way my chest eases at that. I don't know what to call it or what she wants, for that matter. But I want her.

"I guess the better question I should be asking is what do you want?"

Her! But I don't know how to tell her that without words. So I shift her in my hold so I can see her angelic face. The last time I kissed her, I didn't even think about it before acting. This time, I overthink to compensate. Did I do it right?

Well, the way she squirted on me after makes me think I did.

So I lower my head so we share the same air and tenderly brush my lips against hers, deepening the kiss after I'm sure she wants it.

I thought she was addicting before, with her tight body and curves. But I underestimated the effect her kiss would have on me, soft, plump lips and all.

God, she's so beautiful. I don't know why she looks even prettier now but somehow she does. It's like the hope shining in her eyes creates an ethereal glow around her. I can't get over it.

When I pull away from her, I know by the way she rests her head on me, cheek to chest, that she understands what I want. There's a palpable burden lifted from her shoulders and she eases into me.

She eventually falls asleep on me so I settle into the bed a bit more so it's more comfortable for her. But I lie awake much longer, unable to stop my brain from turning over and over like an engine powering itself.

Everything just changed.

And I think I like it.

Which makes me feel uneasy.

Now that I've kissed Mara, I can't stop.

And kissing her so frequently leads to more sex, as well. The lack of condoms since we used the last one I had in the house has become a problem, mainly because cleaning her up afterward is getting tedious. But thank God Mara likes to swallow.

I wanted to show her that sex doesn't always have to be something she overthinks. And she likes to thank me for that on a regular basis. After I've given her three or four orgasms, she gets on her knees for me and makes me see stars.

With her sleeping in my bed every night, I don't have as many nightmares as usual, but they haven't stopped completely. On one side of the coin, it's nice having her in my arms to ease my sleep, and when I do have a nightmare, she brings me instant relief.

But on the other side of the coin, she's starting to notice that they happen semi-regularly. Though she doesn't ask what I'm dreaming about since she knows I won't answer. But I see a million questions dancing in her irises. She knows something is going on.

Or maybe she knows it's something from the past. She's too perceptive sometimes.

Dad took me to work with him because I got sent home for hitting Bryce Quinn. No one believed me when I said he and his friends were breaking all my crayons and throwing them away so I couldn't color. So I'm the one that got in trouble. The school called Dad and he can't take time off work so I have to go with him to the mill.

I know Dad works at the sawmill but I don't know what he does. He works in an office now, not on the floor like he used to. He also wears nicer shirts to work these days. He used to wear tan work pants and a bright green vest.

The bland office is cold since it's really just a steel box at the front of the mill with a bathroom and a desk. Dad points to the empty corner with a fat finger and tells me, "Sit there and don't cause trouble."

It feels like I sit there for hours! *He didn't give me anything to do and there's no TV in here. There's a computer but Dad has to use it to work. The bottom of the computer screen says 11:56 am which means I would have been having lunch at school, right now.*

I'm hungry.

I know this could get me in trouble but my hunger is stronger than my fear.

"Dad," I ask timidly.

"What, Jason?" He doesn't even turn around to look at me, just keeps typing on the keyboard.

"I'm hungry. It's lunch time at school."

He lifts his graying head to look at the clock on the bottom of the screen and huffs.

"Ok. Let me go to the employee lounge and see what I can find for you." He spins in the office chair and narrows his eyes on me. "Stay put."

I nod. I don't want to get in trouble.

But he's gone for so long!

I see the paper and pencil on his desk. The paper is blank so maybe I can draw on it. I start to draw a picture of a truck, it's the one at the lodge I like so much. Dad said if I work hard enough it will be mine one day. It's so cool. I can't wait until I'm old enough to drive it. But Dad said it also needs to be fixed. I hope I can fix things like he does one day.

I look at his computer and the clock says 12:32. Mom says I'm really smart for my age since I can already tell time.

Dad has been gone for a while. Maybe he forgot about me. My tummy starts gurgling. I know he said to stay here but maybe I can find him and he'll remember he was going to get me food.

The door knob turns easily into the cold October day. It's cloudy and the mist mixes with the steam from the mill over the huge piles of logs that are as tall as buildings. I asked Dad if we can climb them and he said that's dangerous.

It occurs to me I don't know where the employee lounge is but it can't be too hard to find. Trusting my instincts I take a right and start searching through the maze of lumber piles. There's so much machinery and logs everywhere. And chips of wood mixed in the mud. I look down and see my boots are covered in mud too. I already know Dad is going to be mad about that. But it's too late for that.

I weave through the mill trying to find a building. I'm sure an employee lounge would be in a building, right? The guys wouldn't want to sit out in this rain everyday. And starting in October, it rains everyday. *I hate the rain. But I like the snow we get in December.*

No matter how long I search I can't find my dad. I can't find anyone. I must be lost so I turn around trying to retrace my steps but everything looks the same. The pyramids of lumber, the muddy ground, the clouds and mist block out the sun so even the sky looks the same. I don't know where to go but I can't stop moving.

It's so cold too.

"Hey," I hear a voice. For a second I think it's Dad but Dad's voice sounds deeper than this one. I turn to my left and see a guy in a yellow hard hat and a bright green vest like Dad used to wear. I recognize his black beard. His name is Bob. He sometimes comes over to the house to drink with Dad and watch football with a couple other guys from work.

"Hey, kid," he beckons me over with a wave of his hand. He's taller than Dad. It's kind of scary. I feel like being that tall would be scary, like I might hit my head on things. "Where's your dad?" He asks. "What are you doing here?"

"I can't find him," I answer. I've never talked to this man before. Even though he's been at the house before, he didn't talk to me. "Where's the employee lounge? He said he would get me lunch."

"Where did he leave you?" Bob aks.

"His office," I tell him even though I'm worried he'll tell on me. "I thought he forgot about me. He was gone for a long time."

"Is that so?" Bob gets a weird look in his eyes. I don't like it. I don't like him. He's weird. He looks mean. He makes me nervous.

"I'm going to go find my dad."

A meaty hand grabs my shoulder and jerks me back. I don't like it. I don't like it. His touch hurt my shoulder. Why did he have to hold me so hard?

"Hold on, kid, I'll help you."

A soft voice coaxes me from my nightmare.

Fuck. I never dream about the day my father took me to work with him. Usually it's about the fight on the porch. Why the fuck is my head messing with me like this?

Sticky sweat coats my half-naked body. My vision clears and I'm back in my bedroom, in a chilly room since the embers in the hearth are nearly out. Small hands hold my face in their grasp with a force like they're afraid I might slip away, fearful yet determined. I look up into Mara's eyes and remember where I am, how old I am, the blowjob she gave me before bed that was so intense it knocked me out.

"Jason," she sighs when she notices the recognition in my eyes. "Hey. Were you having a nightmare?"

I nod and rub my eyes as her hands fall away. Folding the quilts away from me, I head to the hearth and begin building the fire back up with some pre-cut kindling and firewood.

"I know you have nightmares a lot," she announces as if I don't already know she's aware of them. "But you were shaking in your sleep, Jason. You don't usually shake. Usually, you just jolt awake in the middle of the night. Was this one different?"

I could nod, because she's right, but I don't want to acknowledge that. Why does she have to be so damned observant?

I return to the bed and smash our faces together in a determined kiss. Maybe I can distract her from what she's picking up on. One hand on her lower back, and the other pressed against the mattress I start to lower her flat against the bed but she resists.

"Hey," she breaks the kiss and tries to placate me. "Do you want to talk about it? I mean, I know you don't talk. But, do you need to process it?"

Fuck no.

I start to lower her again and run my palm along her smooth outer thigh pushing up the t-shirt she's wearing to bed. No underwear. Perfect. I slip my hand between her legs and start stroking her pussy that gets soaked at the first of my touches. She's so easy to turn on for me. Just for me. Mine.

"Jason," she says but not in the way she usually does when I'm between her legs. She says it like she's annoyed. "You can't use sex to ignore your problems." I ignore her comment and keep stroking her, admittedly less coordinated than usual. "You don't have to talk to me about it but maybe you should write about what you're feeling. Jason."

Fuck. The annoyance in her voice tells me she's going to ignore the way her body responds to me and try to make this bigger than it needs to be. Why does she have to stick her fucking nose in my goddamn business?

I pull my hand away and put distance between us in an instant, running my hands through my hair, significantly longer than when the winter started.

"Jason, please," she pleads, "I don't like seeing you like this. I don't like seeing you shake in your sleep. And you can't tell me what happened in your sleep to make you shake like that which only makes it worse."

Yeah, cause you need to know everything about everyone all the time.

"I just think if you wrote down what you're feeling you might be able to work through whatever it is since you can't talk about it."

I shake my head no. No fucking way I'm writing my *feelings* down like some loser with a diary. Not my style. She's inserting herself where she doesn't belong.

I kick the dresser with the inner side of my foot. Not hard, but enough to rattle the drawers. I don't want to deal with this. I'm already on edge from that fucking dream and now Mara is trying to get me to open up about shit that should stay buried. And it's the middle of the goddamn night. This is not the time. I have all this restless energy, now, so I storm out of the room. Without knowing where I'm going to I somehow end up in the gym in the garage.

As good a place as any, I suppose.

Even though its two in the morning, I decide to do an incline treadmill walk to work off my excess energy that's fizzling and burning under my skin.

It helps. So I head back upstairs to my room ready to silently apologize to what I'm sure is a pissed Mara. But my room is empty, my bed is empty. But I think I know where she is.

Making a point.

So I make a point of my own by sliding into Mara's bed beside her. It's significantly colder in here without a fire in the corner which explains why she's curled up in a ball like a cat.

When she's beside me, she usually sleeps splayed across me like a starfish.

I curl my body around hers telling myself it's to share my body heat with her. But really, it's because I need her. I don't like that I need her but I do. I need her close to keep the demons at bay. I need to feel her so I know she's safe. The warmth of her skin against mine helps me breathe a little easier when it feels like my chest is caving in around my lungs.

Burying my face in the crook of her neck, I fall asleep with her scent in my lungs instead of the pressure that always makes me feel like I'm slowly deteriorating. But not with her. Not when I touch her.

Chapter Twenty-Three

Mara

S AVE YOURSELF-KALEO

It's been two weeks since Jason and I had our heart to heart and it feels like he's been making changes to positively affect our relationship. He still has nightmares and he doesn't talk about it but I see him writing in the middle of the night sometimes and I like to think he's doing that not only for me, but for himself. He just needed a little push to realize he was his own worst enemy. I just roll over and go back to sleep when I notice he's writing. I don't want to disturb him or the cathartic bubble he's created.

The mornings following his nightmares I wake him up with my lips wrapped around his already hard dick. If he's noticed that my blow jobs usually correspond with his nightmares, he hasn't let on to it. The pain etched into his features when he's lost to a nightmare breaks my heart. He looks like a little boy, helpless and innocent. I know that innocence is gone, he's a full grown man now, but I still want to remind him he's cared for.

The more time I spend with Jason, the more I realize he's a man masquerading as a brute when he's just a cinnamon roll who needs affection like the rest of us. I want to give him that so badly.

I've put my insecurities on the back burner, deciding I need to soak up every ounce of the happiness I've been feeling. I don't know if it will last, so I might as well make the most of right now.

Laying beside Jason at night, the pathetic thoughts creep back in and I start to worry if he'll send me packing when the snow melts. It's hard to ignore them when they pound at my mental walls trying to break through my shields. I don't know how to explain the back and forth of my thoughts. One day I'm fine and the next I'm struggling. I'm slow. I'm fatigued and worried with little explanation.

For so long, I was just depressed. But with the joy Jason and Dylan have brought me simply by liking who I am without the rest of the world surrounding me—the expectations and astronomical standards, have brought more good days than bad.

I never realized how much I needed the true acceptance of others before now. I thought I had to conform to the image others wanted to earn acceptance and that would make me happy. Through these two unlikely characters in my story, I discovered I'm a reformed people pleaser who didn't need to change to be happy. I needed to change the people in my life to find contentment.

The people in my life before this happy accident blinded me to the fact that they weren't what I needed. Maybe I'm pathetic for not realizing it sooner. But I'm human.

I'm cleaning out the chicken stall while Dylan is working on Bessie's stall. The chicks are thriving. We're even incubating more eggs at the moment. The last batch of fluffy chicks are skittering around my feet while I try to lay new wood shavings on the floor for them. Afterward, I collect the eggs from the nesting box. There are five today, which is two less than yesterday. But Dylan said it's normal for their egg production to slow down in the winter. Come April, he said there will be a dozen every morning with the number of layers they have.

I wonder if I'll be here to see it.

I stop by Bessie's stall on my way out. Dylan has music playing on his phone, he must have pre-downloaded a bunch of songs before hibernation began. "Need any help?" I ask, leaning against the support beam while Dylan shovels horse shit into a wheel barrel.

"Nah, I got it from here. Almost done. How many eggs today?"

"Five." I hold the basket out for him to see.

"That's ok. We don't need much. In the spring and summer we have eggs coming out of our ears. The chicks won't be laying until about 18 weeks old."

"I know Jason doesn't really leave the mountain in the spring but what about you?" It's been bugging me for months. I've been dying to know what changes for Dylan when the snow melts. This doesn't seem like the kind of life he'd want but here he is, cleaning a horse stall in below freezing weather. Granted, the barn is heated for the animals.

"Yeah, I go to town for groceries and stuff. Sometimes I go out with a couple friends. But it's hard to get close to people when you disappear for almost half a year."

It feels tactless to ask but... "what about relationships? I mean, how do you meet other guys? Especially in a town that isn't as progressive in their beliefs. I know you said there are some closeted guys but..." I don't know what else I'm trying to say.

"You mean, how do I get laid?" Dylan winks at me making this even more uncomfortable than it already is.

"I shouldn't have asked," I confess, feeling like I overstepped a boundary.

"No, it's ok," Dylan placates me. "I really don't mind. Honestly, the action is a little dry in this town. I told you there are a few people in the closet who like to get together when the snow melts. But I've gotten to a point where I don't like being a secret anymore."

"Yeah, I get that," I admit before thinking better of it. My situation was not nearly the same as Dylan's. But by the raise of his brows I assume he is curious to learn more.

I sign heavily and begin. "Sorry. My situation was not nearly the same as yours. I was with my ex for about two years and he didn't actually refer to me as his girlfriend until I caught him cheating and dumped him on the spot. Funny how he never took me to spend time with his family or friends much, but all of a sudden I was the love of his life when I was ending it. I don't know if he was ashamed of me or just keeping things casual. He was probably cheating on me the whole time. Though I guess it's not cheating if you're not official."

"You never had *the talk*?" Dylan stands the shovel against the wall, abandoning his chore momentarily for the distraction of our conversation.

I shake my head. "I didn't want to be the needy girlfriend who needed labels on everything. Alpha-jackasses love to belittle women for insecure behaviors such as making a relationship official, calling him her boyfriend. At least that's the way it was in high school. You'd think I would have learned my lesson."

Dylan perks up at that. "What is that supposed to mean?" He waggles his eyebrows as if he knows where this is going.

"Ugh," I huff. "Just...Jason. And please keep this between us. I just don't really know where we stand. It's no secret to you we're fucking. And I think things are a little more than that, now, but I don't know where we stand when the snow melts and I can leave."

"Let me guess," Dylan lowers to the freshly cleared floor and closes his ankles in front of him, "you haven't bothered to ask him what he wants."

"Gee, am I that transparent?" I drop to the ground and bury my face in my palms.

"You two are such a cliche." He's laughing, actually laughing at our situation. "You're both sure of your feelings but confused how to go about it. And before you ask, no, Jason hasn't told me anything. He doesn't talk much, in case you haven't noticed. But I can tell he's just as unsteady as you in your relationship."

"You're pretty wise for a guy who's never been in a relationship." No sooner do the words leave my mouth before I register just how insensitive they were. "Oh, Dylan. I am so sorry. That was such a bitchy thing to say and I didn't mean it how it came out."

The shadow that passes over his face tells me my words struck a nerve. But it's gone as quickly as it came and I know it's already forgiven.

"It's ok," he assures me with a wave of his hand, "you're right. I've never been in a relationship. But I've observed a lot of failed relationships from the sidelines and I like to think I've learned a thing or two from poor examples."

"Thank you," I bow my head in shame. "And you're right. Maybe being a third party observant gives you a better outlook on things."

"Don't get me wrong, I'd love to find love. I'd love to find a guy who isn't ashamed to shout from the rooftops that he loves me, but it's hard to find that here."

"What about leaving?" Once I've dropped that bombshell of a question, it hangs like a mushroom cloud in the air waiting for a response that I don't think Dylan even knows the answer to. Conflict rages in his eyes. I can see the wheels turning and thoughts battling in his head.

"I've thought about it. I'd love to get my teaching degree so I can be a better teacher and coach than I had. I know that sounds fucked up since my wrestling coach was my first. But I didn't realize how messed up and predatory that was until I was older. I deserved better than that. I deserved a mentor who would encourage me to be who I am instead of messing around with me in his office after hours and keeping it all quiet. I want to be the example that being different in a small town doesn't have to be a sin."

If I didn't already know Dylan was a saint, I'd know with that. The fact that he wants to use his trauma and abuse to change the lives of others for the better is so positive. He's the picture perfect image of healing and moving on from your past. He could have let his experiences break him, but he's choosing to use his pain to heal the world instead.

"That's a really selfless outlook," I praise him. "So why don't you? Why not enroll in classes as soon as the snow melts?"

Dylan chews on his lip mulling that notion over, averting his eyes from me in the process. Finally, he discloses, "I couldn't do that to Jason. Not after all he's done for me. The business is growing and he can't keep up with orders on his own. Especially in the summer. He needs my help. And I owe him."

Excuse me?

"What?" My brows pull together and I lean forward as if I can coax more out of him. "You owe him? For what?"

Dylan looks like a deer in the headlights. Frozen in time with an expression of regret and shock on his face. "It's not my story to tell," he finally says, which does absolute shit to satisfy my curiosity.

"It certainly sounds like it is. What happened, Dylan?"

"Mara, I'm not sure he wants you to—."

"Bullshit," I sound fiercer than I meant to. "Does it have something to do with why he doesn't speak?"

"No, I have no idea why he doesn't speak. Not sure we ever will. This is something different. I shouldn't have said anything."

"But you did. So what happened, Dylan?"

He releases a heavy sigh and leans his head back to look at the ceiling before settling his eyes on me once again. "Ok, fine. But, Mara, you have to keep an open mind. And try to understand. I'm sure there's a lot about our family you don't know."

I wait patiently. If I was in a chair, I'd be on the edge of my seat. The ominous tension in the air tells me this is going to be hard to hear. I have a strong suspicion I'll never look at Jason the same way again. But I hope I'll understand him more after this.

"The beatings started when we were little. I think I was nine so Jason was probably ten." I suck in a breath. That was the last thing I expected. Their family always seemed close, the perfect nuclear family. Their mom was always at school fundraisers with baked goods. "I don't remember why it started. He wasn't a drunk or anything. He was just evil and bitter. And he made our lives as hellish as he felt his own was."

Chapter Twenty-Four

Jason-One Month After Prom

UNSTEADY-X AMBASSADOR

"I have a fucking faggot and a mute for sons, Lois," my father screams at Mom in the kitchen while Dylan and I sit on the porch listing to the bullshit our father is spewing. "What the hell do you want me to say? That I'm happy with our life? That I'm okay with this shit? Neither one of them are right. Maybe I should send them to the cabin this winter to become men. No help from anyone except themselves."

The look Dylan and I exchange says it all. *That doesn't sound too bad, actually.* At least we'd be away from him.

Mom uses her passive, tender voice that she always uses to pacify our father. "They have school, Phil. They need their education."

"Fine." I hear his thunderous steps get louder as they head our way. "Then maybe I'll toughen them up myself."

"Phil," Mom shouts. I hear her little footsteps follow our father toward us and jump to my feet to stand between the son of a bitch and my brother. He's plenty tough from wrestling, but they kicked him off the team this year when they found out he was gay. Not that he was interested in anyone on the team.

But they don't give a shit. He doesn't think the same as them so he's a threat, a danger.

The door flies open so hard I'm surprised it doesn't come off the hinges. As soon as our father locks eyes on me, smoke comes out of his nostrils. He drops the cigarette he was smoking inside and smashes it under his boot. He's preparing for a face-off. He's been waiting for a reason to hit me again and I just gave him one.

"What the fuck do you think you're doing?" Our father grits out in a strained voice. All the years of smoking make him sound like rocks in a blender, now.

When I don't answer—like he knew I wouldn't—he takes a step closer. "You trying to stand up to me, huh? Trying to be the man, now? Protect your fucked up brother?"

He's not fucked up. Everything about him is completely normal except his taste in partners. Which, to be honest, isn't that weird in this day and age. But our town is a decade behind the rest of the world and they don't appreciate him leapfrogging into modern relationships.

"So what are you doing, boy? Answer me when I ask you a fucking question." His voice raises a notch in volume with each word until he's yelling at me. But that's never scared me before and it sure as hell doesn't scare me now.

"You fucking retard." My father swings his fist at my head and I stumble, but I remember a few things from my brief time in sports and tackle him with my shoulder to his abdomen, arms around the waist, trying to take him down. Even though I've gotten a bit bigger since picking up weight lifting, he's still bigger than me. Offensive lineman in high school. Probably could have gone to college on scholarship for it if he hadn't knocked up our mom.

He's clearly caught off guard by my attack which causes him to stumble, but it doesn't take long for the bastard to shove me to the ground and stomp on my chest.

Mom starts hollering, crying for our dad to stop. But when he's like this, there's no stopping the rampage. The sad thing is he's not even drunk. I've heard about dads who get violent when they drink. But at least there's an excuse there, a way to stop it. Our dad was just born mean, bitter, violent.

He shoves me down the front steps with his steel-toed boot and I turn into the fetal position and hold my bruised rib cage hoping that seeing me wounded like a dog on the ground is enough to satisfy his taste for blood and misery.

"You thought you could hide behind your brother?" Our father turns on Dylan, clearly not satiated yet.

"No, I—." Dylan loses the power of speech when our father charges for him next.

Panic sets in. I see the pure terror in Dylan's eyes, hear Mom plead for our father to stop, crying in between sucking in lungfuls of air she can't hold onto. And my chest caves with the weight of it all. I can't see them hurting. He can hurt me all he wants, but not them.

So I do the only thing I can think of.

"NO!" I shout. It's hoarse from disuse like I've been swallowing gravel, but the shock of hearing me speak for the first time in years stops him dead in his tracks long enough for Mom to get to Dylan.

And, more importantly, it redirects our father's focus to me. That rage turned toward the son who refused to speak no matter how many beatings I took. No matter how many bruised ribs I've hidden under my clothes, I've never broken

Until now.

Until he threatened the two people I care about in this world. He's never laid a hand on our mother or Dylan because most of his anger was honed in on me. But when he found out that his youngest son likes other men, not women like men were supposed to in his day and age, I wasn't his biggest problem anymore. He had two disappointments to beat the hell out of.

"What the fuck?" He snarls under his breath. "What the fuck!" His words are clearer that time, heavier, laced with venom. "Are you fucking telling me you've been able to speak this entire time?"

I don't answer, I don't plan to speak again.

"ANSWER ME," he demands. But his orders fall on deaf ears. I stopped caring about his patience years ago. There's no incentive to please him when I'm already used to the beatings.

"You fucking worthless, pathetic excuse for a man." I don't think he even wants me to speak. I think he wants a reason to lay hands on me. So I'll fucking give it to him. This match has been a long time coming.

In answer to my active disrespect, he charges down the stairs for me but I'm ready this time. Fists in the air the way *he* taught me, I'm able to land a blow to his nose before he can take the last step to the flagstone path I'm standing on. Disoriented and probably a little shocked, he stumbles forward with his fists in the air but not as precisely as usual. He's a shell of the man he used to be.

He steps his left foot forward alerting me he's preparing to throw his right hook, so I dodge it just in time and land an uppercut to his ribs. We spar in a continuous back and forth. He manages to land a few punches on me as well but the final blow that connects with his jaw is the last straw for him. He's enraged, blinded by anger and hatred, and his movements become less coordinated and more frenzied. Rookie mistakes a pro like him shouldn't be making. He's just too overwhelmed to think straight which works in my favor.

Seeing that the bare-knuckle boxing technique isn't working, he tries to tackle me to the ground, but I'm ready this time. I refuse to be weak anymore. I refuse to be a punching bag. And I refuse to back down. He's belittled me my entire life.

Retard.

Stupid.

Mute.

Coward.

Liar.

I'm done being any of the things he and countless others have called me. If I don't assert my dominance tonight, he'll always see me as the pathetic boy who takes his beatings like a coward.

So when he loops an arm around my neck trying to push me down and cut off my air supply, I plant my palms against his chest and shove as hard as I can, channeling every ounce of resentment into putting as much space between us as possible.

My efforts work, my father stumbles away from me. But his heel catches on one of the uneven stones and he's falling like a tree in the woods before I can reach him. I feel the panic in a single second as though time is frozen with fear. I'm angry. I'm hurt. I want to make it clear I'm not a boy anymore. But I didn't want to do any serious damage.

Our father's head collides with one of the rocks lining the pathway before I can grab him. A sickening crunch and thud precede the unnatural stillness of his body. Eyes fixed on me, unblinking, lifeless. I know before I even get to him to feel his pulse that the man who's abused me mentally and physically my entire life no longer inhabits this body.

The silence behind me speaks loud enough, Mom and Dylan are just as petrified as I am.

I have to think fast. It was an accident. If I try to hide it, it'll look like it was intentional. Thankfully, I have witnesses to back up my story.

"I'm gonna call 911," Dylan breaks the silence.

My mother's hands are on me the following second. Her warm palms against my cheeks turning my gaze from the dead man before us to her. Her kind eyes—my eyes—stare back at me. I look just like my now deceased father from the strong jaw and hair color to my build, but my eyes came from the only parent that truly mattered.

"Jason, sweetheart, listen to me." My kind, gentle, would-never-hurt-a-fly mother's voice is all business now. "You are not a bad person. You are not to blame for his actions that lead to this point. You are a good man!"

I focus on her eyes. I focus on her nose. I focus on the words leaving her mouth. Otherwise I'll spiral.

"We will tell the police that you two fought and he stepped outside to get some air. We heard a noise and came outside to find him like this. Do you understand me? I will not have my boy go to jail for second degree murder when you were simply defending yourself. I won't even have you in front of a jury who might find you guilty of manslaughter. We both know this was *his* fault."

Footsteps reverberate on the hollow porch. "They'll be here in ten minutes," Dylan announces.

"Good," my mom says without taking her hands off me. "Go grab the bottle of whiskey on the shelf."

My brows bunch in confusion until Dylan returns and our mother sets to work pouring the amber liquor down his throat. Maybe four shots worth. Then she lays the bottle beside him not far from his hand so the whiskey spills out.

She's making it look like he was a drunk. People might believe that he stumbled on a path he's walked a thousand times. *Might.* But they sure as hell won't think twice about a drunk man tripping over uneven stones after a fight with his son. I'll be the victim, not the murderer.

Logically, I know I didn't kill him with intent. But it's still my fault he died. I pushed him. I pushed him every day of my life. I pushed him to fight me instead of Dylan. I pushed him down causing his head to hit the rock and split open.

I stare at his body as if I expect him to rise from the dead with glazed over eyes and try to eat my brains. The stubborn son of a bitch would, too. But his eyes start to cloud over, the gash on the side of his head continues to seep blood. Small bits of rock and dust are embedded in the open wound. Even his limbs are laid in a crooked, unnatural fashion. The telltale purple-yellow discoloration of a bruise is starting to emerge on his jaw where I'd connected my fist to his face.

I'd been afraid of this man my entire life, feared being in the same room as him. Now, he lays dead and I feel foolish for ever being afraid of someone so mortal and insignificant.

Our deaths are just one misstep away. No one is immune to the side effects of humanity.

Blue and red flashes draw my attention from the woman who showed me more love than I deserved to the road where two county sheriff's deputy vehicles pull up against the curb. We don't live in city limits so this is their jurisdiction.

Mom and Dylan fed them the story. Everyone knows I don't speak. But I was required to write a statement and sign it. Even I wasn't exempt from due process. But as my mother predicted, no one questioned a drunk man tripping over a rock and bashing his head on stones. No one suspected I had anything to do with it other than the fight we had before his death. It was too easy to walk away from all of this without suffering the consequences.

My father was a bastard, a horrible man who deserved to suffer for his actions. But did he deserve to die? Nothing like being faced with immortality to make you question the past. Even when you know you were the victim in the story.

Six months after the "accident" that killed our father, our mom suffered a heart attack in her sleep and died. It felt like some cruel joke. Like our father dragged her into the afterlife so she would have to suffer with him. Or maybe it was meant to make me suffer for the life I took before his time was up. A life for a life. Either way, I felt responsible and I knew whatever power there was in the world was sending a message. I just wish I'd paid the price of it instead of a woman who deserved more than she got.

Perhaps living is the price I have to pay. If that's the case, I'll suffer in silence for my crimes.

That's the way it's always been.

Chapter Twenty-Five

Jason

You Know You're Right-Nirvana

It was a long day. The blower on the heater went out so I was crawling around in the attic most of the day trying to fix it with what I have instead of working on orders that need to be ready in a little over a month. I did what I could to keep it going until the snow melted enough for us to get into town and get a new part for it. If we could even find one.

The fireplace in the living room did a great job of heating the downstairs, but since Dylan didn't have a fireplace in his room, I needed to get the heater working so he didn't freeze tonight.

After a long day of working on the heater, Dylan made elk chili with the last of the ground elk sausage from our Thanksgiving kill. We'd have to go hunting soon since we were almost out of all our frozen meat. We didn't stock up enough for three people since we didn't anticipate our unexpected guest.

After dinner, Dylan went to bed so Mara and I decided to have our nightly routine in our room instead of the living room.

Fire burning warm in the fireplace, Mara tucked under my arm while she read from a book out loud, blankets pulled over us. She wore one of my t-shirts while I lounged comfortably in flannel pajama bottoms. I'd rather we were wearing nothing but we'll get to that later. For now, I just enjoyed listening to her voice.

She asked me once if my mom ever read aloud to me, like it was some weird oedipus thing. But, much to her relief, my mom didn't read aloud to us past the age of four. Listening to her read had nothing to do with my mom and everything to do with the woman I found myself addicted to despite my best efforts.

Maybe if I stopped fighting the universe for bringing us together, I could acknowledge that it means something.

Maybe if I could stop punishing myself for the past, I could allow myself to be unabashedly happy.

Easier said than done.

As Mara ends the chapter, she places the ribbon she uses for a bookmark between the pages and shuts it with a satisfyingly soft thud. The sound of a hardback closing was akin to the wings of a bird flying by or snow hitting the windows. Subtle and peaceful.

Mara's hand slides to my thigh over the comforter and I relish that. Her touch sends shivers up my spine as though she were conducting electricity through her palm directly to my chest. It makes my cock twitch and my breath stutter. You'd think after two months of sleeping together almost daily, I'd be sick of her.

But I'm not. Quite the opposite, I can't get enough of her. I could spend all day buried between her legs with either my face, my hand, or my dick and it would never be enough. I could hear her come over and over like some people play the same song on repeat and never get tired of hearing it.

I need to be inside her constantly.

I need her.

Lacing my fingers with hers, I lift her hand to my mouth so I can press my lips to the back of her hand. Convey with the lightest touch what I can't say aloud.

"Jason?" Mara's voice holds the sound of hesitation instead of lust. Can't have that.

I lower my lips to her shoulder and kiss a blazing trail from her shoulder socket to her neck to the back of her ear.

"Jason," she giggles, trying to sound uneffected. "I need to tell you something."

What's wrong?

I wish I could ask. She has me worried, now.

Oh god, she's pregnant! We've been pretty careful but we did have unprotected sex a few weeks ago when she said it wasn't the right time of her menstrual cycle. What if she miscounted?

Jolting forward, I lock eyes with her and shoot a hand to her belly to see if I can feel anything. To let her know I know where this was going.

"What?" Her brow furrows. Then realization dawns on her. "What? No!" She shoves my hand away. "I'm not pregnant. But now I'm wondering if I should be using the treadmill every morning."

I retract my hand and lean back against the stack of pillows waiting for whatever is coming. The tension is killing me. Mara usually has no problem expressing her thoughts freely. So what could have her tongue in such a bind that she can't even speak.

That's my MO.

After sucking on her bottom lip until its tinted rose, she confesses, "Dylan told me what happened to your father." *Oh shit.*

Her eyes drop to the bed then flick back to me, the hazel kaleidoscopes peering at me through thick lashes. "Please don't be angry with me. I wanted to know what happened. I think it's only fair you know that I know. And I wanted to tell you that you shouldn't blame yourself—."

In a flash of fabric I throw the covers off and storm across the room, pull the door open, and cross the landing at the top of the stairs to Dylan's room in a matter of seconds. I've barged inside and hauled him out of bed before he even realizes what's going on. The vacant, perplexed expression on his face makes it look like he's trying to figure out what day it is, let alone who has their hands fisted in his shirt. I throw him against the wall and square up before sending my fist flying through the air to connect with his jaw. I don't hit him hard enough to break anything, just to scare the living shit out of him.

To punish him. How dare he fucking tell Mara one of my darkest secrets. We swore we'd never talk about it again. We swore we'd never tell anyone what really happened. And he broke that promise.

"Jason!" Mara's voice filters past the rage, "Dylan, I'm sorry. I didn't think he'd be mad at you. I thought he'd be angry with me."

I barely register her voice.

Dylan isn't one to take a beating lying down. He never came face to face with our father's fists like I did. But he learned to stand his ground in school and especially on the wrestling team. Which is exactly what instincts take over.

He rams his body into mine, using his limbs and leverage to bring me to the ground so we're wrestling back and forth on the wood floors that creak beneath our combined weight. This isn't like playful wrestling most brothers do. We're damn near trying to kill each other.

I want him to hurt as bad as I do.

I vaguely hear Mara shouting for us to stop, calling both our names. The panic in her voice should shake me out of my trance but tunnel vision is taking over and all I can focus on is my brother's betrayal.

Dylan lands a few well placed punches, but so do I. We'll both be bruised up and sore in the morning if we make it out of this alive.

I manage to shove him off me with my feet planted against his hip bones. He flies into the air and smacks into his dresser while I scramble to my feet, leaning into my right leg with my shoulders wide preparing for another attack. I wind my arm back to give it more impact when Mara steps in between us. I don't register it quick enough to stop my arm from shooting my fist forward, too focused on the attack and not on the recipient.

Thank god Mara is quick as she ducks at the perfect moment so my strike doesn't touch anything but open air. Dylan stands back looking rightfully aghast. Mara mirrors that expression when she rises to her full height again. Her eyes sear me with hurt, and fear.

She can't fear me.

I wanted her to when she first came here, but not now. Now she can't fear me because I need her.

But I can see in her shock that I royally fucked up. And I just pray I can fix it.

She darts past me before I can catch her but I sprint out of the room as soon as my brain starts working again. I catch her before she can even take the first step on the stairs and pull her back into me by the upper arm so our chests clash.

"Get off me, Jason," she spits fire at me.

I should let her go, I should do the right thing, I should respect her wishes. It's not like she can really go anywhere.

But I'm not that guy. I'm selfish and desperate and I need her to see that I didn't mean to swing at her. I need her to know she's safe.

"Fuck you," she hisses. "You stubborn, closed minded juggernaut."

That's a new one.

She slams the palm of her hand into my chest right over my heart. "How could you do that? How could you attack your only family? The only one who's stuck by you. He didn't do anything wrong."

I drop her arm and shoot my eyes to the ceiling in frustration before looking back at her. I wish I could tell her how I feel. I wish I could argue with her and tell her my own brother betrayed my secret. But I can't overcome my own roadblocks.

"I know you're the only two alive who know what really happened, and now me. I asked him what happened. *Me.* He didn't want to tell me and I made him because I want to know *you.* I want to understand you. But you don't speak so you can't tell me shit." She lifts her arms, palms facing up, then slams them down to her sides. "You should be the one to tell me these things but you don't. You don't even write. You don't communicate with me."

I do, I want to tell her. So I draw closer to her again until she's backed into the railing at the top of the stairs.

I do communicate with you. In my own way. Why can't she understand that? Why isn't it enough?

"Jason, we both know this is more than just fucking around with each other. It's not casual. You've seen my insecure sides. I've been vulnerable with you. And I've gotten jack shit from you. You're closed off and I don't really know you. Knowing you enjoy reading and like your eggs scrambled isn't the same thing as knowing the man beneath the surface. It's not fair you get to see me at my weakest and I don't get to know a damn thing about you."

Her weakest? Yeah she's insecure about her past relationships but that's not the same as killing someone. That's one of my darkest secrets that I planned to take to my grave. Besides, that is not the point. The point is that my brother that I trusted implicitly betrayed my confidence.

"What? Are you angry I know something personal about you?"

I run my fingers through my thick hair and turn away from her. This is infuriating and getting us nowhere.

"Oh I see, you think it's not enough. You think your secret isn't the same as how vulnerable I've been with you." I thought she was past this. I thought I'd made it clear I didn't see her as the girl she thought she was.

"Then how's this for even? Want to know my darkest secret?" Eyes locked in a fierce battle of wills, she drops her bomb. "I was on the road the night you found me because I was going to drive off the bridge and end it."

Time. Time ceased for I don't know how long. I stopped breathing and stopped trying to think straight. My mind jumped from thought to thought.

She was going to kill herself?

Did she change her mind or not make it before her accident occurred?

Why hasn't she tried again?

What could have made her feel so lost she wanted to end her life?

My mind was a mess of unfinished thoughts, a culmination of shock and fear and relief all at once. I found myself so relieved that she's still here. That I found her.

I've tried to ignore that it felt like fate that brought me to the bridge the night of her accident. Maybe in more ways than one.

Tears welled in her eyes, glimmering under the low lights. I rushed toward her and took her cheeks in my hands, desperate to feel her, feel her breath, feel her pulse. I want so badly to tell her I'm so thankful she's still here and that I found her. That we've had this time.

But most importantly, I want to tell her I'm sorry. *I'm sorry.*

So I sign it. I don't sign often but for her I will. If it's what she needs from me to make a stride forward. I hope she sees it for the gesture it is.

"I don't understand sign language," she sighs.

"He said he's sorry," Dylan's voice comes from over my shoulder. We both look to him and the defeated, hurt expression on his face that I feel all too guilty for. I took this too far. I acted just like our father and let my anger get the best of me. Before I can apologize to him too, he shuts his door and I hear it lock.

Fuck.

I turn back to Mara with pleading eyes, begging her to forgive me and to understand. None of this is easy for anyone involved. But I want her to know me, if that's what she wants. It took this clusterfuck for me to realize it, but I have to try.

I pull Mara close, tenderly, angling my hand on her cheek so my fingers weave through her blonde locks behind her ear, and bring our foreheads together. Her skin is so hot with the heat of all her emotions. Her breathing is erratic and unpredictable. A soft sniffle tells me she's fighting back her tears.

Fuck. Mara tried to kill herself. And somehow fate intervened and brought us together instead of letting her leave this earth.

I feel so guilty my inability to control my emotions pushed her to share when she wasn't ready.

I want to say her name. I want to tell her it'll be ok. That I'll do better. I'll be whatever she needs me to be.

"The day I fell through the ice, I thought it was some kind of cosmic balance, that I was supposed to die that day since I didn't die that day on the bridge. But you keep saving me." Her voice sounds so raw with emotion.

Her voice lowers to a whisper like she's afraid of awaking some monster. "Jason, that day on the ice, did you shout my name?"

I lift my head so I can look into her misty eyes.

And I nod. An admission I'm not comfortable with and I don't know how to explain. But she deserves honesty.

"And you don't think you can do it again?"

I shake my head no. I've spoken twice in the last decade and they both felt too unnatural. It's not that I don't know if I can. Every time I've tried to speak—the few times I've tried—no sound came out. It's like my voice box is littered with cobwebs from disuse. Broken.

"Have you tried?" The hope in her voice guts me like a knife.

I nod again. Resolution settles in her eyes.

"You owe Dylan an apology," she scolds me. "You should be mad at me for pushing the subject, not him."

I rub my middle and pointer finger over the space between my eyes on the bridge of my nose. I know I fucked up. Big time. I have so much to apologize for. So much I need to say. To both of them. My anger shouldn't be directed at anyone but myself.

"I'll sleep in my room," she announces in the silence. But as she tries to walk past me I pull her into me once more and silently beg for her to stay with me. I hold her gaze and shake my head. Then start toward *our* room, hoping she'll come with me.

"Jason," she looks unsure. So I kiss her with as much passion as I can muster through all the hurt and confusion. If I can't tell her how I feel, maybe my actions can speak on my behalf.

A little reluctantly, she follows me into the bedroom and I tuck us into bed, spooning her small frame with my body so I can bury my face in her neck and breathe her in all night. So even in my dreams, I know she's here.

She's here. She's alive.

I've had to remind myself of that too many times this winter.

Chapter Twenty-Six

Mara

JASON IS GONE BY the time I wake up the next morning, probably working off steam in the garage gym. Like usual.

Last night plays on repeat in my head with the steady beat of the drumming in my temples. My body is sore, I'm tired, my brain is exhausted. I haven't felt this way in a while. It's too all consuming to ignore but I'm no longer in a position where I can stay in bed for god knows how long. So I rip myself out of bed and start getting ready.

I can't believe I told Jason about my suicide attempt. And I can't believe Dylan heard it too.

That should be the least of my worries considering Jason attacked his brother last night. But I have a feeling Jason will do whatever it takes to make things right with Dylan. They are too close and have been through too much together to let this tear them apart.

Besides, Dylan doesn't seem like the type to hold a grudge. He loves his brother, that much is evident. And doesn't love overpower everything else?

While I'm washing dishes after breakfast, I notice both boys standing in the open door of the shop. Dylan holds something in his hands while Jason leans against the doorframe with his hands tucked in his coat pockets. Something about the way he stands looks so unsure, like a child waiting to be told they misbehaved. He looks so innocent I just want to hug him and brush my fingers through his hair.

No, Mara. That's coddling and he doesn't deserve to be coddled after the way he behaved.

Snooping through the window, I see the two brothers embrace one another in a man hug which makes a heavy weight lift from my soul. They're too important to one another to stay mad for very long. I just hope Jason found a way to adequately apologize. Dylan deserves that much from him.

They head back to the house, traipsing through the snow. We had another snowfall last night. Doesn't look like I'll be able to get down the mountain anytime soon. Not sure I want to, either. It feels like we have unfinished business. It feels like *I* have unfinished business. Like I was sent here for a reason and it hasn't been fulfilled yet. I can't shake the feeling of dissatisfaction.

As soon as the pair walk through the door, kicking snow off their boots, I observe, "That was a fast recovery." Leaning my hip against the sink, I cross my arms over my chest and stare them down.

Dylan looks between me and his brother and shrugs one shoulder. "We're brothers." He states it like it answers every question under the sun. "We can't stay mad at each other long."

"Mmm-hmm." I go back to washing the pan in the sink but continue to talk to them with my back turned. "You both need haircuts. I'm not saying I'm a pro but I think I could do a pretty good job if you're willing."

I hear a subtle chuckle behind me and I'm not sure if it's from Dylan, Jason, or both. But Dylan answers, "Why not. If you fuck it up, it'll grow out by the time I have to see other human beings again."

"Thanks for the vote of confidence," I flick soapy water at him as he dodges past. "Let's do it before dinner. Do you have clippers?"

"In the bathroom upstairs. I'll bring them down later. I think your man wants your attention right now."

I turn my head over my shoulder to see Jason standing only a foot away from me. Downcast eyes and worried brows clue me in to how vulnerable he's going to be, or at least it feels that way to him. I dry my hands on a towel then turn to face him, resting my hip against the counter waiting for whatever it is he has planned to try and make up for last night.

Slowly, almost hesitantly, Jason extends a piece of paper gripped in his hand toward me.

What is this?

I take the paper from him and unfold it to see what is clearly a man's handwriting—Jason's handwriting.

He wrote me a letter? I thought he doesn't communicate with anyone. Not even like this.

Dear Mara,

Fuck, this feels weird. I haven't written in years. But you asked me to try. So I am.

First off, I want to apologize for last night, for almost hitting you and for losing my temper. Last night, I morphed into a version of my father, the man I've hated for so fucking long. I didn't even realize I was becoming him until last night and that's not who I want to be. That's not who my mom raised. I've been angry for so long and I don't want to be. I'm trying. I'm trying for you.

Secondly, I'm sorry for making you feel like you can't talk to me. I'm sorry you had to hold so much in for so long. I wish I could change so much about our story but I can't. I wish you and I had had a better start. And that you'd had a better life. You don't have to tell me what led to you driving to the bridge. It's none of my business. I want to be here for you if you need to talk about it. I want to be more for you. I want to be enough.

I know there's so many obstacles and my speech issue doesn't help. But I hope you can accept it for what it is.

Lastly, I'm glad you're here. I'm glad we got a second chance. I didn't realize how much I needed you until now. You were right, last night, we are more than just casual. We're more, Mara. We're more.

Sincerely,

Jason

PS Sincerely sounds weird. Scratch that.

I giggle at the post script. I can't believe my eyes. I can't believe he *wrote* to me. I have no idea what his voice sounds like but in a way he's showing me. His voice doesn't have sound but it has meaning. It has character.

I look back up at Jason and the worry etched into his features. I've never seen him look so helpless. I eliminate the space between us in two quick steps and wrap my arms around him, hands clasped behind his neck. Our lips come together in a searing kiss that binds us together.

"Jason," I utter as I stroke one hand through his hair. His arms band around me as he nestles his face in my neck and breathes like I'm a life force he thrives on.

"Thank you." I have no other words for this gesture because I know it must have been hard for him. He's trying. It's not perfect but it's a huge step in the right direction. The fact that he acknowledged our relationship means the world to me.

We're more.

Those words will be branded on my soul for eternity.

While the roast is in the oven, I set to work trimming the boys' hair. I think they just agreed to it because we're all so bored. Cabin fever is a real thing and we are seeking anything new to entertain ourselves with.

It's clear Jason's last haircut was quite a while ago, longer than Dylan's based on the length of his hair.

As far as tools go, I have a pair of scissors and clippers with only the two, four, and seven length attachments. Looks like I'll be getting creative.

Dragging one of the dining chairs into the center of the kitchen I ask my willing victims, "Ok, who wants to go first?"

The two brothers exchange worried glances before Dylan makes an executive decision. Waving a hand as if he's presenting a grand gift to his brother, Dylan declares, "She's your girl, you get to be the guinea pig."

Jason rolls his eyes then takes the chair like a man, unafraid and confident. But that doesn't stop Dylan from asking, "Have you ever cut hair before?"

"A couple times in college," I answer while assessing Jason's hair, running my fingers through the long strands fully knowing what that does to him. Maybe I'm being a little devious. "Some of the guys in my hall needed haircuts but starving college students don't really want to pay for haircuts. So I was nominated to give it a try. I watched a few YouTube videos and did a pretty good job if I do say so myself."

I start to wet Jason's hair by dipping my hand in a bowl of water since I'm lacking a spray bottle.

"I'm going to be honest," I lean over Jason's shoulder, "I like your hair a little longer. But it seems a little hard for you to manage. How about I just give it a trim?"

He smirks up at me. He knows *exactly* how much I like his hair. Then nods in agreement so I take the scissors in hand and start trimming off an inch or so, shaping it a little bit better so when it's down it looks less like a mop. Less unintentional and more like he styled it that way on purpose.

"When was the last time you had a haircut?" I ask Jason. His hair was more like Dylan's length in high school.

He holds two fingers in the air in a peace sign which confuses me, at first I think he means two months which isn't accurate since we've been stuck at the cabin since November. Then I realize, "Two years?" He nods. "So this sexy hipster man bun thing wasn't to look like a lumberjack, just pure neglect." I can't help the laugh bubbling out of me. Only Jason Alder would look sexier when he neglects his appearance.

"What about you, Dylan?"

"Got one at the start of November before the snow fell. I knew it would be a while so I try to get it under control before we go into hibernation."

His hair is much more awkward looking at the moment, the disheveled phase between short shaggy hair and the 70s face framing look.

"Who do you usually go to to cut your hair in town?"

"Remember Ally Herm?"

"Yeah, I used to be friends with her."

"Used to go to her, she went to beauty school after high school."

"I thought she was going to University of Washington for pre-med."

"Yeah, I think being a rocket surgeon was a lot harder than she thought it would be. She came back to town after one semester and enrolled at the local cosmetology school and became a hairstylist. She was pretty good but I had to stop going to her after this one," he points at my current client, "slept with her. She wouldn't stop asking me about him so I tried a real man's barber and I gotta say, women like me a lot more than straight guys."

I peer down at Jason from where I'm trimming the pieces around his face with what I can only imagine is a stupefied expression. "You slept with Ally Herm?" And then never called her again, apparently.

He nodded.

"Shit, sorry dude," Dylan sucks air between his teeth. "Guess you haven't had the body count talk yet." Jason shoots him an unamused look past my shoulder. If I know Dylan, though, he probably wasn't the least bit affected by it.

After I finish with Jason and Dylan comments on how symmetrical everything looks—right before Jason pulls his hair back into a bun again—he admits he feels more confident in my skills now.

"Alright, how long or short do you want it?"

"I want it long on top and short on the sides like a 1920s gangster," he says with all seriousness.

I chuckle and shake my head, "I'll see what I can do."

Trying to make his dreams come true with my limited tools is a challenge I wasn't quite prepared for, but I think I managed to bring his vision to life. As Dylan fiddles with the longer strands atop his head while staring into a mirror, the smile on his face tells me he is quite pleased.

"Wasn't sure this would look good on me or not. But I gotta say, I think it suits me. Do I look like I could pull a tommy gun on you at any minute?" His eyes narrow into a squint while his mouth forms a hard line that doesn't suit his bubbly personality.

"More like a squirt gun, but ok."

As I grab the broom from where it rests against the wall, Jason rips it from my hands, wraps an arm over my shoulders and pulls me into him so he can plant a romantic kiss to my temple. This openly affectionate side of Jason will take some getting used to but I think I like it.

After the chaos of the previous evening and the tenderness of this morning, I was ready for our nightly ritual of reading before bed. After showering and brushing my teeth, I slipped into our room ready to lay beside the man I've come to find comfort in.

As soon as I step inside, Jason's body is against mine with his hands planted on my lower back. He presses his lips to mine then, looking down on me with passionate fire in his eyes. I melt internally at the sight of this man who was so closed off, punishing himself for the things he couldn't control, opening up to me in his own way. Affection is his way of communicating now, of reassuring me. And I know he does it because of what I shared the other night. Maybe I got too personal, maybe I shouldn't have said anything at all. But I can't deny the weightlessness I've felt since confessing my secret. I feel like I need to explain further but he hasn't pushed me on the matter. I know he'll be there when I'm ready to talk about it.

"Hey," I say as soon as Jason releases me from the kiss. "Nice to see you too." I run my fingertips up and down his bare back savoring the curvature of his body. His playful smile seems so innocent on the face of a man who scowls ninety percent of the time.

"Sooo," I drag out the word. "Ally Herm, huh?" He rolls his eyes at that. "No shame there. She's pretty. Just surprised. We've never had that conversation. Exactly how many girls have you slept with in town?"

Jason walks away from me with a cocky grin that edges me on. Oh how I hate not knowing things. And he's very aware of that.

"Ok fine, I'll guess." I follow him to the bed. "Five?" No response. I reach the edge of the bed. "Ten?" Nothing. I lift myself onto the mattress. "Fifteen?" I wait on my knees at the end of the bed, waiting expectantly. "*Twenty?*" Still nothing. "Come on, Alder, are you some kind of Casanova or just like being mysterious?"

He meets me halfway on the bed where I sit on my heels. He's on his knees but still towers over me as he cradles my jaw in both hands. He points a finger at my chest as if to say *you first*.

"Fine. You're the third guy I've ever been with. Unless you count fooling around with Max Crown behind the bleachers. But we only got to second base."

He laughs a silent laugh that makes his upper body shake a little. I know he has a voice and chooses not to use it. But I wish I could hear him laugh. A *real* laugh.

"Alright. Your turn. How many?"

Looking a little reluctant, Jason scratches the nape of his neck before he holds his hands in the air and flashes all ten fingers twice then holds two fingers in the air after. As he drops his arms down to my thighs my mouth gapes.

"You've been with twenty-two women?" I ask incredulously. "Does that include me?"

He nods.

"Oh my gosh. I feel so inexperienced. If I'd known I'd be locked away with a sexual savant all winter I might have tried to increase my numbers a little bit before then."

He pulls me into him so our chests flatten against one another in a possessive way. I have a feeling he'd rather I have slept with no one besides him. Rather hypocritical considering. Not that I'm shaming. I just feel inadequate.

"Did you sleep with anyone in high school?"

He stares into my eyes for a moment, the gray of his eyes growing dark for a split second before shaking his head no.

Then it hits me, prom night would have been his first time.

With me.

"Jason," I breath, "I—I didn't know—I didn't think—." What else is there to say?

Before I can finish that incoherent babble, he stalks over to the dresser and picks up the pencil to write on the sheets of paper he keeps there. He's only gone a moment before he returns and hands it to me.

Two letters in one day. I feel spoiled.

You would have been my first. I'm sorry you weren't. But I felt I had something to prove after that night.

However, you were my first kiss. And I don't know why, but that feels more important.

That does something to my fragile heart. Because I agree, it feels more significant. It feels like a form of trust. Sex can be as emotional or vacant as people want. And I like to think ours carries a deeper sentiment than anything either of us have experienced in the past.

I've heard people say that you can learn to love anyone if you spend enough time with them. There's something to be said about forced proximity. But I'm choosing to believe whatever is happening between Jason and I is bigger than that, that our connection was forged long before this winter.

Chapter Twenty-Seven

Mara

GLYCERINE-BUSH

A heavy thud against the window jolts me out of my dreamless sleep like a shot to the heart. For a second I can't recall where I am. I've never been in a coma but sometimes when I wake up I'm so numb I imagine that's what it would feel like.

I crawl out of the warm bed and head to the double doors that lead to the balcony. That's where it sounded like the noise came from. Peering through the spiderwebs of frozen tendrils on the glass I see a bird of indigo and gray hues lying lifeless in the snow.

What the fuck?

Did a bird just fly into the window and kill itself? I've heard of birds doing this before but I didn't think it was an actual occurrence. And why was it even flying around in this weather?

I crack the door and stick my foot into the frigid winter air to poke the bird with my sock-covered toes. No movement. Must be dead.

If that doesn't seem like some kind of ominous sign, I don't know what is. Maybe I need an old crone in a cloak chanting something in the woods to seal whatever spell this is.

After dressing in a pair of jeans and pulling one of Jason's sweatshirts over my head, I head downstairs braiding my hair with each step.

"A bird just committed suicide on the balcony," I announce to Jason and (surprisingly) Dylan who are standing in the kitchen drinking their morning coffee. Their perplexed eyes turn to me as if I spoke a foreign language. "A bird flew into the glass upstairs and it's dead." The two men exchange a look that screams *what the fuck* before Jason walks past me up the stairs, but not without running his hand down my arm as he passes.

"We'll that's fucking creepy," Dylan voices my inner monologue.

"That's what I thought. I feel like it's a bad sign or something."

"Don't let it go to your head," Dylan waves it off. "We're not on any ancient burial grounds or summoning demons in the garage, are we?"

Although I try to laugh it off, the whole encounter has me feeling a little spooked.

Jason returns downstairs and washes his hands in the kitchen sink. I ask timidly, "Is it gone?" He replies with a slow nod.

I have no idea if Jason is superstitious or not. He doesn't seem that shaken by the idea of a bird killing itself on our balcony. Maybe it's a common occurrence around here.

"So what's on the agenda today?" I ask after starting the pancakes for breakfast.

Jason walks over to the back door where his shot gun is propped against the doorframe then holds it toward me.

"You're going for a hunt?" I ask.

He shakes his head and maneuvers his pointer finger between our two bodies.

"*We* are going hunting?" He nods yes. "But I don't want to shoot an animal."

"You just want to eat them," Dylan remarks. My returning scowl is answer enough. "We've been over this."

"Yes, and I'm comfortable with the knowledge my food has to get on my plate somehow, but not actually watching it." Both boys roll their eyes at my continued pretend ignorance toward where all our meat comes from. "Can't I just play with baby chicks all day?"

Jason shakes his head and I can't tell if he's trying to tell me I can't play with the animals all day, or if he's just exasperated with my antics.

My argument dies after breakfast when he brings the snow gear to me at the kitchen table in a clear request for me to join him. I agree and start to bundle up. I refuse to watch if we do find a deer or elk, but I want to spend more time with Jason. I hope I don't come off as clingy but I want to enjoy as much time with him as I can. Not just because our time is running out, but because being with him is the most content I ever feel.

Snow crunches under our boots as we walk side by side. The layers of frozen to fresh to frozen snow beneath my steps make each one less coordinated than the last. It's a good thing I'm not trying to appear infallible to Jason like I used to, because this would be a miserable failure. I used to hone my image like a delicate craft. There's freedom in not caring what others think, but I'm still chasing it.

We've only been walking for ten minutes but the ache in my chest from shortness of breath makes it feel like we're running a marathon. I didn't realize until this winter how immobilizing snow gear can be. Bulky material banded around every limb with limited range of motion.

"Will we be going far from the cabin?" I've learned to frame my questions in yes or no formats to make communication easier between us.

Dylan told me they have a hunting cabin for the fall but they can't get to it in the snow. Apparently, that's where Jason was coming back from the night he found my car in the snow bank. I doubt we are going all that way. But if I know Jason, he has a plan, and probably somewhere close by he can hunker down and wait for a deer to approach.

He shakes his head to tell me we aren't too far away from wherever he likes to hunt.

Jason only packed one gun—thank goodness—because I don't think I'd be able to carry a gun in this condition. Too cumbersome.

Not long after leaving the lodge, we come to a collection of ferns poking out of the snow beneath twin pillar pine trees rising toward the clouded sky. Even though winter is getting close to giving way to spring, today is particularly cold.

We sit in silence for sometime which feels comforting at first. But silence always leaves too much room for wild thoughts to creep inside my head. I don't know if Jason ever experiences that in his own silent life.

"What do you think about all day?" I ask before I can stop myself. I know talking will scare away potential targets but I can't help myself sometimes.

Jason looks at me a shrugs.

"Sometimes, I feel like I can't control my thoughts." I continue even though it probably sounds like babbling to him. "Silence feels like a wide open gate letting every bad memory come back to me. I relive the cringiest moments of my life. It'd be nice if the good memories made an appearance every once in a while."

I chuckle nervously to myself when a specific cringe-worthy moment comes to mind. Jason's eyes land back on me as his head slowly swivels in my direction.

"This one time, the entire class passed around yearbooks in my eighth grade English lit class. We had to sign everyone's book. There was a kid I didn't know very well, we never shared any work groups. I had no clue what to say and instead of just using the basics like 'have a great summer,' I wrote 'you look nice.'" I scrunch my face remembering the humiliation of the following moment. "He thought that was me coming on to him so he found me after school and leaned against my locker while asking me if

I wanted to hang out at the park. He swooped in and kissed me so fast I didn't see it coming. Anddd that was the story of my first kiss. It was with Ryan Parrish and I didn't even want it."

An invisible string pulls the corner of Jason's mouth up in a half smirk, clearly enjoying my embarrassment.

My story reminds me of what Jason shared with me the other night. About how I was his first kiss. The way my heart flutters thinking about it, thinking about how he trusted me enough, or maybe was just attracted to me enough, that he wanted his first kiss to be me...twice. I don't know what he saw in me in high school but I know what I saw in him. I saw someone who didn't conform to the expectations of society. I saw a guy who was completely content with the person he chose to be. And I envied that.

He was so vulnerable with me the other day. I want to reciprocate. Being that open with him doesn't come as easily as I'd like. But not because of anything he's done. My own inhibitions stifle any progress I want to make on that front.

But I put on my big girl pants, take in a lung full of crisp air, and try.

"I don't know why I feel the way I do," I confess. "Somedays I feel fine, I'm happy and content, the next, I don't even want to get out of bed. I know mental health awareness is big now but usually people are depressed for a reason. Loneliness, PTSD, breakups, a series of unfortunate events. What do I have to be depressed about? Plenty of people don't do well in college, look at Ally Herm. But she came back and found her calling, I guess. So what, my parents didn't love me enough? That's a little too on the nose. And I shouldn't be bothered that a guy I didn't even love cheated on me. I'm glad to be rid of him. None of that is good enough a reason to feel this way."

I didn't realize I was staring at the snow until I saw Jason's leg shift against the tree trunk which draws my attention back to him. His stormy eyes are fixed on me as though he's hanging on to every word I say.

Talking about it is so much harder than I thought it would be. My chest feels tight and my eyes well with tears. One even slips past the barricade and descends my cheek leaving a streak of warmth in its wake.

"I don't want to feel this way. Sometimes it's so overwhelming. Like the night I drove to the bridge. I just felt...unwanted." There. I said it. "I felt like it would be easier on myself if I wasn't here anymore. It felt like an easy way to erase the horrible image I'd earned and just be a faded memory, you know?"

One hand on the back of my neck, Jason draws our foreheads together so we share a breath. The heat of him splits the cold between us.

"I'm sorry, I wasn't looking for sympathy. I just thought you'd want an explanation. And, in case you're wondering, I haven't thought about following through again since being here." His shoulders drop the slightest amount, just enough to notice.

"Thanks for not judging," I tell him. I don't see judgment in his eyes, I don't see any pity either. I only see affection. I like to think his gestures mean he's glad I'm here.

After leaning my body against Jason's for a while, sharing as much body heat as possible, and freezing my nose off, the sound of the snow shifting ahead of us alerts us to the presence of the buck in the distance. He has two points on either of his antlers. He's so much smaller than the elk Jason killed on Thanksgiving. But equally as majestic. Which makes it harder to know his life is about to end. I understand the logic behind this. We need to eat. But I still marvel at the buck's beauty and appreciate the sacrifice of his life for our continued existence.

Maybe I'm growing numb to this life, but I don't even flinch when Jason pulls the trigger and the buck drops to the ground. I don't even blink. All of this is starting to feel like a natural part of my life.

And I like that.

Except when I have to help carry pieces of deer back to the cabin. That will never be part of my picture-perfect vision.

Chapter Twenty-Eight

Jason

TEMPORARY **T**EARS-**NEEDTOBREATHE**

The look on Mara's face when I held one quarter of the deer towards her was priceless. I gave her the smaller of the pieces and I went back for the other half on my own while she and Dylan started processing the meat. Once it was headless and skinless, she seemed to do better with butchering the meat for storage.

When I come back inside from disposing of the feet and processing the skull and antlers for a future sell, I'm met with Mara's baffled tone.

"You're telling me this is an illegal deer?" Her pitch rises with her surprise. I shake my head to myself.

"Technically, yes," Dylan answers while stuffing more meat into the grinder for sausage.

"Technically—" Mara's words are cut off by the sound of the meat grinder whirring through the air, mechanical and *loud*.

"Dylan just told me it's not deer season anymore," Mara turns her blazing stare toward me with a knife pointed in my direction. I hold my hands up in mock surrender. "This deer is *illegal*."

"Well, we hunted during the proper time frame but only enough for two people through the winter," Dylan reminds her of the peculiar circumstances. "Besides. How would anyone know? No one comes up here even in the summer, unless we bring them ourselves."

Great, a reminder of the girls I've brought here. That's the last thing Mara needs.

"Do you bring prospective romantic partners to the cabin?" Mara asks teasingly.

"Um, no," Dylan states finitely. "Usually find a hotel room to meet people at in town."

"I've never had sex in a hotel room," she confesses. It's all I can do to stifle the subtle laugh that leaves me at that particular confession. Didn't realize that was on her bucket list. Come to think of it, neither have I. Maybe we can cross it off together when the snow melts. There's a lot of sex-related things I'd like to cross off my bucket list with her.

After we finish with the deer Dylan heads out to the barn to tend to the animals. He was working in the shop this morning but the goats seem to like him best, seeing as they don't try to eat his clothes when he walks into their pen, so he was nominated to milk them tonight.

As for Mara and I, I find her in our bedroom stripping out of the clothes she was wearing beneath the snow gear. They're probably laced with sweat after the tiresome workout of hiking in the snow and transporting deer chunks back to the cabin.

A band I've never heard before plays on the speaker. She must have borrowed a CD from Dylan. She's down to her underwear and the long sleeve thermal I leant her when I step into the room and shut the door. Her head lifts to look at me at the sound and a smile graces her lips. It's so beautiful, genuine, innocent. After I became sexually active and word spread about the size of my "eel" women always smiled with purpose toward me. Their smiles held requests, selfish intentions. I didn't mind it then because I thought I was the lucky one getting laid on a regular basis and not having to woo a woman into bed. It was easy.

I didn't realize how shallow those smiles were until Mara came barreling back into my life. When she smiles at me, there's nothing selfish about it. She's truly happy to see me. I'm sure she wants sex, too, but that's just a perk, not the root of it.

I take my time crossing the space between us in slow strides until coming to stand directly in front of her. She waits motionless for me to take the lead, to make the next move. I gingerly run my hands from her hips over the curve of her waist, along her rib cage, taking the shirt she's wearing as I go. My fingers scale over the outer shell of her breasts, eliciting bolts of lightning through me when I feel she's bare underneath. I brush my thumbs over her hardened nipples before wrapping my fingers around the hem of the shirt and gently bring it up over her arms and head.

Next is her underwear, I scale down her body kissing as I go. Once I reach her hip bone, I take the side of her panties in my teeth and use them to tug the pesky garment down her body, inch by inch, massaging her ass and the backs of her thighs in the process. Her skin is pure silk, warm and salty. She's perfect.

As soon as she steps out of her panties, I run the pad of my tongue through her slit one time as I rise to stand over her once again, appreciating her naked glory.

Then it's my turn, she leans in and kisses the area where my neck meets my jaw as she slips her delicate hands beneath my flannel and pushes it over my broad shoulders. I just have a white t-shirt underneath so I do the one handed pull at the back of the shirt to strip it off that seems to make girls go wild. Her eyes heat with the movement before her hands work at my belt, expertly unfastening. Her fingers curl into the waistband of my pants and boxers as she uses her might to pull them over my quads and down my legs, all I have left is my socks which she slips off one at a time, kneeling before me like I'm her god, her salvation. I love when she looks up at me through her lashes. She's a stunning temptress.

I yank her up by the hand to plant my lips on hers as soon as her mouth is close enough. One hand on the back of her neck, my fingers lace into her hair and tug a little to tilt her face toward me more. I use just enough force to draw a hiss from her that tells me she liked it. I keep my fingers bunched in her soft waves as I walk her backward toward the balcony doors.

I'm so fucking hard for her. After what she told me earlier, after seeing a couple tears leek from her eyes, I need to be inside of her and fill her with as much affection as I can. I want to remind her she's alive. She's living.

As soon as I unlatch the door, I force Mara onto the snowy balcony into the freezing cold using my body as a battering ram. She shrieks at the sudden chill of snow on her feet but I press on. We stand completely naked, chest to chest, in the open air. My arms band around her waist while her hands rest on my biceps. The contrast of her hot flesh against the frozen air does something to me. And to her, if her painfully peaked nipples are any indication.

Without warning, I flip her around so she's facing the forest and flatten her upper half so her voluptuous breasts are smushed into the snow on the railing. I helped my father make the railing, the top piece is made of a two by eight board. Never have I been more grateful for this balcony.

A moan somewhere between pain and pleasure leaves her when her body makes contact with the dusting of snow on the railing, just before I bury myself deep inside her, all the way to the hilt. Then her moan is pure lust, it fuels my actions like kindling to a fire.

"God, you're so big, Jason."

I don't give her any time to adjust, I don't start slow, I'm ruthless in every thrust that drives me deeper into her, grinding her nipples against the layer of glassy ice on the railing. Try as she might to muffle the sounds bubbling out of her, Mara's groans for more are music to my ears.

Hands gripping her waist in a bruising hold, I increase my pace as one hand glides along her abdomen to the apex of her spread legs. Putting pressure on her clit, vigorous circles drive her into a state of bliss as I work her from every angle.

The cold doesn't bother me too much now that I'm working up a sweat with her. I doubt it bothers her that much either. I switch from my thumb on her clit to two fingers that increase the tension until she's writhing under me. As soon as her body clenches around my dick, I know she's coming. She doesn't even have to tell me. I've learned every nuance about this woman, everything that makes her tick and how to work her until she's limp with satiation. As soon as her body relaxes, I pull out and spin her in my hands before hoisting her into the air, plopping her round ass into the snow on the railing.

Mara takes a moment to look over the railing at the drop she would endure should she fall. Fear darkens the corners of her eyes. But I would never let her fall.

Her attention returns to me when I slide back inside her warmth in one long, torturous thrust until it's unclear where I end and she begins.

"Jason," she whispers breathlessly. I resume my relentless pace, pivoting at my hips so I thrust my entire body into the motion. She's practically bouncing on the railing but I keep my hands firm around the narrow of her waist to keep her from going anywhere. I see how much the thrill gets her off, she likes a little bit of risk in her pleasure, it makes her pulse skyrocket. Her eyes are shut tight as she chases another orgasm that's just out of reach.

"Harder," she demands. So I pick up the pace.

"Harder," she asks again. So I increase the pressure until I'm worried she's going to spill over the side of the balcony.

"Harder," she pleads. It's then I realize she wants the pain, she wants to be punished, not because she likes it but because she feels she deserves it. Because pain is control. Because pain is part of life. I want to wrap her in my arms and tell her it's alright but I know she doesn't want that right now. Mara has to feel everything in her own time.

Just when she thinks I've given her all I have to give, I launch forward and suck one pebbled nipple between my teeth, biting down just enough to draw a cry from her lips but not hard enough to actually hurt her. I've heard women's nipples harden to a painful point when it's this cold. I don't want to push her too far. Just far enough that she erupts.

And she does. Her body spasms in my grasp as my bite washes an orgasm over her, rocking her nerves into oblivion. She's shaking like a leaf when I pull out of her and point my come into the snow sucking air between my teeth. My body is just as rattled from this encounter as hers.

Ok, maybe not as much as her. She's dead weight in my arms as I slide her off the railing and carry her into the warm bedroom. The heat of the fire practically burns compared to the icy balcony.

I don't break contact with Mara as I bury us beneath the covers to preserve heat. Her body feels ice cold but it's not long before the aftershocks of her orgasms subside and she stills in my arms, warmth returning to her skin. As soon as her breathing evens out, I know she's asleep. I don't sleep, though, I just embrace her in my hold, afraid to let her go.

It's two hours later when Mara wakes and dusk is starting to settle on the world. I've never been able to sleep during the day but it was tranquil to feel her steady breaths against my side while her body curled into mine. She blinks bleary eyes until reality comes back to her. Lifting her head a bit, she takes me in, though we haven't moved at all in the last two hours.

"Hi," she whispers into the toasty air. "How long have I been out?" I hold up two fingers to indicate the hours. "Oh, I'm sorry."

She has no reason to be sorry, so I pull her into me further hoping she understands.

"I feel like I wasted the last half of the day. I guess that hike really took it out of me. Thanks for going back to get the rest of the deer. Sorry I wasn't more help."

She needs to stop apologizing for everything.

"Do you ever want kids?" Well that came out of nowhere. "Not with me, not right now," she clarifies quickly, like the idea is so terrifying. "I just mean in general. If you have kids, one day they'll be able to help you with all of this, you know? Isn't that the point of having kids, anyway?"

I pull a piece of paper from the nightstand where I had been jotting down notes while she slept. I quickly scribble out the words *Maybe. Someday.* and show it to her.

My tap against her shoulder is my way of asking *what about you?*

"I never used to want kids," she admits. "But...I think a lot has changed about me. I think I'd like to be a mom one day. I'd like to be the mom I wish I'd had. I'd like to raise good humans who respect others and know how loved they are. Maybe I'm just trying to right the wrongs of my parents. I don't know.

"I used to want a big city life and no kids and to travel to as many states and countries as possible. But now, I don't think that's who I am anymore. I like the simplicity of how you live up here. I like the lack of chaos and pressure. Maybe it was just immersion therapy, but I think I could live like this and be happy."

My heart flips at that. With spring approaching, I've been trying to figure out what Mara wants. If she wants to go home, back to her life, and pursue her dreams...

Or if she wants to stay here. With me.

It feels foolish to think that because she's never seemed like the hermit farmer she's become during this winter. But hearing her confess that she actually likes this life, maybe she would want to continue to live here.

And in the summer, it's not like we couldn't go into town as often as she wants. With roads open, we can travel, we can go to town for dinner or something. Whatever she wants.

Maybe she could have the best of both worlds.

Maybe I can keep her in my world.

Chapter Twenty-Nine

Mara

S LEEP DEPRIVATION-CHANCE PEÑA

"It's definitely melting but not quite safe to drive on," Dylan announces upon walking through the back door, stripping his heavy coat and boots off.

The temperature has been rising steadily the past couple weeks. There's certainly less snow than there has been in months, but I guess not quite enough to drive into town. Which means we are one day closer to facing the subject of whether I leave or stay. I think Jason wants me to stay, I think we've made so much progress and become a real couple, but he hasn't made any indication that he wants me to stay. For all I know he could drag me out of bed tomorrow and drive me back down the mountain.

I just need to put my big girl pants on and talk to him about it. This whole not-talking-about-our-feelings thing is the worst book trope out there. Communication is key. And if he doesn't want me to stay, at least I'll have my answer and only a couple more days of living with someone who doesn't want me.

If that's the case, of course.

Best case scenario, he wants me to stay and we drive to town to get my things and move me in permanently.

I swore I wouldn't live with a guy again before marriage after my ex and the fiasco of our break up. Then again, I didn't really have a choice when it came to Jason. But we've proven we can handle it.

"Do you guys have a first day of freedom tradition, or anything?" I ask as Jason prepares sandwiches for all of us with the bread I made this morning. While Dylan takes his seat at the kitchen table.

"We usually just go to town to restock groceries and liquor," Dylan laughs. "We bulk up on provisions like flour and milk, things like that, in case we get a freak snow storm that locks us up here again. Hasn't happened to us yet, but I remember it happened once when I was a kid and we were already home in town, glad we weren't stuck at the cabin."

"Worried about a false spring?"

"One can never be too careful."

Jason and I are cocooned into bed after dinner when I dig deep in my core to muster the courage to ask what neither of us has acknowledged.

"Jason," I ask from the bed while he adds another log to the fire across the room. "Do you want me to stay here? After the snow melts, I mean?"

His head whips around in a flash, his long hair fanning around him in the process. The sharpness to his eyes makes me second guess myself. Maybe that's not what he wants at all. Maybe I'm overstepping his boundaries.

And that's when the rambling starts. "I mean, I don't have to. I can go back to town. I just didn't know if you wanted me to stay or not. You know what? Forget I said anything. I'm fine going back to town. Though I guess I don't know if you still want to see me again or not after that. I know the sex has been good but there's more to life than sex. You have to actually see a future with someone to live with them, or so I'm—"

Before I can dig my grave any deeper, Jason has flown across the room to the bed and captured my mouth in a searing kiss that brands me as his.

Question answered.

I break away to clarify, "Is that a yes? You want me to stay?"

I've never seen him smile so brightly, it's beautiful. His smile has an infectious effect on my soul that makes me feel like I'm full of carbonation, bubbly and happy.

Jason nods vigorously shaking hair into his face that I brush out of the way with trembling hands he steadies with his own.

"I'm happy here." I feel the need to assure Jason. I want to shout it from the rooftop, to be honest. "I'm happy with you."

All of this makes me think of the three little words that every couple should be saying right about now but we haven't admitted to each other. We just overcame one hurtle, I don't want to add anymore weight to this moment and just enjoy the fact that he wants me.

He wants me to stay.

He wants me.

In one powerful, fluid motion, Jason flips us so he lies on his back and I'm straddling him. I lean down and kiss him like my life depends on it. But it's broken when Jason lifts me forward and scoots down the bed so his head lays between my spread thighs.

Oh god. I've never done this before, or not like this, I should say. It feels way more intimate and vulnerable for some reason. I feel like he can see every inch of me even though technically his view is more impaired. Still, when I'm impaled on his tongue, I melt into a ball of putty, pliable and willing to mold under his touch. He spears me expertly as only he knows how to do. He is the Mozart to my body, a skilled master of his craft. And every time he touches me in *just the right spot,* I feel like I'm being wound tight as a knot.

My entire body is wrapped in sexual tension as his tongue delves into me over and over and over again. It's the worst and best kind of tease that makes my muscles clench but he's dangling me over the precipice refusing to let me come. I lean forward gripping the headboard like I'm holding on for dear life, trying not to squish his head between my thighs as they clench tighter with each thrust of his tongue.

Then one hand presses on my lower stomach to lift the clitoral hood and his other starts massaging it in vigorous circles.

"Jason," I hiss. "Yes, yes, yes. Yes. *Yes. Ahhh.*"

It's so intense and sensitive I combust in seconds. But somehow he makes the orgasm linger, drawing it out so painstakingly long that my body can't handle the pressure. One, long, continuous climax wracks my body with unbearable euphoria. I can't help the cries that escape me and pray that Dylan isn't nearby to hear them. But that thought is just a blip in my mind that's overcome with how all-consuming that orgasm was, and how overly sensitive my body feels after that.

As soon as the rush has worn off, Jason removes his tongue and takes my hips in a vice grip to lift me and lower me onto his hard cock. His beautiful, thick, veiny, monstrous cock that I can't seem to get enough of.

He doesn't expect me to start riding him like a bronco after that. So he lifts me on his hips so I balance on my knees that are pressed into the mattress and starts fucking me from underneath. Each lift that slams into my core is powered by lust, adoration, and strength. I can see the might in every flexed muscle that works to drive me over another edge and forces me into a mindless, bodiless state of existence where all I can do is feel every thrust, every time his dick slams into my g-spot, every ecstatic inch of friction.

"Jason, *fuck*, I'm gonna—."

It happens so fast I can barely catch my breath before air lodges in my throat and my body spasms with another orgasm that's just as powerful—if not more powerful—than the first.

Jason pulls out of me just in time as his come flies into the air painting my breasts and stomach with his arousal. A low rumble vibrates in his chest, making me feel like the room is shaking around us.

I'm in a state of love and lust as I stare into the soulful eyes of this man that I just know I want to spend every moment of my life with.

After I've been thoroughly cleaned and cuddled, we lay in a heap beneath the bedding. Skin to skin. Chest to chest. Dopamine is coursing between us. I lazily trace a finger over various tattoo designs on his chest and shoulder. It looked like a mosaic suit of armor built of different images that I'm sure hold some significance to Jason.

Before drifting to sleep, I inform the man I'm falling in love with, "One day, you'll have to tell me what these mean."

The following morning Jason and I are in the kitchen making breakfast together. It feels so domestic, like a 1950s magazine ad of a husband and wife cooking together on Sunday morning before church. Granted, we aren't married and the pearl necklace I had on last night has been wiped away, but the atmosphere is still the same: wholesome and romantic.

I peer up at the clock that reads 8:36 am.

"Dylan isn't up yet?" Jason's eyes lift to the ceiling as if he could use X-ray vision to see through it into his brother's room. "I'll go check on him and make sure he's ok."

I climb the stairs to the landing and knock on his door once, calling, "Dylan?" At the lack of a response I turn the knob and enter the room only to be met with the sight of Dylan fully naked facing his headboard, presumably in the middle of something I don't want to see any more of.

An unexpected squeal leaves me. "Agh. Sorry. I'll—sorry."

"What the f—." His head whips over his shoulder. "*Mara.*" Fear etched into his tone, he throws himself flat against the bed as though that will shield me from seeing him naked. The idea is ridiculous though since his bare ass is sticking up in the air. I throw a hand over my eyes and dart out of the room, pulling the door shut behind me, and race back downstairs.

Jason is already at the bottom of the staircase with a worried look on his face.

"I'm permanently scarred for the rest of my life," I tell him.

"Oh come on, my ass isn't that bad." Dylan appears at the top of the stairs. "It's not like you saw the family jewels."

The heat of blush seeps across my nose and cheeks. "It's more so knowing what I walked in on. You have a very nice ass, Dylan."

Jason pulls me down the last step into his embrace at that remark, possessive and territorial as he is.

"Relax, bro, she's not my type." We all know this but Jason still keeps an arm banded around me as he steers us back into the kitchen to finish breakfast.

"What do you expect from me, I have to listen to you two fuck every day for months. It's a painful reminder of how utterly single and horny I am in isolation. Thank goodness the ice will be melted soon so I can go to town and get laid."

"About that..." I flash him an awkward smile. "You might have to listen to us a little longer than you thought. Wait that came out wrong. I don't want you to listen to us. We'll try to keep it down from now on. But when the ice melts, we're going back to town and getting my stuff so—."

I don't get to finish my sentence before Dylan swoops me up in a brotherly hug and spins me around the room.

"You're staying!" He announces jovially before crying, "Woohoo!"

Laughing, I request, "I'm excited too but put me down. It's way too soon after seeing you naked to hug."

He respects my request and lowers me to my feet as Jason walks up behind me and kisses the top of my head sweetly. I peer up into his gorgeous eyes and see my own smile reflected.

I'm so happy. It feels impossible. I feel like I'm waiting for the other shoe to drop. Maybe I'm too used to disappointment to accept happiness when it's so easily dropped into my lap.

"Honestly, the ice might have melted enough by this evening. We can check it out then and see if we can get to town."

"Let's just wait until tomorrow," I tell him. "I want one last day before I have to tell my parents where I've been since November. They probably think I'm dead, after all."

I'm so blissfully, unnaturally, imperfectly happy. I've felt like an unwelcome guest even after Jason and I started sleeping together. With everything out in the open I feel completely at home here. Cleaning out the stalls and taking a moment to feed the chicks scraps of food is part of my daily routine. Cooking with Dylan and Jason brings me so much joy. Reading in Jason's arms feels like home in a way words can't bring justice to. Everything about my life—our life—is perfect in its simplicity. I dare to think the dreaded words that could jinx everything.

What could go wrong?

I'm jostled awake in the early hours of the morning when the gray of early light begins to filter through the curtains pulled over the balcony doors casting the room in dreary shadows. The fire in the hearth has fizzled into a soft glow of embers that do nothing to brighten the space.

Jason stands over me and points to the alarm clock on the nightstand but the screen is blank. He gestures with his hand slashing it across his throat.

"The power is out?" He nods to confirm. He pulls me out of bed by the hand and I slip on a pair of sweats and a sweatshirt before heading down stairs. If the power is out that means our only source of heat is the fireplaces. We're fortunate to have one in our room but Dylan isn't as lucky.

Speaking of the devil, he's already downstairs on the couch when we make it to the main floor, bundled in a thick wool blanket with a fire going already.

"Hey, lovebirds, finally realize the power went out?"

"Yeah," I answer. "How long has it been out?"

"Since four." He lifts his phone so the screen brightens and shows us it's 5:23 in the morning.

"How did you know when it went out?"

"I sleep with a white noise machine and when it stopped working I woke up. Haven't been able to sleep without one since I was a kid."

I start to walk toward the couch and slam my thigh directly into the corner of the side table beside the couch. I let out a grunt then a hiss and declare, "I can't see anything this early. Do you still have a flashlight in your nightstand?" I direct the question to Jason and he nods so I head back upstairs to search for it, missing the first step of the stairs in the process and further proving my point.

I stroll over to his side of the bed and start rummaging around in the drawer until my hand brushes the round plastic cylinder. Thankfully, the light bursts from the object when I flip the switch, shining directly into the drawer where something catches my eye. The notes that Jason writes when he can't sleep lay still at the bottom of the drawer facing toward me.

I've never experienced real temptation like this before, the pull to do something you know you shouldn't but can't seem to resist. In the seconds I stand staring at the letters, certain words and phrases catch my eye. After seeing those, I can't look away, I can't pretend I didn't see them.

I'm used to the dreams about my father, they've plagued me since his death. But the ones about Bob? They don't happen often. And they're so vivid, too. I'll never be able to unfeel the way he touched me, the way he felt, the way my dad didn't believe what I told him happened. He called me a liar. He said I was talking out of my ass and didn't believe a word I said. So I stopped saying anything.

So much changed me that day. And I hate the fact that I am who I am today because of all the evil things my father accused me of. And because of what Bob did to me. It took me too fucking long to realize just how fucked up the whole thing was. And now I have to suffer for the rest of my life for it.

Chapter Thirty

Jason-Age 8

"HEY, KID," HE BECKONS me over with a wave of his hand. He's taller than Dad. It's kind of scary. I feel like being that tall would be scary, like I might hit my head on things. "Where's your dad?" He asks, looking around the empty corridor between stacks of logs a mile high. "What are you doing here?"

"I can't find him," I answer. I've never talked to this man before. Even though he's been at the house before, he didn't talk to me. "Where's the employee lounge? He said he would get me lunch."

"Where did he leave you?" Bob asks.

"His office," I tell him even though I'm worried he'll tell on me. "I thought he forgot about me. He was gone for a long time."

"Is that so?" Bob gets a weird look in his eyes. I don't like it. I don't like him. He's weird. He looks mean. He makes me nervous. His eyes are too dark and his mustache is too long, hanging over his upper lip.

"I'm going to go find my dad."

A meaty hand grabs my shoulder and jerks me back. I don't like it. I don't like it. His touch hurts my shoulder. Why does he have to hold me so hard?

"Hold on, kid, I'll help you."

He steers me in the opposite direction of my dad's office, the direction I was going before turning around. Bob keeps his hand clamped on my shoulder so hard I can feel the bruise forming under my skin.

"Is the employee lounge this way?" I ask Bob in a quiet voice.

"Don't worry, we'll find him."

I hear him messing with his pants and the belt buckle. I've seen some of the guys do this before, adjusting themselves in their pants. I never asked why. I don't have to do that but maybe it's because I'm not as big as they are. I try not to look cause Dad said that's rude and "perverted"—whatever that means.

"I don't think he's—." Bob shoves me into the uneven stacks of logs which hurts my spine. Before I can cry out, he smashes his hand over my mouth to stop any sounds I make and uses his body to pin me in place.

I'm trapped.

I don't like this feeling. I don't like not being able to move. I want my dad.

I want my mom!

"I've been eyeing you for years," he says coldly with an evil looking smile while fumbling with his pants. "You're gonna do what I say, and you're not going to tell your dad, because otherwise you'll embarrass him and you know he wouldn't like that. It'll be our little secret, kid."

He removes his hand from my mouth but I don't have a chance to scream before I'm choking on whatever he shoved inside it.

I'm running back through the weaving paths between logs until I spot my dad's office. I'm almost there, I'm almost safe. I run with so much fear and force I can't breath and my lungs hurt. As soon as I reach the door I turn the knob, pull it open, and dart inside tracking mud with me. I'm too upset and scared to worry about that, though.

"Where the fuck have you been?" I've never been so glad to hear my dad's voice, even if he sounds enraged. "I've been looking all over for you. You were supposed to stay here. Why can't you following something so fucking simple? Why couldn't you listen to me just one time?"

"Dad," I heave while gasping for air through agonizing pain in my throat, "I'm sorry. I didn't mean to. I thought you forgot about me and I was hungry." Then I notice the sandwich on his desk. I don't think I'm hungry anymore, though, I feel sick. My voice sounds weird after…after.

"I had to talk to one of my guys. Did I tell you to stay here for ten minutes and then go snooping? No! I told you to wait here." His arms are flailing and his voice gets rougher and meaner with each sentence. "You're useless, Jason. You don't listen to anything I say. And why the hell are you covered in all this damn mud? Look, it's all over my office now. You're going to be the one to clean this up."

"Dad, This guy found me while I was looking for you. He was mean, he pushed me around."

Slap.

My dad slapped me. He's never hit me before.

"I don't want to hear any of your bullshit. You're a fucking liar, Jason. You said you didn't hit that kid at school and you did. You said you'd stay here and you didn't. Now this? Stop lying, you little shit."

"I'm not, Dad. I'm not. Really. He held me against the logs and—."

I'm up against a wall again, only this time it's my father's hands fisting the cuff of my shirt and his angry red face that fills my vision. "I don't want to hear it, Jason. Get some rags out of the closet and start cleaning. I don't want to hear a peep out of you until it's done."

I just stare at him. *Why doesn't he believe me? Why would I lie about what that guy just did to me? Why won't he listen to me?*

"GO." My father points to the narrow door of the closet with a meaty finger. "Not another word."

I can't believe it. Why is it ok for Bob to hurt me and my dad does nothing about it? Why is it ok for my *father* to hurt me? Why am I the one who gets hurt when I'm not even lying? Why do bad things keep happening whenever I speak up and tell the truth?

No one ever believes me.

Mom and Dylan believe me. But maybe Bob was right and they would all be embarrassed by me. Ashamed. I shouldn't tell anyone what happened ever again. I don't want to humiliate my family. And who would believe me anyway?

So I get the rags from the closet and the cleaning spray like my father told me to, drop to my hands and knees, and start to clean up the mess.

Chapter Thirty-One

Mara

SAVIN' ME-NICKELBACK

That was the last time I spoke, until the day my father died. And the day Mara fell through the ice. I think she wants me to speak but it's been so long. I've tried and my voice doesn't work like that anymore. Besides, if I did I'd probably ruin everything. I want to keep her, I don't want to push her away. And if staying silent keeps her here, then maybe she can learn to love like me the way I am.

If not, then I'm already used to losing people.

I don't even know what to say.

My mind is racing over the horror I just read and the heartbreaking words the man I love wrote about his childhood. About the dreams that have been plaguing him.

I had no idea it could be so bad.

Jason was sexually abused by his Dad's friend when he was a kid.

I don't know how old he was but it sounds like he was pretty young. Whoever this Bob guy is deserves to rot in hell for what he did. Anyone who harms a child deserves the lowest circle of Hell. How could anyone be so sick and twisted and cruel enough to do that to a child?

I think to myself that I have to tell Jason it's not his fault, there is nothing he could have done and he is not to blame. He's a victim.

But then he would know I was snooping and found the letters he's been writing. He clearly didn't want me to see these or know what happened. He didn't want anyone to know what happened. I don't even think Dylan knows about this.

Still, the overwhelming part of me that loves him wants him to know that he was a victim of child abuse, he's not responsible for the actions of two fully grown men who should have listened to him when he spoke up. If he thinks we're going to think he's lying, he's wrong. If he thinks I'll leave because of this or because he was too scared to speak again, he's wrong.

But the decision of whether or not to tell him what I found is made for me when the door opens and I turn to see him glaring at me with such fear in his deep eyes. Those eyes dart between me and the letter in my hand. I only read one, and I think it was the most important one to read.

Then, his expression shifts from scared and ashamed to utter hatred. All the times he looked at me with disdain because of our past, it was never as icy and pure as the look he's giving me now. I crossed a line I can't come back from.

"Jason," I say on an exhale, "I didn't mean to. I was looking for the flashlight and found this. I'm sorry I shouldn't have read it but—."

He storms across the room and rips the pages out of my hands before tossing them into the fireplace like a grenade about to go off. They instantly catch on the glowing embers and shrivel into ash before my eyes. I didn't mean to upset him this much.

"Jason, I'm so sorry, please." I try to take his hand in mine but he pulls it away in a snap and doesn't even bother to look at me again as he exits the room.

Following after him, I plead. "Jason please talk to me. I mean—you know what I mean." He's down the stairs now but I reach his arm and touch his bicep before he jerks out of my reach. "Jason, listen to me. It wasn't your fault. You didn't do anything wrong. What they did to you is disgusting and horrible and none of it was your fault."

Dylan steps inside the house with a bundle of firewood tucked into his arm. The tension in the room is thick enough to cut with a knife. His gaze bounces between Jason and I assessing the situation with interest and worry.

"What's going on?" He asks timidly, almost afraid to hear the answer.

"I found something Jason didn't want me to see," I confess, knowing he'll want something but not wanting to tell him everything. "I'm sorry Dylan, it's not my place to tell you."

I look back to Jason with hope in my eyes. Hope he'll forgive me and we can work through this together. Hope this doesn't ruin us. Hope that he can forgive himself. Because that is the most important thing, that he understands he's not to blame.

"Jason, can we please talk about this? Can we go somewhere private and work through this?"

He shoots back up the stairs and Dylan and I follow, though I wish Dylan would stay downstairs. Jason might be more willing to talk about this if Dylan isn't around.

But when I locate him in the bedroom, he's loading my items from a drawer in the dresser into a brown paper bag. Shirts, pants, a pair of underwear, and the gun he and Dylan made me.

No. He can't be doing what I think he's doing.

He marches back down the stairs ignoring Dylan and I as we call for him to stop and think, to calm down. He's so enraged he can't think past his own emotions. He takes a set of keys off the hook by the door and storms outside barefoot in just his sweats and a thermal shirt and throws the bag into the backseat of the truck Dylan used to scout the roads. He tosses the keys to Dylan who's also poorly dressed for the cold air and walks back toward the house. I chase after him because he won't even look at me and I need him to look at me, I need him to *see* me.

"Jason, wait," I grab his hand and he turns around so fast I almost run into him. Fury carved into every line of his expression. "Please, Jason, I love you. I *love* you. I want to help you." I know admitting this now sounds silly and desperate but I don't care. I'm clutching his hand like a lifeline to my chest. He rips it from my grasp and continues his trek back inside.

But I'll be damned if he thinks he can storm off with the last word...so to speak.

"You're a coward," I fire my bullets, "you're a coward because you took the easy way out instead of facing your demons and becoming stronger. Instead of taking the power back, you let your past ruin what could have been a beautiful future. And now you have to live with your choices."

Jason takes the last step over the threshold, slamming the door behind him and sealing the decision he's made.

I thought having the last word would make me feel stronger, like I had the upper hand. But when the ultimatum was placed at his feet, Jason chose the option that didn't include me. And now I have to live with his decision too.

Before the tears can overtake me, I ask Dylan, "Can-can you drive me back to my parents house?" He doesn't answer me with words but guides me with gentle hands on my shoulders to the passenger seat and helps me in before climbing into the driver's side behind the wheel. The truck starts with a mechanical whir and then jolts forward with a start, descending down the mountain and out of Jason's life forever.

I can't control it much longer, I'm vibrating with emotions that feel more powerful than I could have ever imagined.

He doesn't love me. He doesn't even want me anymore. I fucked the whole thing up and we both have to suffer for it. Why couldn't I keep my nose out his business? How could I be so fucking stupid? How could he shake me off so easily and throw me out? I thought that after everything we've been through together, he would have wanted to at least cool off and try to work things out after some time had passed. Apparently I'm not worth it to him.

As much as my heart is breaking over the loss of a relationship that never had a chance, it's also fractured for the little boy who was abused and never got the help he deserved. For the boy who's spirit broke and innocence stripped. He deserved more. Who would Jason be if his father had just listened to him?

Tears slip down my cheeks in endless streams as I struggle to breath while keeping the sobs from flooding the vehicle. Too ashamed of my current state, I angle my body toward the passenger side window in a feeble attempt to conceal the ambush of emotions overtaking me.

Dylan doesn't ask what happened, he stays silent the entire drive, he doesn't even play music. I wish I could thank him for that but I know if I try to speak I'll break apart completely.

Forty minutes later, we're back in town and Dylan is parking the truck on the circle driveway of my parents house. I completely forgot to see if my car was still by the bridge on our way down. I guess it doesn't really matter.

I can hardly bring myself to look at Dylan but I know it will probably be the last time so I lift my head and peer at him through damp lashes. As soon as I do, he envelopes me in a hug that feels like it should heal, it feels like it should fix everything and make it all better. But he doesn't have that kind of power. All it does is remind me of the life I've lost today.

"Th-Thanks," I stutter through controlled sobs.

As I start to climb out of the truck, Dylan stops me. "Mara, I don't know what happened, but he loves you. You have to see that. You mean more to him than anything in the world."

I don't think that's true anymore. But it's nice of him to say that. He kisses the top of my hand in farewell before I shut the door and he drives away.

I try to get myself under control on the short walk to the front door of my parents house. Do I knock? Do I walk right in? I decide walking into their house would cause an alarm so I ring the doorbell. A minute later, my mom opens the door and the shock that mars her face is enough to tell me she never thought she would see me again.

"Mara?" She utters on a whisper. "You're alive?" She doesn't even sound that happy about it, just surprised.

"Yeah, Mom," she gestures for me to come inside, "I have a lot to tell you."

Chapter Thirty-Two

Mara

CEILINGS - LIZZY MCALPINE

Borderline personality disorder. That's what my therapist diagnosed me with. And, to be honest, it makes sense. She described it as the middle child between bipolar disorder and depression. Where you have ups and downs but not quite as rapidly as being bipolar and not as consistently down as depression is. Which explains why I can feel so content in my life, so at peace with things and then all of a sudden a spiral of sadness consumes me out of nowhere.

Labeling how I feel both makes it feel all too real, and gives me a sliver of hope that this isn't forever. Putting a label on it helps me define my actions as more than just being emotional. Through lots of self reflection and research, I've accepted that this isn't something that has a magic cure, but I can learn to cope with the bad days and hold on to the good days through skills I'm learning in therapy. I spent so much time denying that this would be a part of my life forever, I thought I could fix it like I've had to fix everything else in my life.

But I've had to accept a lot of hard truths in the past two months.

My parents were shocked, to say the least, when I showed up on their doorstep—alive. At first, they thought I'd been kidnapped but no ransom call ever came. Then they assumed I'd just run away from home. They should have known me better than that. I don't make impulsive decisions often. But after they didn't hear from me for months, they assumed I was gone forever. I didn't bother to ask if they held a memorial for me or even tried to figure out where I went. I don't think I want to know even though deep down, I do.

I told them as much as I could while composing myself so I didn't break down into tears. I told them about the accident and how Jason found me. I told them about how I spent the winter at their cabin on the mountain and they kept me alive until the snow and ice melted enough for us to drive safely back. I didn't tell them anything personal about my relationship with Jason and the inevitable end. And they didn't ask why I looked so distraught upon my return. Just the way I wanted it. All I wanted was to cry for the next decade and hide away.

But my mother insisted I should go to therapy. One of her girlfriends suggested a woman in town and that's how I found Nita. She's wonderful. Non-judgemental, objective, insightful, and informative. She balances the scales of emotion and logic in a way that makes sense to me. It feels like I'm talking to a friend but without the social constructions of expectations. I'm not afraid of what she thinks because frankly I don't give a fuck. But when she does have something to say, it's always helpful. She's helped me to understand what I'm feeling and dealing with without telling me what to do. She's guided me into a state of self-awareness that I wouldn't have been able to find without her.

She's also the only person I've told about what really happened with Jason. I didn't tell her Jason's secrets because they aren't mine to tell, even to someone who's bound by law to keep secrets. Just that our crash and burn came from me sticking my nose where it didn't belong and his inability to see past his own insecurities.

Nita reminded me that I am not to blame for that. I know that, but it's still reassuring to hear that. She also reminded me that we can't force others to see things our way, to do what they don't want to. And as much as I'd like to be the most important reason for working on his issues, I can't be. It has to be his cognitive choice.

I just wish I had been enough.

But I keep that to myself because she'd probably tell me I am enough, he is the one who isn't strong enough to make a change. And that I deserve better than someone who doesn't give an equal effort.

I could have continued my free-loader existence at my parents house but Nita also suggested a sense of independence would be beneficial for my healing. And routine would be helpful to balance my ups and downs. So I took a job at a local coffee shop called Mt. Hood Coffee Roasters (that name didn't require a lot of brain cells to come up with). It's mediocre work that numbs my mind and keeps me busy. I spent the first couple weeks facing every person I've ever met in town, and all their questions about the last few years.

"Oh, you're back with your parents?"

"We thought you ran off. What happened?"

"Really? The Alder brothers? Those freaks?"

"I can't believe you're still alive."

Neither can I.

I took all of my willpower not to berate every person who badmouthed Dylan and Jason in the shop. Despite how things ended, I'll still defend those misunderstood boys to anyone who dares to speak ill of them. They aren't freaks. They shouldn't be outcasts. They're the most authentic and honorable men I've ever met. I just wish others could see it.

I haven't seen either of them in town since I've been back. I didn't expect to see Jason ever again, but I thought I'd at least see Dylan getting groceries or at the bar, maybe. A part of me even thought he'd find out I worked at the coffee shop and would come to see me. But it's been radio silence for two months. I haven't seen Dylan since he hugged me, told me Jason loved me, and left me at my parents house.

I've thought about leaving again several times, too ashamed to stay, too heartbroken to think about the man I loved living a short drive up the mountain in the same county as me. Does proximity make it harder to forget? Or will I be emotionally scarred by the events of this winter for the rest of my life? I don't know where I'd go if I left or what I would do to make a fresh start. It's not like I make enough at the coffee shop to get my own place in town either. The town is so small there aren't any apartment buildings so the only housing is rental houses that no one can afford on a single income let alone minimum wage. And the idea of roommates is just as bad as living with my parents so I'm coasting through life, at the moment, and my current circumstances.

I work the morning shift on Saturdays, so it's only one in the afternoon by the time I make it back to my parent's house. I've never really called it home because it doesn't feel like home.

The cabin on the mountain where a brooding, pigheaded man lives feels more like home.

I try not to think about the things I miss but sometimes I can't help it. When I walk into the kitchen and start making lunch I miss how we used to make all our meals together, eat them together, clean together. I've read found family books before but having one is indescribably more significant than it feels reading about it. It's hard to explain how unexpected friends can fill a void you didn't realize existed in the first place.

The housekeeper stocks the fridge with pre-made meals for the weekend in organized, identical containers so my mother never has to do more than operate the microwave. But I asked her if she could start getting sandwich ingredients from the store on her weekly trips so I could make my own. Making breakfast and lunch for myself has been a little comfort that gives me a sense of normalcy. Nita thought that was a great idea and commended me for it.

I'm layering Turkey and cheese onto sourdough bread (I miss making bread too) atop the marble countertops when my mother walks past the kitchen and wrinkles her nose at the menial task she considers beneath us.

"How was work?" She asks me. It's part of our new routine. She thinks the idea of me working when I don't have to is absurd, but tolerates it regardless. Every day when I get back from work, she asks how it was and I supply the same answer each time.

"Fine." Today I add, "One of the steamers stopped working which caused some back up but we managed."

Judging by the perplexed look on her face, I doubt she knows what a steamer is.

"When is your next session with Dr. Riley?"

"Monday." It varies based on my work schedule.

"And how's that going?" Even though she's the one who suggested therapy, she acts like it's a stain on her reputation. Now that I'm not the accomplished straight A student excelling in multiple extracurricular activities and volunteering on the weekends, I'm useless in her world. I was ornamentation on her wall of bragging rights but my color has faded so what's the point of even having a daughter now? I guess my purpose has run its course.

"It's good. Nita is wonderful. She's been really great with helping me move on from this winter and a lot of the things that happened before it."

"Before it? What on earth do you need to talk about in therapy before your trauma this winter? You didn't have any issues before then."

Is she serious? If you listen close enough, you can hear something in my brain snap.

"I don't know, how about the pressure of being perfect for you and Dad and never feeling good enough? Or the fact that my boyfriend cheated on me? Oh, or the part where I was so lost I decided to drive off a bridge and got into an accident in the snow instead?"

I didn't mean for that last part to slip. But in the heat of the moment my momentum propelled my tongue into speaking faster than my brain could keep track of.

She stares at me wide-eyed and slack-jawed, like I've just transformed into a different species before her very eyes.

Of course, that's the moment my father chooses to return from his golf game at the country club and walks into my little outburst.

"What's the meaning of this?" He speaks with more curiosity than annoyance, which is new for him. He hasn't asked me much about this winter other than confirming I wasn't taken advantage of by the "outcasts." I put a hard stop to that rumor immediately. As angry as I might be, I'm not going to let people believe Jason is a rapist. Or Dylan, even though I'm pretty sure the whole town knows I'm not his type. But I've observed that when people want to crucify someone, the facts don't matter.

My mom ignores Dad's question to keep her focus on me.

"Mara, I...we didn't kn...why didn't you say anything?"

My dad comes to stand beside his wife but doesn't touch her, not even a reassuring hand on her back. Just a twin pillar of solidarity as they face my latest indiscretion.

Mom takes a seat on the barstool on her side of the counter, laying folded hands on the clean marble. Keeping her back ramrod straight, she looks like she belongs in a boardroom not a kitchen.

My dad takes the seat beside her looking equally put-out by this inconvenience and curious about how this will go down.

"Alright, Mara, let's start with never feeling good enough. Am I to understand we've made you feel like you haven't been successful?"

"It's not about my success, Mom, it's about feeling important." I wasn't mentally prepared to have this conversation. Nita has been encouraging me to confront my parents about how I've felt through the years but I've been too chicken. I guess the universe decided it was time to have this talk.

"Nothing I ever did warranted attention from either of you. Unless we were in front of your friends and you had the chance to brag about me like I was *your* accomplishment, I didn't get any recognition for my achievements."

"When was the last time you were in my office?" It's my dad who speaks up much to my astonishment. He usually takes a backseat during serious conversations that don't involve work.

"Umm," I draw out the M while trying to think back. I don't go to his office unless I have to. "I don't know, a few years."

"Did you know I have a picture of you at the cross country state championship on my desk?"I went to state my sophomore year of high school. "Before you assume it's just for show, I keep it facing me on my desk, but any time a client asks if I have kids, I'm more than eager to show them the photo of my daughter placing at the state championship."

This is a side of him I haven't seen before, not to mention the most I've heard him speak in this house without twenty guests. "I—I didn't know you cared." Maybe I'm a bitch for letting it cross my mind, but a small part of me wonders if he's just telling me what I want to hear. Like when he tells Mom her favorite skirt doesn't make her look fat.

"I'm very proud of you, Mara. I apologize for not telling you enough." Although his voice carries a tone of professionalism, he sounds sincere.

Dumbfounded doesn't even come close to how I'm feeling. Never in a million years did I expect my dad to be the one to tell me he's proud of me, let alone for this conversation to be so productive. I thought they'd put up a fight, tell me I'm imagining things, whatever takes the blame off their shoulders. And Dad proved me wrong in two minutes flat.

"Now, Mara," Mom grabs my attention again, "is that boy cheating on you why you moved home?" I gave them as many vague answers as I could when I left college and moved back. My go-to was "I'm trying to figure out what I want to do with my life." That didn't earn me any brownie points in their eyes.

"The main reason, yeah," I'm not ready to tell them how much of a failure I was in college. One battle at a time. "It was more like the straw that broke the camel's back. I caught him cheating on me and made a rash decision. Felt like I didn't have anything else to stay in California for."

"Honey," I've never heard her use a term of endearment with me before. Paired with the sad look she's giving me, I want to break down and cry under the motherly concern I've craved for so long. "I'm so sorry. I wish I'd known."

"What would you have done?" I twist the lid back on the pickle jar that was forgotten on the counter and return it to its designated place in the fridge.

"Come see you, help you move if you needed me to. I don't know. But having been in your shoes, I just would have wanted to be with you, I suppose."

"Mom, I had no idea." Mom was cheated on? She's never told me about her life before marriage. "I wish you'd told me more about your life before you married Dad. This is part of the problem, I feel like I don't know much about you both aside from what I've observed." The two of them share a look and I swear this is the most they've ever seemed like an actual team instead of separate entities in the same space.

"Fair enough," she nods her head. "Maybe we need to start having more mother-daughter time. Would Wednesday afternoons work for a weekly lunch? I recall you don't work that day."

I'm both impressed she knows my schedule by heart and taken aback by how formal her offer is at the same time. But I agree. As daunting as weekly lunches with my mom seem, it is what I asked for, essentially.

My dad's voice chimes in. "Well, if those are the days you don't work, perhaps Wednesday evenings would be good for a family dinner instead, time for all of us to be together."

"Good idea." Mom rubs his shoulder affectionately and I swear it's like I'm having a conversation with two completely different people than the parents who've raised me thus far.

"What is this?" I blurt out, gesturing between them with my index finger. "You've never touched each other in front of me before. You don't have productive heart-to-hearts in the kitchen after golf. What is happening?"

"Mara," Mom scowls at me incredulously. "Just because your father and I aren't affectionate in front of you very often doesn't mean it doesn't happen. We've been together for twenty-five years. And many more to come. We just try to keep our private life private, including from our daughter. As for heart-to-hearts in the kitchen, our daughter has never brought up anything so serious before. If you want more of this, all you have to do is ask."

She makes it sound so simple. I guess I can shoulder some of the blame as well. As stand-offish as they've been most of my life, I haven't exactly made my feelings known or made an effort to connect with them on a different level.

"Now, Mara," Dad's voice lowers to a scary quiet decibel I usually only hear when he's made a decision the rest of the world has to adhere to. "I won't force you to talk about what happened the night you disappeared, that's what you have Dr. Riley for. But I am asking you to promise that if you ever feel that way again, you'll tell someone. It doesn't have to be us, it could be Dr. Riley, it could be a stranger on the street. But please don't follow through without finding help first."

Promise. Coming from a lawyer, that's a pretty strong word choice. I nod, not feeling strong enough to acknowledge what he's asking. He gives me a single, curt nod, then stands bracing both hands on the countertop.

"This has been a productive conversation, ladies. If you'll excuse me, I would like to freshen up after my game from this afternoon." With that, he strides toward the staircase and disappears out of sight.

What an oddly official end to this unofficial family intervention.

Chapter Thirty-Three

Mara-One Month Later

CAN'T CATCH ME NOW-OLIVIA Rodrigo

Weekly dinners started out a bit awkward, we didn't really know how to start conversations with one another that didn't feel like checking boxes off a to-do list. They started with my parents asking if I'd thought about going back to school, what I wanted to do with my time, if I enjoyed working at the coffee shop. I asked about their work, social circles, and charity functions. It took us a couple dinners until we started sharing life events with one another, things they'd missed out on in my younger years, and things I'd never known about their youth.

Turns out, my mom was quite the catch at the university she and Dad met at. And he was a nerd with his nose buried in books. But he won my mom's heart when her car broke down and he drove her back to their shared home town for Christmas break. Apparently, it was his taste in music which was a shock to me since I only ever heard music when they had guests over and always classical composers. Dad and I both have a soft spot for Led Zeppelin while Mom prefers the Beatles.

As different as this all is, it's been a nice change now that we are more comfortable with our redefined relationship. I still have no idea what I want to do with my life, which I know gets under their skin, but I'm starting to think I do have a future, even if I don't know what it is.

I thought about going to a local college but I don't know what I want to study because my feelings haven't changed even though my situation has. I don't want to be a career woman, I want to be a wife and mother. I want to learn as many skills as I can to pass on to my children. I want to value my home and the life I create instead of grinding so hard in the corporate world I miss out on the memories.

I don't judge other women who don't want the same things as me because we all have different strengths, and I've discovered business and deadlines are not one of mine. I succeeded in school because my drive wasn't for success but for attention. My goals in life have drastically changed, and it's taken lots of therapy to realize that's not only ok, but commendable. Every role a woman plays in this world is worthy of appreciation whether it be making and raising babies or building a thriving career.

Hooray for personal growth.

It's Sunday, so I'm working the morning shift again which thankfully doesn't start until nine in the morning on Sundays. It's nearly one now so I still have one hour to go and I'm already exhausted. Despite all the growth and progress I've been making, healing is not linear and I still have bad days. Last night was one of those. I couldn't shut my brain off as it replayed my final morning at the cabin over and over and over again like a sick horror film designed specifically for my torture.

I just can't get the hatred in Jason's eyes out of my head. Through everything we went through to get to a good place, to find what I believed to be love, I still can't wrap my head around how it ended so quickly.

I hate him.

I love him.

I miss him.

I'm angry he isn't willing to work on things and runs at the first sign of trouble.

I spend way too much time going over the what-ifs and maybes of that final day, wishing I could change everything and savor the happy moments in his arms before it all went to shit.

The ring of the bell over the door jolts me back to reality where I'm not in a snow-laden cabin in the arms of a sexy man. I'm serving coffee to people who talk shit about me behind my back.

I've never wished I could teleport more than when I look up from the dishes I'm sanitizing and see Bryce—high-school-douchebag-boyfriend Bryce—step inside the coffee shop. Judging by the amused expression on his sour face, he knew I would be here. I'm not even remotely prepared to deal with his brand of bullshit, today. But a customer service position doesn't let you pick and choose your customers.

"Well, well, well," he says mischievously, "Mara Meyers. I heard you were back in town. Actually, I heard quite a lot about you, recently."

I bet you have.

"Bryce," I don't even sound convincingly sweet. "It's been a few years. Nice to see you. Are you back in town for the summer?"

I'd like to say I remember the day I broke up with him so vividly but I honestly haven't thought about him since. I remember he was pissed, he couldn't believe *I* was the one dumping *him*. And I reminded him that it wasn't feasible to maintain our "relationship" long distance.

"Yeah. I am. I'll be here all summer long." He drags out the l in all like that should matter to me. "I heard you spent the winter with the Alder boys, is that true?"

Here we go. "Yeah. I was in an accident and got stranded on the mountain." I've perfected the simple answer to everyone's questions about how I got stuck up there. "Can I get you something to drink?"

His eyes narrow at my dismissal of his baiting. "Sure. I'll take a twelve ounce americano."

Grinding the beans and pulling the shot drowns out the noise for a blissful minute but Bryce's focused eyes never leave me. I don't give him the satisfaction of looking up at him but I can tell, I can feel the pressure of his gaze like a hot blast of air.

I finish the drink, pouring the shot into the twelve ounce cup and adding the proper amount of water. The rest of our encounter passes without issue as we exchange the drink for money. "Thanks, Mar." The way he says my name gives me a sickening feeling at the base of my stomach. With that, he departs the shop.

I have the ominous feeling this won't be the last I see of him.

The last bit of my shift passes without any more trouble. I finally clock out at the end of the lunch rush. I stayed an extra fifteen minutes to help my boss with the huge line that formed five minutes before my shift was supposed to end.

We've been having nice weather lately so I wore a smocked dress today, a dress similar to the one I wore at the cabin for Thanksgiving. I like the way the off the shoulder cut looks on my frame, I feel like it emphasizes all my best features. This one, however, is pure white, adding to the feminine aesthetic the style provides. I love it. Embracing my femininity is one of the things that stuck with me after I left the cabin.

It took me a month after starting therapy to get behind the wheel again. I didn't think I'd have any PTSD from the accident since the end of my stay at the cabin felt more traumatic, but as soon as I got in my car (that was towed from the bridge and repaired) to drive myself to my first session, it all came rushing back to me. My mom had to drive me.

Now, I can successfully drive myself from point A to point B without having a panic attack. Baby steps.

I'm walking to my car when the breeze picks up rustling my hair and sending a chill down my spine. That's the trouble with summers in Oregon, they get warm but they can shift in an instant. This state loves the cold.

"Mar." That voice grates against my skin. I hate that nickname too.

I lift my head to see Bryce leaning against the passenger side of my car, planting one foot on the sidewalk and the other propped against the car door. I want to tell him to get his dirty shoes off my car but I don't want to start anything with him.

"Bryce," I say with as little emotion as I can suppress. "What are you doing here?"

"Wanted to see if you would go somewhere with me." *Not a chance.*

"Sorry, I have a late lunch date with my parents," I lie easily, stopping short of my car to keep a safe distance from him. I'm infinitely annoyed he won't leave me alone. Our history is just that, it should stay in the past. He's just bored and looking for something to occupy his summer. He's never been very good at being alone.

"Oh, come on, I'm sure you can explain you're catching up with an old friend and they'll understand."

Don't engage, Mara. "Sorry, our schedules are so busy this is the only time we get to all be together."

"They didn't matter this much to you in high school." He's digging.

"Things change." A lot of things.

I try to walk between my car and the one parked behind it to get to the driver's side when he steps closer to me and grabs my elbow. Not hard, not threateningly. But the fact that he thinks he has a right to touch me at all ignites a fire in me. And I'm not very good at controlling my temper.

"Come on, baby, I just want to catch up." I highly doubt he wants to talk at all.

"Don't touch me, Bryce," I jerk my arm out of his grasp. The way his nostrils flare and his pupils dilate tells me that was the wrong thing to do.

Bryce grabs me with both hands by the upper arms in a bruising hold and gives me a quick shake. "What the fuck is wrong with you? You'll be a whore for the Alder boys but not for me? We have history. I was always good to you."

I jerk myself away again but his hold is stronger than my attempt to get away. I can't believe he's doing this in the fucking street where everyone could see.

"Fuck you, Bryce, I'm no one's whore. And you were a piece of shit. Always have been, always will be. So get the fuck off of me." I shove my hands into his chest which is enough to break his hold.

Just before he can step forward to try again, a large body comes between us. I'd know that body anywhere. The way his shoulder blades pinch at the center, the way his neck muscles strain, the way his hair is tied back to keep it out of his face. I spent hours memorizing every detail of him.

And I can't believe he's here.

Jason slams a fist into Bryce's face without hesitation. Bryce doesn't see it coming and barely puts up a fight. I should jump in the middle and stop this but I'm too stunned to move. Not to mention, Bryce has had this coming for years. If anyone deserves to take a shot at him, it's Jason.

"What the f–." Relentless and determined, Jason doesn't give Bryce the chance to finish his sentence before slamming his fist into his other cheek, systematically backing him into the wall of the coffee shop with each punch. It's amazing to think this is now the second time I've watched Jason beat someone up, but this time I just stand back and watch because, to be honest, Bryce deserves it and so does Jason.

Jason pulls his arms back like a wind up toy providing him lots of momentum for each punch that rattles Bryce. He isn't even fighting back at this point as Jason pulverizes him.

Seeing that Bryce is on the verge of collapsing, I finally decide to step in and stop the fight before anyone else notices and gets involved.

"Jason," I shout once, but I'm not sure he can hear me over the blood and adrenaline pumping through him. So I risk a step closer and place a firm hand on his shoulder, calling his name one more time. "Jason!"

That gets his attention. He ceases his attack to turn his head toward me and I freeze. I never thought I would see those stormy eyes again, feel the overwhelming magnetism that draws me to his orbit. Yet, here he is. I don't know if my anger is stronger than my relief to see him again.

Jason steps away from Bryce to admire his handy work, the blood and bruises form open wounds on his face and chest.

"What the hell are you doing here?" I ask once the fog has cleared from my brain.

I didn't expect a verbal answer, but I also didn't expect Jason to lift me and toss me over his shoulder. It's very reminiscent of Shrek carrying Fiona through the woods.

"What the–Jason. Put me down."

He carries me away from the scene of the crime, leaving my car on the street. I hear Bryce struggle to speak as we walk away but he manages to say. "You're fucking crazy, man."

I writhe in Jason's grasp the entire way until he opens a car door and deposits me inside on the bench seat of a truck. He runs to the other side and slides into the driver's seat, turns the key in the ignition, and peels away from the curb. I know where he's going before we even take the first turn: the mountain.

Jason's hands anxiously grip the steering wheel, he's vibrating with tension. I guess the come down from all that adrenaline is still wracking his body. His knuckles are bloody, split over the joints that impacted with Bryce's face the most.

Then recognition dawns on me and I blurt, "This is your dad's truck." He knows that, obviously, but I'm surprised it's both running, and that he's even driving it. He always seemed conflicted about the truck, probably because of who it belonged to before him.

I can't sit in here without thinking about what we did on the hood of the truck. Or–more appropriately–what he did to me.

God, two minutes with him and my body is already singing with desire for him. The traitorous bitch. I can't help it. Every inch of me remembers every inch of him. It would be so easy to forget everything that happened and climb him like a tree, erase the past few months and pretend none of it ever happened so we could live happily ever after.

That's the easy way out of this, not the right way. The right thing to do is never the easiest thing to do but hopefully it has the best results, despite however many obstacles that path entails.

I don't know if Jason is here to try and apologize, to work things out, maybe just to be a big baby and kidnap me so I have no choice but to stay with him. I wouldn't put it past him.

We sit in silence the entire drive, I don't give him the satisfaction of begging for answers when I know he won't give them to me. Because–once again–that would be too easy.

It's when he pulls off the road after we've already crossed the bridge that I start to realize where we are headed. The woods look so different without the fluffy white snow to blanket it. Lush, green, full of life. The ferns on the forest floor are in full swing and the sun beams through the gaps in the tree trunks. The forest seems so alive with color and light when it was so diminished a few months ago, set to slumber beneath the winter snow. It's almost like it was resting, waiting for spring to take over and blossom again. I've been in these woods so many times, driven around on the mountain before. But it feels like I'm seeing it for the first time with fresh eyes uninhibited by reality.

The sparkling water of the pond glimmers ahead as the truck comes to a stop on the grassy bank a few feet from the shore. It seems like yesterday this place was frozen over and I fell through the ice. It seems like yesterday Jason was cradling me in my sleep in front of the fireplace to keep me warm as my body temperature rose. I thought it was beautiful under the cover of winter. But with the color of spring, this place is magical. The way the light dances off the water illuminates the entire world. It's as if Thomas Kinkade painted the view before me. Birds chirping in the trees, a light breeze sending ripples over the surface of the crystal clear water. Golden rays of sunlight striking the surface.

It's breathtaking.

Jason steps out of the truck, comes to my side of the car, opens the door and extends a hand for me to take. *What a gentleman.*

I hop down on my own accord and stare him directly in the eye when I say, "I'm capable of walking myself." Storming off, I mutter under my breath, "neanderthal, brutish caveman." The words trickle into nothing the closer I get to the pond and feel the cooling effect of the breeze on my exposed skin. I hate how irritated I am right now. It would have been so much more satisfying if I was calm and collected, unaffected by his actions. But I'm subject to my own whims.

Jason approaches from behind, stopping a few inches away. I can feel his warm breath in my hair, the energy crackling in the small space between our bodies that comes alive whenever he's near. Every part of me wants him to wrap his limbs around me and hold me until the pain goes away. The one percent of me that isn't flustered right now knows that's not going to solve anything.

I'm so fucking angry. I was making peace with everything, I was working on myself. I was trying to forget about him and all the hurt he caused.

I was also trying to forget about the security and fulfillment I felt in his presence. The overpowering love I acquired for him. It wasn't a gradual development. The love I felt (feel) for Jason hit me like a freight train, knocking me off my axis. What I felt for him was so strong and all-consuming, it makes it that much harder for me to forget it. If it was easy, we wouldn't have ballads that perfectly explain what it's like to try to forget this love. Heartbreak has been the root of so much art and beauty in the world, as well as so much pain.

Hell, Troy and Greece went to war over love. People have killed for love, or lack-thereof. We're all searching for something that feels as rare as the holy grail and just as desirable. But how much destruction comes from the pursuit?

I spin around in a flash and start hammering on Jason's chest, overwhelmed by the myriad of emotions raging a storm in my soul.

"You son of a bitch," I fire at him. "I was healing. I was getting better. I was getting stronger and you ruined everything." Am I talking about the past three months? Or the time I spent with him? Because I was healing this winter, his rough edges softened mine. His healing hands soothed the bitterness in my heart. And he threw me off a cliff at the end.

"Why couldn't you leave me alone. You made your choice. You fucking coward." He just lets me pound at his chest. Although I know my assault isn't nearly hard enough to do any real damage, it can't be pleasant either. But he tolerates everything I need to unleash. Some people go shooting or ax throwing to release tension. Apparently, I find punching the love of my life more cathartic.

"You stubborn, selfish, bastard. I loved you and you just–."

"Mara."

Chapter 37

Jason

MISTAKES-JIM CLACK

She freezes the second I speak, just like I knew she would. Last time she heard my voice she was falling through ice on this very lake. I didn't know how to start this conversation but she was working herself up too much and I need her to listen to me, I need her to be patient with me. I'm still not very good at this.

After a moment of stunned silence, those big eyes staring at me expectantly, she whispers, "Did...did you just say my name?" It's almost like she's afraid of the answer, afraid to hear she's hallucinating.

But she's not imagining anything. I've been working the last three months to get to this point. The minute Dylan left with her, I instantly regretted everything that happened. It's like I replayed it in my mind as a bystander observing it and realized how utterly despicable my actions were. How uncalled for and down-right cruel. I was too wrapped up in my own shame to think clearly.

I thought about driving after her but decided against it, she needed time, the wounds would be too fresh. I knew if I went after her right away, she wouldn't be willing to listen, let alone forgive me.

That's also the moment I decided she's right, I've been a coward and I've let trauma rule my life for too long. My father ruined everything good in my life while he was alive, and he was still infecting it after his death. He doesn't deserve that kind of power beyond the grave. The only way I could make amends was if I made an effort. The only way she might even consider forgiving me is if I made a gesture so big it overpowered every horrible thing I've done.

She has to know this is all for her. Because even though it took me way too fucking long to realize it, I love her and I can't stand a second away from her. Waking up without her everyday has been pure torture. I haven't slept for longer than a couple hours at a time. I haven't been able to live in the cabin without seeing her everywhere. The couch I laid her on when she was freezing after her accident. The kitchen she danced around in and where I lost control of my desire for her. The bed where I kissed her for the first time. Even the damn chickens remind me of her. I've spent three months loving her while she's spent all that time trying to forget everything we shared.

She's my everything. And if she lets me, if she gives her heart to me again, I'll give her everything I have to give. I want to be her home. I want to be her healing. I want to be her harbor.

And I want to tell her that with my own voice.

So, taking a deep breath and fighting through all the chaos in my head, I answer her question. "Y-yes."

She looks like she's seen a ghost. As soon as enough of the shock fades for her to think clearly, she continues.

"How? When? Jason, I don't understand. I thought–." Her words trail off as the gears in her head visibly turn over everything she knows to be true and how contradictory this is to what she's known.

"I-." Fuck, this is hard. It was easier when I was reading books in the shop aloud, by myself. I haven't even spoken to Dylan yet. I wanted her to be the first to hear me, so she knew it was for her. I think he knows I've been working on it, but he hasn't actually heard me speak. "I've been t-trying. I want-ted to try for y-you."

I really wish I didn't sound so stupid. I sound like a moron. Not speaking for years is like not working out for years. You can't just walk into the gym again after a decade and expect to deadlift three-hundred pounds. Likewise, I had to retrain the muscles involved in talking and work on the mental blocks preventing me from overcoming my fears.

"How?" One word and yet she's asking so much. I don't even know where to begin. So I speak as honestly as I can, hoping it tells her enough.

"Th-the way you sa-ved me. Reading." It's coming easier now.

The sheen of tears glosses over her eyes as I continue.

"You were right." Ok, one sentence without stammering down. "I was a c-coward." So much for that.

Fuck, keep going, Jason.

"I've been af-raid for t-too long. They can't r-ruin my l-life anymore. They t-took everything from m-me. They can't. Take. You. Too."

Mara sucks air in like she's been drowning while listening to me. I've been so focused on getting through every word I didn't realize her palms were pressed flat to my chest. I don't think she realizes it either. I've been lost in her pleading hazel eyes and the way hope is shining in them. I don't know if I can repair what I've broken but I'm sure as hell going to try.

"I'm...sorry, Mara. I'm s-sorry f-for everything."

"Jason," she breathes my name like a prayer. "I'm so proud of you." Mara's anger melts away as she lifts onto her toes and wraps her arms around me so fast I barely have time to brace for the impact. As soon as she does, I return the hug, holding her to me with my arms banded around her back. If it's possible, I'll never let her go. This is all I've wanted. I'm not foolish enough to think we can fix everything in a day, or that she'll trust me again without a lot of work on my part. But All I can do is try.

I breathe in her scent like an addict who's been fighting withdrawals. She is intoxicating. My own personal methamphetamine. Maybe comparing her to hard drugs isn't that romantic, but I don't know how else to describe my need for her. They say absence makes the heart grow fonder but I've always known I need her, I just didn't know what it would take to keep her.

"I know how hard this must be for you." I nod, because even though I'm speaking again, it's not easy. I still have the training wheels on.

"I missed you...so much."

"I missed you too." She blinks and a tear rolls down her rounded cheek. She's so perfect. She's so beautiful it kills me. And I can't forgive myself for hurting her.

But I can try to make up for it every day for the rest of our lives.

"I'm so sorry, Mara." It takes me twice as long to get a sentence out but for her I'll make a fool of myself any day. "I'm sorry I-I h-hurt you. You are...the best...thing th-that has ever h-happened...to me."

I wipe the tear from her cheek with my thumb and lower my forehead to hers. God, just being near her feels like it has healed every ache, every wound, all the tension her absence has caused. I've been a mess since she left and it feels like it's all disappeared now that I'm holding her again. I can only hope she understands this was all for her.

Ok Jason, be strong and don't falter. You can do this. I have to get this out without stuttering. I don't want the first time she hears it to be a disjointed mess.

Here goes nothing.

"I. Love. You."

Mara pulls away so she can stare into my eyes like she's looking for something. Her lips part and her breathing hitches in her throat. I can hear her stop breathing for a moment at the same time her body locks up in my arms. Fuck, I hope I didn't do that wrong. She's told me she loves me but maybe she doesn't feel that way anymore. She did say she "loved" me. Past tense. Maybe I've missed my shot and this is just her way of telling me goodbye.

Before my mind can doubt her intentions anymore, she pulls me into a kiss that seals our fates. That kiss alone tells me everything I need to know and all my worries are drowned in her warmth, her touch, the energy coursing from her body to mine.

Pulling her hips into mine like I'm afraid she'll float away, I channel all of my love and devotion into the kiss. I might be holding her too hard but I can't bother to care right now because she's here, she's in my arms, and I think we are on the verge of fixing what I destroyed.

As determined as I was to try, I wasn't confident I could get her back. I didn't let myself hope because if none of this worked, at least I was prepared for rejection. I deserve rejection after what I did. But Mara loves with her whole heart, she's so much more than the shallow person she presents to the world, the girl who doesn't care about anything or anyone. She's full of love she wants to give and she just wants to be loved in return. I don't know if she thought it was weak to show how much she needed affection but she put on the unfeeling mask for so long I think she convinced herself that was her reality. Now that someone is here, willing to love her–now that I am here and laying my heart on the line for her, she's accepting that she is not only worthy of love, but it's within her grasp.

Mara breaks away long enough to whisper into the breeze, "I love you too." And I'm done for. I don't know how to describe the inordinate happiness I'm feeling. I've lived comfortably in misery for so long I forgot what it feels like to be happy.

The love I feel for Mara is stronger than my hatred, stronger than my self-deprecation. Stronger than anything I've ever felt.

Spurred on like a deer in the rut, I slide my hands over Mara's ass, under her thigh, and lift her into the air so her head is level with mine, if not an inch or two higher. She anchors her legs on my hips while one arm loops around my neck and the other hand caresses my beard. Even the lightest touch from her sends shockwaves through my entire body straight to my groin. I can't get enough of her and I plan to make up all the time we have spent apart.

Walking forward, I start splashing into the water still fully clothed, boots on and everything. The bottom of the lake is a mix of river rocks and soil beneath my shoes as I wade farther out into the water at a brisk pace. As soon as the water touches her legs, Mara squeals and breaks the kiss, peering down at the chilly water. It's a little cold, not freezing but bearable. There are no bodies of water in Oregon that are warm even in the summer.

"You're insane." She giggles into my neck then starts sucking at the sensitive skin. If the goal is to mark me, she's succeeding. But I plan to mark her as mine, too.

I keep walking into the water until the surface of the water sloshes just beneath her breasts. The wetter the gauzy white material gets, the sheerer it becomes until I can see her pink, peaked nipples through the fabric.

Fuck, I've missed her so much. I miss her laugh, the way she smells in our bed at night, the sound of her voice as she reads aloud to me. I've missed her delicious pancakes, the feel of her body wrapped around mine, the sound of her breathy moans, the way she says my name. I don't care if it's with lust, irritation, or love, I just miss her saying my name at all.

I kiss her into a stupor in the gently rocking water as my hand that's not supporting her slips beneath the fabric of her beautiful dress to stroke between her legs. Obviously she's wet because we are in the water, but I know she's as ready for me as I am for her.

"Ah, Jason." Fuck yes, I love when she says my name like *that* the most.

I slide two fingers inside her glorious pussy so easily. It's like her body missed me as much as I crave her. "Fuck," I say when I feel how tight she is. I've realized swear words come easily to me, they flow off the tongue smooth and quick. "You feel s-so good."

"God, I love your voice." I can't even begin to describe how happy that makes me. "It's so sexy."

I love her dirty talk. Even though I don't think complimenting my voice would be considered dirty talk. But it is to me. There are so many things I've wanted to tell her, especially during sex. Like how fucking beautiful she is, how much I love the way she rides me, how she's not afraid to tell me what she wants. And I intend to tell her everything. All of it. Forever.

I start pumping my fingers in out of her, steady at first, savoring the way her body reacts to my touch. Something I love about Mara is how she gets lost in sex, how she succumbs to what her body craves and lets herself experience it fully. Her eyes flutter closed and her lips part as her breathing gets heavy. She's weightless in the water as I press our fronts together, grounding our combined weight as we sway with the tide. All the while driving her higher toward an orgasm with my fingers, kissing her neck and clavicle so I can taste as much of her as I can get right now. There's plenty of time to taste the rest of her later.

As the speed of my fingers increases, she starts to grind herself on me. I angle my torso so my hip bone is in the perfect spot to strike her clit against with every movement. Her breath stutters when I do that and I want to hear it over and over again.

"That's it baby," I say flawlessly. "You're doing so good." I think my words against her slender neck have the same effect on her that my name on her tongue has on me. She shivers as my words slither down the curves of her skin. She's tanner than the last time I saw her and the golden glow accentuates every indentation and line of her body. The dip above her collar bone, the swell of her breasts, the tendons in her neck that I can't stop kissing because I can feel how fast her pulse is beating beneath them.

When her grinding is more feverish and shes practically fucking my hand herself, I whisper into the shell of her ear, "You're so fucking sexy baby." That sends her right over the edge as she plummets into an orgasm that draws a cry from her perfect lips. I can't wait to stick my cock in them later after she's come about a hundred times.

Her breathing slows a bit, her heart rate goes back to almost normal, and she buries her forehead in my neck. The sun has warmed the upper halves of our bodies while the lower halves have acclimated to the temperature of the water. I brace Mara with one hand around her lower back and the other cradling her head to me. There's something about feeling her weight on me that feels so secure. Although I'm the one holding her, it feels like she's saving me.

"You're mine," I tell her with conviction. That's when I dig into my pants pocket and pull the ring I made for her from it, holding it between my thumb, index, and middle finger so she can examine the intricate detail etched into the metal. I made it similar to how I designed her pistol. A matching set. "Be mine forever."

Although I say it like a request, I'm secretly praying she'll say yes because at the end of the day she is her own woman with the right to do whatever makes her happy. I just hope I am what makes her happy.

"I-I don't want to g-go a sing-le day without you."

Her eyes go so wide I'm amazed they're still in her head. When the surprise on her face morphs into the biggest smile I've ever seen, I know her answer before she kisses me.

"Yes," she practically sings, like she's telling the entire world how much she loves me. "Yes, Jason, yes." I slip the ring onto her ring finger, it's half a size too big but I can fix that later, and she doesn't seem to mind as she admires my work and how destined it looks to be on her finger. It was literally made for her. Not too wide or too thin. Feminine with a hint of me in there. I'll make a matching one for myself whenever we get married, wherever she wants to get married. Just as long as she's with me.

I walk us back out of the lake onto the dry shore toward the truck, clinging to her all the while. As soon as we reach the truck, I pull the door open and slide onto the bench seat with her still on me so she's seated in my lap. The fatigue from her orgasm must have worn off because she begins frantically unbuttoning and unzipping my pants as soon as we are inside. I didn't even get to close the door, not that it matters.

I lift at the hips so my pelvis is straight and together we slide my soaking wet pants and boxers down my thighs so my cock springs free of its confinement. I think Mara forgot what it looks like for a second because she stares at it with rapt fascination before ducking forward to seal our mouths in a passionate kiss.

Not going to lie, the way she was looking at my dick sent a jolt of pride firing through my ego.

Mara lifts onto her knees so her breasts are pressed against my t-shirt as she lines herself up with my tip. Slowly, painfully slowly, *rapturously* slowly, she lowers herself onto my shaft inch by inch. Her jaw snaps open once all of me is inside her and the rest of her body curls into me.

"*Fuck,*" she seethes through gritted teeth. "*You're so big. And I'm not just saying that.*" I laugh, and it feels good to laugh out loud so she can hear it. I've kept so much hidden away for the sake of fear and now I get to share it. I hardly ever laughed before she came along anyway. There are so many things I want to give her, my words, my time, my heart, and especially my laughter. Just like I want all of hers, too.

"It's good to hear your laugh." *It feels good to share it with you.*

As much as I want to say everything that comes to mind, old habits are hard to break. Sharing everything with her will take some getting used to. But it's one-hundred percent worth it.

Mara starts to lift, pivoting at her hips, and lowering back down. Over and over she takes all of me and creates beautiful friction between us as she starts to ride me. She's so fucking *hot*, she's beautiful and stunning and remarkable but all I can think when she's riding me like there's no tomorrow is how hot this girl is. And she's all mine. Breasts bouncing, chest heaving, pussy squeezing me in a vice grip. I have to tell her.

"You're so h-hot when you ride me like that." Talking to her is getting easier. And it would seem doing so drives her wild. She gets lost in the moment, in my words.

I yank on the stretchy top of her dress so her breasts are on full display, reveling in the perfect melon shape and dusky nipples, the way they move with her driving me insane with need. I want to fuck her, I want to chanel how much I've missed her into my movements.

As if she can read my thoughts, Mara leans back bracing her elbows on the dashboard so I buck my hips up to lift hers, tightening my hold on her as I start to pound into her from below. Every thrust pushes us closer to finishing, I just want to stay inside her forever.

And now we have forever.

My thrusts are so intense I'm worried she'll be sore later but if I know my girl, she'll probably like that. She claws her nails down my arms, begging for a release and more all at the same time. She gets louder and louder as each minute passes. Knowing she's the kind of girl who needs more than just vaginal stimulation, I move my hand so my thumb can reach her clit and press down before stroking up and down, coaxing her.

"God, Jason, I can't handle it." Her eyes pinch closed and her head tips back. She's about to come.

"Agh, you're amazing. *Fuck.*"

"You take it so well, b-baby. Come for me."

Knowing she's on the verge of climaxing, I give myself permission to do the same as we both moan and grunt into oblivion, falling through space and time until we are dizzy with satisfaction. Mara falls forward onto me so her face rests on my chest as we breathe into one another, trying to catch our breaths. I stroke the back of her silky hair while we come down from the high of that orgasm. There are plenty more in our future.

"I'm so s-sorry, Mara." I say as I continue my steady pace of stroking her gently. "For everything. F-for how I be-haved. For–."

"I forgive you." Three little words, most people think the L word is the most important but those words, *I forgive you*, mean more to me than anything else ever could.

I hold her in a tight embrace afraid to let go. She curls her arms around me as well and we just stay like that for who knows how long, cherishing this moment in time.

I love this woman so much.

"I noticed you don't stutter as much when we're having sex," she points out. "Maybe we should do it more often so you can practice." I mirror the mischievous smile on her face as she laughs to herself, making me laugh too. Then I duck in and kiss her, holding her face between both hands. And I don't think I'll ever be able to let go.

Eventually, we manage to peel ourselves away from one another and head back to the cabin. I know she needs to go home and get her things, and tell her parents what's happened. And that will be a trial in itself. But for one more day I want to live in our happy little bubble away from any real world problems. Afterall, that's what this place was meant to be. It's an escape from reality to create the life we want, not the one society wants us to have.

I didn't give Dylan any inclination where I was going when I left this morning. I sat in my truck outside the coffee shop for two hours trying to find the courage to go in and see her. Then I decided I should just wait until she's done with her shift so I didn't get her fired. I know she doesn't need a job so if she's working, she wants to be.

Dylan came back from running errands a month ago and told me he saw Mara was working at Mt. Hood Coffee Roasters. I thought that would be a better place to approach her than risk running into her parents at their house. I can't thank my lucky stars enough that I was there when that douchebag tried to harass her. I won't even let my mind wander down the road of *what if I hadn't been there* because I know I'll just get angry. I don't want to be angry right now, I want to bask in this reunion.

As we pull into the driveway of the cabin I wonder if it looks any different to her, the snow was pretty melted last time she was here, but the flowers weren't in bloom yet and the sky was covered by a thick layer of gray clouds. Now, the landscape is full of color and life. Even the wood seems brighter, glowing with the warmth of the sun.

Mara unlatches her door and hops out, an eager, hopeful expression on her face that fills me to the brim with joy. I hoped she would feel that way.

She stares onward toward the cabin while I watch her intently. She can probably feel me staring at her but I don't care, she looks right here, she looks like she's part of the landscape. Since the lake made her dress see through, I gave her one of my flannels I keep in the back seat to cover up. Her hair is tied back with a white bow, a feminine juxtaposition to the masculine flannel hanging off her shoulders. She's perfect.

"I feel like I'm home." Some of the best words I've heard leave her lips, second to *"I forgive you."*

I stare up at the cabin appreciatively for a moment as I snake an arm around her shoulders, folding her into my side.

"You-you are h-ome."

The front door opens and Dylan steps out, looking down at the bowl of scraps in his hand that I assume he's taking to the barn. As soon as he spots us, he doesn't even stop walking, just greets us by saying, "Well, it's about damn time." He changes course so he's walking straight for us when I decide it's time to let him in on my secret now that Mara is back.

"Hhi" I say slowly. It needs work. But my single word has the desired effect and the unshakable man stops dead in his tracks, eyes as wide as lightbulbs while he swallows a lump in his throat. It takes him a moment to process that what he just heard wasn't in his head. So I follow it up with, "Dylan."

At the sound of his own name he crosses the space between us in a flash and pulls me into a brotherly embrace. I knew he'd be happy but I didn't expect as much emotion as he's showing. I can't wait to tell him how grateful I am for him, how important he's been in my life all these years. And, inevitably, the cause of my silence for so many years. I don't think I'll ever be ready to have that discussion but he deserves some answers. He deserves the truth. I know he'll want to blame himself in some way, tell me I should have told him or Mom, but I think in time he'll understand and accept the past for what it is.

"Love you, brother," he smacks my back and steps away. "I'm proud of you." Knowing I don't like being the center of attention, he shifts his body toward Mara. "As for you," he pulls her into a hug next, with the same brotherly affection he gave me. "Welcome home."

Mara-Five Months Later

IF YOU LOVE HER-FOREST Blakk

Jason and I were married at sunset at the place we feel most connected: the pond that means so much to both of us. I wore a simple white strapless dress and flowers in my hair while he wore a linen button up with dark denim jeans. It was simple, beautiful, and everything I could have imagined. Dylan was certified online to officiate the ceremony and my parents were the only guests in attendance.

The night Jason and I reunited, he took me back to my parent's house so I could explain what happened and he could meet them properly. Anxious doesn't even begin to cover how I felt going into the introductions. But, to my surprise, my parents were very receptive. I saw the hesitation in their eyes when I told them I was leaving home...again, to marry the man I spent all of high school tormenting and all winter learning to love. But, I like to think they saw the love between us and accepted it for what it was. I think they saw how genuine our affection for one another is and didn't want to get in the middle of it.

It immensely warmed my heart that our relationship was more important than their hesitation. The more they got to know Jason, the more they liked him. As weird as it might be for them to tell their high society friends that their daughter is married to the mute kid who isn't a mute anymore, they seem authentically happy for us.

We spent the summer basking in the sun and the rose colored glasses of our honeymoon phase. Dylan took off for a week to visit some friends in Portland so we could have some privacy after the wedding. Bless his selfless heart. But I think it was purely selfish because he didn't want to listen to our endless "love making" in the heat of my return and the excitement of our marriage. We toned it down quite a bit after he got back.

And that is when he broke the news to us that he was moving to Portland to attend Portland State University in the fall and work on his goal of becoming a teacher. I couldn't have been happier for him. Of course, we were both sad we wouldn't see him every day, but seeing how thrilled he was about starting his future made up for it tenfold. I'm still not sure if Dylan ever told his brother about those plans before they were set in motion, but Jason was nothing but supportive.

Granted, that meant Jason was also losing a business partner, and I certainly wouldn't be any help in the shop (unless he wanted a handjob). Thankfully, supply and demand is a beautiful thing and eager customers–mainly rich guys across the country–were willing to pay top dollar to be pushed to the front of the line, especially after all their friends received the firearms constructed over the winter and saw the immeasurable quality of Jason's work.

I learned that Dylan helped only in the basic manufacturing department, Jason was the one doing all the customizations. Maybe one day Jason will take someone under his wing in the summertime and pass his knowledge onto someone else like him. Someone who was let down by the school system and finds fulfillment in working with their hands. Someone with the same goals as him.

As for me, I continued my sessions with Nita. I have no idea what I want to do with my life now but I've accepted that that's ok. I can take my time to find my passion and create the life I want.

Even though Jason's business brings in more than enough for our simple life, I kept my job through the summer and fall. I wanted to get out a few days a week, interact with people, and do something for myself. Especially considering I was signing up for another winter of isolation on the mountain.

With my husband.

I never get tired of saying that. Just like I never get tired of hearing him call me his wife, especially in the bedroom.

My husband spent the better part of the summer teaching me how to fish. I quickly learned I am not a natural at outdoor sports, as evidenced by how long it took me to learn to aim a gun. But we have nothing but time to practice and he has all the patience in the world. And I don't really care how many fish I catch as long as Jason is standing near me.

Despite the fact that he can speak, now, I don't mind our comfortable silence. The times we spent on the bank of the river fishing in silence are as meaningful to me as the times he whispers sweet nothings into my ear. Everything about our life is exactly as I imagined it. I wouldn't change our story for anything.

It's the first snowfall of the year which means we have a couple more days until we are trapped on the mountain for the winter. I stand on the porch with a mug of hot chocolate in my hand and a thick wool blanket wrapped around me. Beneath, I'm only wearing a simple black nightie which I've grown fond of since sleeping up here in the summer. It helps that Jason is basically a space heater so even on the cold nights I'm pretty warm in this. The amount of exposed skin means he's all over me, but I'm not complaining.

The puffy white flakes are falling so slowly, as if gently carried down from the heavens. It's not a storm like my first night on the mountain, it's a gentle dusting as the sky coats the world in the fresh powder that will transform the barren earth into an enchanted forest come spring. The image before my eyes is so magical, so peaceful. Every breath I take feels like it embodies my happiness, pure and fresh.

"Baby," Jason says through the open door. "Come inside. It's c-cold."

I take one more look at the darkening world beyond the front steps and smile before turning inside, ready to retire in our favorite way.

I'm nestled between Jason's legs on the couch so my back rests against his chest. His voice vibrates over my shoulder as he reads a book to me while I sketch in a notepad. I've been sketching more and more. I don't know if anything will come from it, but it brings me joy and the world is my oyster.

Jason has been the one reading to me lately, so he can practice speaking. It's getting easier and easier for him to speak, and his words are becoming more solid every day. I can't even begin to express how proud of him I am. Some people spend the rest of their lives allowing fear to control them. I almost let fear and doubt end my life. I'm grateful for every day I've been given and every word Jason speaks. Nothing could sound quite as sweet as his voice because it's not just words coming out of his mouth, it's courage and strength.

I managed to convince Jason to read one of my favorite books, even though it's a contemporary romance. He closes the book as he finishes the chapter where they hike to the waterfall and lays the book on the end table beside the couch. As soon as his hands are free, he locks them around me, enveloping me in his warmth. I'll never get enough of this, of him.

"I've been thinking," he announces over my shoulder.

"Well this can't be good," I tease. He pinches my nipple in response and I let loose a little squeal of surprise.

"I'm s-serious. I think we're missing something here."

I turn a bit in his arms so I can look at him over my shoulder, lost in the infinity of his eyes. "What's that? I already told you you can't get another car until you're done with the truck." He's had his eye on a 55 Chevy Bel Air that's still for sale on Craigslist but I'm insisting he finish the restoration on the truck first.

"Not a car," he laughs. Then he leans forward so his lips are a hair's breadth away from my ear. "I think we're missing a l-little soul to teach about our life, this life. Someone I can share this with that hopefully l-looks more like you than me."

I spin so fast in his hold I'm surprised I didn't take an eye out.

"Are you serious?"

"Of course I am," his brows narrow even though his smile is infallible.

"I thought you didn't want to be a dad yet?"

"I didn't," he confirms. "But you want to be a m-mom. And the more I thought about you holding a little baby, one that's h-alf you and half me, I started thinking that life sounds pretty good. I've already accomplished the imp-possible, with you. I can do it again."

There are no words. Nothing can adequately describe how full my heart feels in my chest as if it could spring out at any moment. It's overwhelming, untapped, pure elation that I didn't know one person could feel so fully.

I shift to straddle his hips and take his jaw in my hands so I can stare into those deep, soulful eyes I love so much.

"Jason," I utter through my uneven breathing. "I love you so much. I can't even tell you how much this means to me and how much I want it." Touching my forehead to his I say, "You are more than I could have ever imagined for myself. You're going to be the most loving father."

"And the most protective," he laughs. God, I love that sound.

"What do you say, wife, should we start practicing?" He eyes me knowingly, I can already feel his erection digging into me beneath our clothing. A full and hearty laugh leaves us both until he ceases it with a kiss that can be felt in the soul of the earth.

We deserve this. It took so long for us both to learn we deserved to be happy but now that we are here, I know this is where we are meant to be. Together.

Epilogue Part II

Jason

IF SOMEONE IS WILLING to give you their heart, take it.

If someone sees you as their home, keep them safe.

If you love every piece of her, she'll love every piece of you.

And If you love her like that, you'll never need more.

Ackowledgements

D EAR READERS,

If you've made it to the end of my book I want to thank you. If you've shown any support I want to thank you. And if you're the kind of person who reads acknowledgments, we are kindred spirits.

First and foremost I want to thank my husband for his endless support. For all the times he stayed home with our daughter so I could lock myself in my writing cave and work. For encouraging me to move forward with this book.Thank you for inspiring so many parts of this story.

Another independent author in particular helped me navigate the self-publishing process and cheered me on every step of the way. Laetitia, I feel blessed to call you a friend.

To my beta reader Jess, thank you for dealing with my imposter syndrome and giving me such helpful critiques.

To my beta reader and friend Jenna, your feedback was both helpful and entertaining. Thank you for believing in this story.

To Kelci2D, I feel infinitely blessed that we connected. I can't thank you enough for the amazing artwork you contributed.

Thank you to Rowan for the breath-taking hardcover design. And for always cheering me on.

Lastly, though she is a toddler who can't read, to my daughter. Thank you for bringing a sense of purpose and belonging into my life. Thank you for all the smiles, snuggles, and pure joy of being your mother. I love you, ladybug.

About the Author

Marisa Haartz is an independent author living in Arkansas with her family, dog, and two cats (even though she's not a cat person). She holds a degree in psychology which looks very sophisticated on her wall while she writes steamy books about lovable unlovable characters.

When she's not hallucinating while typing, she's hallucinating while reading, or she's playing adult dress up. AKA fantasy cosplay.

You can find Marisa on social media as @marisahaartzauthor